MW01518083

Kingmaker

By Chris Loblaw

Copyright 2012 Chris Loblaw

ISBN 978-0-9869650-1-2

All characters appearing in this work are fictitious. Any resemblance to real persons, living or dead, is purely coincidental.

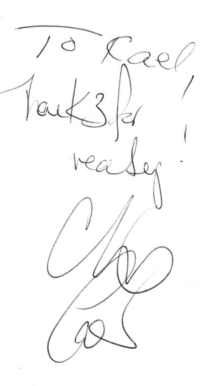

For the wonderful women in my life who support me:
Jennifer J., Jennifer R., Jolene, Cindy,
And the love of my life Kristen
Thank you, ladies

Chapter 1

The last week of February had been a cold and sloppy mess, and Mallory was looking forward to the end of winter and the warm weather that would slowly return after March break. What she wasn't looking forward to was the stack of required reading and study assignments that she had to complete over the break. She sighed in exasperation and asked Kean a question.

"Can you remind me why I chose to take the classes with the highest amount of work, and then join the University preparation program, which was totally optional?"

Kean kept writing his notes as he answered. "Because you wanted to be challenged. And your mom really liked the idea, and that got you a new iPod".

"I didn't do it for the iPod."

"Sure."

"I didn't! I'm not a materialistic brat."

Robert piped up from within the library stacks. "Can I borrow it then? I could really use a new iPod."

"NO. Hands off my stuff, Robert."

Robert emerged from the books and smirked at Mallory. The change that he had undergone over the last 5 months was amazing. Robert had switched schools after the big battle. He couldn't stand the idea of being at a different school when the only kids who were special like him were across town. And after the first few weird days of hanging around together, they had all started to get along. The shy boy who had accidentally become one of the creators of the devastating Old Vic spell was now joking around and comfortable around his two friends.

They had all formed a deep bond of friendship and camaraderie that day, when they had used their magical abilities to defeat the wicked Herlech Gate, and the friendship was deeply rooted into their everyday lives. They shared the victory and they shared the dark memories that still lingered in the back of their minds. The nightmares had lessened over time, but there were still nights when all three of them would see the hateful mage engulfed in magical backlash and destroyed by the wild energies he had tried to master.

There was a more gentle sadness that accompanied the battle for Mallory and Kean, the memory of their friend from the stars, Sterling. Mallory and Kean had connected to Sterling in an emotional way that they would never manage again, and his absence was palpable as they went through their days. Along with that longing, there was a comfort in knowing that Sterling was back with his loved ones and safe.

The kids were different than they had been at the start of the school year. It had only been 5 months, but the changes were noticeable. Kean had found a real interest in competitive sports, and the practice and rigor was shaping his body, lending definition and strength to his muscles, and giving him a natural grace when moving through a room. Kean didn't seem to be aware of the effortless coordination he had. He certainly wasn't aware of the burgeoning attention he was starting to receive from his female classmates. Mallory would mention it occasionally, as she was the one who witnessed and overheard most of the giggling and coy looks that those smitten girls were giving Kean, and each time she mentioned it, Kean shrugged it off. Mallory wanted to tell him that his disinterest in pursuing these girls would only make them more enamored with him, but that was a surprise that Kean could discover on his own. Kean had one physical change that was directly caused by the magical battle last September. The crosshatched pattern of cuts that the subway car window left on his right shoulder had healed into a network of pale, straight scars with a slight bluish tinge to them. To the mundane eye, it looked like a masterfully executed tattoo with silver blue shading to give the tattoo dimension and complexity. The colouring was entirely magical. It was embedded by the magical backlash, and it would itch and glow faintly if Kean was near an active arcane source. Backlash was the brute force realignment of the probabilities sent askew by a spell's interference and the tattoo was a constant reminder to Kean that the universe was quite happy with the way reality was functioning. It did not take kindly to his magical manipulation.

Kean rubbed at his shoulder absentmindedly, and he switched into magesight to check if there was any magic being used around them in the library. A quick scan of the room showed nothing active happening.

Mallory noticed Kean rubbing his shoulder. "Is there something happening?"

"No, just thinking about the scar made it a little itchy."

"Have you told your parents yet?"

"Nope. I've been able to keep it hidden so far, but that's going to be impossible when the warm weather gets here."

"Are you going to confess to getting a tattoo?"

"I don't have much of a choice. It's too weird looking to be a normal scar, and saying it was a scar would raise bigger questions and cause bigger problems. Like, how did I get a bunch of cuts on my arm at the same time, and why did I keep the cuts hidden from them instead of getting medical attention?"

"Are your parents opposed to tattoos? They seem incredibly easy-going. I can't imagine it's a big deal for them."

"I don't know. It's never come up."

"Well, if I was in your position, I would be in a considerable amount of trouble. My mother still gives me grief for this, and it's just a boring patch of hair."

Mallory twirled the thick braid of hair she was speaking about. The meter-long lock of hair started behind her right ear and ran down past her collarbone. It was a pale grey colour and eerily smooth to the touch. Holding the grey lock in your hands also sent a cold feeling of sadness and loss through your heart, like you were staring into the grave.

The lock of hair was Mallory's memento from the time she spent communing with the ghost of the abandoned train station, whisper. The connection Mallory had formed with that sad ghost had been made permanent when the hole in reality had been torn. No matter what Mallory did to the lock of hair, it would return to its original state by the next morning. Even shearing it off at the roots would only remove it for one night. Kean had called it "corpse hair", but a punch on the shoulder and a glare from Mallory had put an end to that name. Mallory referred to it as her Whisperlock. Most of the time, the whisperlock was braided and tucked into the mass of the rest of Mallory's hairdo. The rest of her hair was still unruly and willful, but Mallory had started to pay more attention to it and she was making a concerted effort to tame it into some kind of manageable arrangement. She was making more of an effort to present herself in a more composed fashion, but was still stuck in the strange divide between childish clothing and adult style.

Robert was more aware of his appearance as well. The old wire-rimmed glasses that had sat perched on his nose since grade 6 had finally been replaced with a new set of stylish frames..He had walked into school about a week after the battle, with the new glasses and a brand new set of clothes that didn't look like they had sat on the floor of his bedroom for a couple of days. Robert had walked straight over to their table in the cafeteria and loudly greeted Mallory and Kean.

The change in his behaviour had startled them, and Mall had forced herself to stifle a giggle of surprise. Instead, she had complimented Robert on his new look and he had beamed with pride. What they couldn't see behind the glasses was the oscillating shimmer that had overlaid Robert's irises. It was hard to see normally, but when he used his spell magic, the shifting lines that traced through his eyes would writhe and emit a visible light. Robert had been the most affected by the cataclysm. His magic had become restrained and focused in a way that hadn't happened to Mallory and Kean.

When they talked about their spellcasting, they talked cautiously. And never about the actual process of how they cast their spells. Their mentor Heisenberg had made them very aware of the perils of trying to explain their magic. If a mage recorded the methods they used to conjure spell energy and manifest it, they would find their gift vanishing with the conclusion of the spell. That's why spell books were useless relics of lost gifts, and why learning about your abilities was so difficult. They could talk in hypothetical effects and the things they could interact with, but most of the time they kept their silence.

They spent one afternoon a week at Heisenberg's tea shop experimenting with their magic. Somehow, Heisenberg had talked the school into allowing him to be a part of the co-op program. Kean, Mallory and Robert were the only 3 students working and learning at the tea shop.

Robert had found that his magic was linked to the invisible waves in the air around everyone. Robert could interact and understand radio waves and other types of broadcasted information. He was working on bending those waves to his will, and he called this new ability "wave riding". Mallory and Kean had wondered f Robert felt a sense of loss over the other possibilities that were now closed off to him, but he had no regrets.

"The two of you were casting spells before the big showdown. You knew what you were doing, more or less. I didn't know I had magic until that day. I don't have anything to miss."

Kean noticed the time on the library clock and started packing up his school books.

"Come on, we've got to get out to the bus stop. It's co-op time."

Mallory grumbled. "Ya know, it would be nice to actually get paid for working a job."

"We serve about 1 drink a week, and that's on a busy week. If you consider the space we get to do our experiments, and the amount of hot white chocolate a certain someone drinks, we're being pretty well paid." Robert responded.

"Well fine, I'm glad the two of you are so flush with cash that you can do things for free. I'm on a tight budget here, people, and it takes a lot of moola to keep up a stunning appearance like this."

Mallory huffed, threw her hair behind her and stormed out of the library dramatically.

"I think her mom turned down the request for more allowance."

"Yup, think so." Kean answered.

Kean and Robert crammed the last of their homework into their backpacks and dashed off after Mallory. They made it to the bus stop just as the bus hurtled towards them and stopped suddenly. The transit drivers of the Greater Antler Branch Transit Commission drove like they were in a race with the devil to each and every stop on the route. The handles inside weren't comfort options for the unlucky travelers left standing; they were life-saving necessities. The kids boarded the bus amidst the throng of other students on their way to the mall or downtown for lunch, and they held on for dear life until the crowd thinned out enough to allow them to sit. The drone of commuting lulled them into a half-asleep state. Their drowsy feeling carried them from the bus to the subway, and lasted until the subway pulled into College station. It was still a chore to keep from thinking about the hunt through the subway tunnels and the confrontation with Herlech every time they rode the subway, and sometimes they purposefully got off the subway early to find the sky and chase away the memories. This time they had managed to doze past the memories. At the stairs leading up to the main floor of the station, Heisenberg stood waiting for them.

"This is a little weird. You never meet us at the train." Mal said.

"I thought, my students, that we could have a little field trip today. That is, if you're properly dressed for a quick walk through our lovely metropolis above."

Heisenberg folded up the newspaper that he had been reading, tucked it under his arm with a flourish, and trotted up the stairs. The kids fell in line behind him and followed him out of the subway station and into the blast of cutting icy wind that howled down the street to greet them. It seemed like the city could always find a blast of unpleasant weather to greet the out-of-town visitors with. Robert yelped with surprise at the intensity of the wind.

"Now now, I know for a fact that it is 5 degrees colder in your home town than it is here."

"But we've been bundled up and warm on the bus and the subway for the last hour so this feels really cold."

Kean shivered and agreed. "And the wind is always stronger and colder here. It's probably the lake."

"Oh you two. Honestly, you're both so delicate. If you had scarves, this wouldn't be bothering you." Mal scolded them, tugging on her long colourful scarf to emphasize her point.

They marched off down Yonge Street and down across to a smaller back street. It took a few blocks before Kean realized where they were headed.

"We're going to the collapsed station, aren't we?"

The three kids stopped and waited for Heisenberg to confirm. They were dealing pretty well with the trauma of being in a life or death fight with a psychopathic mage who had been blown from this plane of existence by their efforts, but the site of the battle still frightened them.

"Yes, we are. Only the surface, I assure you. The abandoned station itself is fully collapsed and will remain unusable for decades. The city only cleaned up the minimum amount to allow the upper station to resume use. They then bulldozed over the hole in the ground and left it as an empty lot. Well, almost empty."

The kids stood rooted in place, unwilling to follow along.

"Very well, we could just turn around and head off to the Tea shop. I'm sure what I was going to show you is of no real consequence or threat. It would have been nice to find out what exactly it is, and use our deductive prowess and arcane acumen to address this strange occurrence, but perhaps we can just leave it for another company of magicians. A more courageous group."

Mallory squinted at Heisenberg.

"Are you callin' us yella, mister?"

. "Am I? Why would I do that?"

"You do remember that we are still considered children, so dragging us to strange occurrences would probably count as endangering the wellbeing of a minor."

"It's perfectly safe. At least, I'm reasonably certain it's perfectly safe. It hasn't killed me yet, if that's any consolation."

"No it is not!"

Kean snorted, laughed and gave Robert a little push. "He's going to keep bugging us until we go, so let's just go."

"That feels like peer pressure." Robert said.

"Oh I'm not your peer, lad. Let's go!" Heisenberg said as he turned on his heel and marched off again.

Two short blocks later they arrived at the empty lot. Nervously the kids looked around for something out of the ordinary. On first inspection, they only saw dirt, gravel, and random street trash that had blown in past the scrub fence. Heisenberg gestured them over to a bench that sat across the street from the lot. They all sat down and continued looking at a boring, empty lot.

"So what are we supposed to be seeing here? Is this kind of a therapy session, where we're exposed to something we thought would be scary but it turns out to be boring and pointless?"

"Look more closely with your magesight, Mallory. Start at the point above ground where the building behind the lot stops and the billboard above it begins."

They all switched to magesight and scanned the point in the sky that Heisenberg had directed them to. Robert was the first to see the tip of a thin magical line flicker in and out of existence.

"I see it!"

"Good. You've got a quick eye, Robert. Do the two of you see it yet?"

Mallory and Kean nodded, and Heisenberg continued.

"Now, starting at the tip of the line, follow it down into the ground. Take a moment of pause then, before you continue following the line into the earth. There are still landmarks below the ground that will trigger your memory of the event, so be prepared for that."

The three of them traced the thin line of magic down its path into the dirt below. When the recognizable elements of the collapsed station became visible to their magesight, Robert and Mallory lost their nerve and switched off their magesight, Only Kean traced the line to its very end, well below the collapsed station deep in the earth.

"It's long. A few hundred meters at least. What is it?"

"That is the question. I don't quite know. And that isn't the least of its mysteries. Watch the line closely now, at any point that you prefer. Are you all watching? Good. In 3,2,1."

As they sat watching, the thin line flared into a bright, glowing iris that opened to a span of a meter across. The space between the edges was impossible to see into, full of shifting light and patterns that made Kean's head spin. As the energy increased, the three friends felt the energy reach out and attach itself to them. As it started to gently tug and pull on them, a sense of terror washed over them. Heisenberg shouted in alarm at what he was seeing, and he threw an arm across the three kids to keep them in place. The pulling lasted what felt like an eternity, as the seconds ticked by. Their panic lessened as they all realized that the draw from the iris wasn't intensifying past the weak force it started with, but Mallory was still on the edge of shrieking and swearing about it when 3 minutes after it started, the magical iris flickered and went dormant again. The energy tendrils vanished.

Chapter 2

"WHAT THE HELL, HEISENBERG! DID THAT REALLY SEEM LIKE A GOOD SURPRISE?" Mallory shouted.

"Not cool, H. Not cool at all." Kean added.

Heisenberg stammered an apology.

"I ..I am so sorry for that. I hadn't thought that it would have any interaction with you. It's done nothing to me each time I've been here."

Robert was the only one of the kids not furious at Heisenberg. He was still staring at the hairline slit of magic in front of them. What had initially appeared to be a straight line was composed of irregular curves and deviations.

"It's a scar. A spellscar."

Kean, Mallory and Heisenberg looked at Robert as he continued to talk.

"When the backlash collapsed onto Herlech, it tore a hole in reality, and the hole is still there. But why did it open up again?"

"Because it is the anniversary of the battle. Exactly 5 months ago, the three of you were in the station below, trying to avoid the debris as the station started to fall down around you."

"Wait, it's not exactly 5 months. It's about 4 and a half, at most." Kean said.

"If you use the calendar, then yes, that is correct. But this interesting anomaly adheres to the lunar month. And today is exactly 5 lunar months since the event. The anomaly has been activating each month on the anniversary. Each time it opens, it stays open for a little bit longer. The first month, it was open for less than 30 seconds, and now it is up to 3 minutes. It hasn't had any effect on the world around it, until today."

"I guess we're the special ingredient, huh?" Mallory said sarcastically.

"Mallory, I am really quite sorry. If I had known that it would reach out to you, I would have kept you away from it. You know that I tend to err on the side of safety. What I didn't take into consideration is that the three of you might still have some connection to the spellscar, as Robert describes it."

"Why is it connected to us?" Robert asked.

Kean responded. "We made it. Or helped make it, at least. Our magic went in to ending the Old Alex spell, which blew Herlech through the hole into oblivion, or wherever."

"So is this a problem? Please say it's totally fine."

"Yes, Mallory, I suspect it is a problem, one that will keep growing is left untended. And there is an additional element to consider. There was something else the scar was reaching out to. When it was fully open, there was a faint tendril reaching off into the distance, towards the southwest. The trail faded into illegibility too quickly to identify its destination."

"Could it be, you know, Sterling?"

Mallory asked the question that was on everyone's mind, barely daring to hope that the answer was yes. Heisenberg shook his head.

"No, it wasn't a person. The tendrils that reached out to you blended into your auras and took on your spell colours. The long trail was unmodified. It isn't Sterling. But it also isn't Herlech, and that is good news."

"Wait-Is it even possible that Herlech is alive? I thought the backlash destroyed him. I keep having nightmares about Herlech dying." Robert said.

Kean agreed. "I do too. Some nights I feel like I killed him myself."

Heisenberg took a long look at his three students and friends. He moved off of the bench and crouched down in front of them so that they could all look into his eyes.

"My friends, you did nothing wrong at all. Herlech Gate was intent on creating pain and misery to the world, and he would have done terrible things to all of you had he been able to gain the upper hand. Whatever his eventual fate, it was his own fault. I am proud of how you stood against him. Now then. We've been in the cold for too long. Let's go back to the shop and continue this conversation over a hot chocolate."

Heisenberg led the crew of mages back through the streets to the little tea shop. Sitting around the counter of the tea shop, slowly sipping their piping hot chocolate, they continued to discuss the spellscar and its implications.

"To be honest, you've done a better job describing the thing than I have, Robert. I've spent hours watching that magical line waver and flicker, but I never quite managed to identify it as a scar. It is a scar, and that troubles me."

Robert was intently leaning forward as he asked his question. "Why? What's so bad about a scar?"

"It means that the rules have changed. It is a magical side-effect that is not only refusing to fade away, but is actually increasing in activity. And it's doing so on its own. There isn't a mage willing the scar into activity."

"And our mementos of the battle aren't fading either. Mal's hair, my shoulder scar, and Robert's EM vision. If they were just backlash effects, they should have started fading away, right?"

"But Herlech had those scars on his neck, and those looked pretty permanent." Mallory replied.

Heisenberg nodded. "It's true. Unfortunately, we have no idea how long Herlech had been scarred, and if there had been any fading or change. And it may be that if the backlash causes an actual physical wound, then the results stay around as long as it would if it had been caused naturally. Your shoulder may have been destined to stay scarred, Kean, but the difference is that the magical traces should have vanished by now. And Robert, you've been able to use your new ability with more control and effectiveness recently, hasn't you?"

"Yes. I can move the waves a little bit now. It's kind of neat."

"Your new ability is the most interesting change, Robert, because it's supplanted your initial spellcasting gift. So we are in a world where the limitations that we had assumed to be in place are no longer as strict as they might have been."

"Is the spellscar the problem? What if we got rid of it?"

"How would you propose to destroy the spellscar?"

Heisenberg addressed his question to all three of them, and they sat and thought about the prospect for a minute. Mallory was the first to offer a solution.

"What if we described it into non-existence?"

Kean looked confused. "What do you mean?"

"I mean that magic stops working if you explain it, right? So why don't we explain the scar away?"

Heisenberg turned to the whiteboard at the end of the counter and drew a diagram of the scar, with lines leading off to each of the creators of the scar.

"It's a good idea, but there are two significant complications with the plan. First, to fully negate the spellscar, you'd need to nullify the contributions by all the connected parties. That would include the three of you, and Sterling, and Herlech. Without them, there's a very good chance that you would only nullify your own magic and leave the scar fully active."

Robert examined the diagram on the board, and he traced the line from the scar that led nowhere.

"This is the other complication. What is this, and why is it connected to the scar?"

"Yes. The missing element. On that topic, I have something I need to show you."

Heisenberg tapped the keyboard of the laptop in front of him and turned on the television in the corner of the room. The television screen filled with the images on the laptop's desktop. Heisenberg launched the web browser and navigated to some kind of live webcast of a strange and intricate looking object.

"I was sent this link yesterday, by a friend of mine who's a history buff. This is an ancient device that was, up until recently, believed irreversibly damaged by prolonged exposure to sea water. But when the device arrived at its current location, it was intact and undamaged."

The kids stared at the unassuming device being displayed on the screen. It sat on a padded pedestal in the middle of what looked to be a very small room. The webcast cycled at regular intervals through a series of 8 camera perspectives, giving the viewer a chance to see the full panorama of the device. It was a cuboid shape, nearly entirely symmetrical, but slightly taller than it was wide. On the front face, a filigree of highly polished metal was inlaid in an intricate pattern. Encircling the edge of the front face were tiny gossamer pictures made of lines and small dots of brilliance. Two more smaller patterned circles were set within the face. Radiating out from the center of the front face were 3 metal arms, the end of each matching up with one of the circles. Around the back of the device, a string of attached panels of dark material extended from a barely visible hinge. There was a digital display attached to the bottom edge of the pedestal, showing the room temperature, the current time, and two other measured numbers labeled 'v/m' and 'a/m'. The itch on Kean's shoulder told him to switch to magesight, and he was stunned by what he saw.

"It's magical, but there's no spell colour at all. It's like a spell without a caster."

"It is indeed. This may be the first actual magical artifact. The very thing I swore could not exist is now sitting in a room 2 hours away from here."

"What are the last two readings on the display?" Mallory asked.

Robert answered the question. "Volts per meter and amperes per meter. It's how you measure electromagnetic radiation. This thing is giving of EM waves, somehow."

"Isn't it super-old?

"Looks like it. How old is it actually, Heisenberg?"

"Well that depends on what version of history you believe in. Up until 5 months ago, this particular device was known as the "Antikythera Mechanism". It was retrieved from an ancient shipwreck off of the coast of the Greek island of Antikythera, and it looked like this."

Heisenberg opened a second browser window and loaded up a webpage showing a corroded chunk of metal that was roughly the same shape as the beautiful device in the other window.

"The Antikythera mechanism or "A.M." was sent on loan from the National Archaeological Museum of Athens to Western University in London Ontario 5 months ago. The university had planned to study the remnant of the mechanism as an amazingly early example of ancient computing devices, and to investigate the very faint EM radiation being given off by it. But when it arrived, it was fully intact, and putting out considerably more radiation than initially estimated."

"Let me guess- it arrived in London on the same day that we had the battle." Kean said.

"The very same. This may be the other element that is sustaining the spellscar. It's been very difficult to gather any further information of the A.M. All of the previously published information on the internet has been modified to conform with the current version of the device."

"So someone is covering this up?"

"I thought so, until I called an old friend of mine at the university. He asked around and no one thinks anything is out of the ordinary. They all seemed hard-pressed to even acknowledge the old version of the device. As far as they're concerned, this complete A.M. is the right one, and it was always supposed to be here."

"Then how did you get a picture of the old one?" Mallory asked.

"The magic of Wikipedia. They track all recent changes made to an article, and they keep the original version of the article for reference. The new descriptions of the device have been slowly making their way into the article over the last few months, but the old information is still there."

"They're censoring Wikipedia?"

"I don't know if you could accurately call it censoring, without knowing the intentions and motivations of the editors. What I do know, is that we need to have a closer look at the miraculously restored A.M. and find out a little bit more about what it's doing. And when I say "we" I mean the three of you. You're going on a class trip tomorrow!"

All three of the kids looked at Heisenberg in disbelief. Kean was the one to voice their suspicion.

"We can't just skip a day of school to go to London. My parents will freak out. Mal is still grounded from the first time we skipped school."

"I am not. You make it sound like my mother is ultra-strict."

"So how long were you grounded for?"

Mallory rolled her eyes. "A full month."

"See? How long were you punished, Robert?"

"I wasn't. I told my mom where I was going to be so I didn't get in any trouble."

"And I had to clean the whole house that weekend, but I was still allowed to leave the house after school. Your mom is a little uptight, Mal."

"She has her…moments. So yes, I agree. Skipping school would be a terrible idea."

Heisenberg laughed. "No worries! It is an officially sanctioned field trip for the grade 9 and 10 students of your school, arranged with the principal. Nothing illicit about it."

Mallory squinted at Heisenberg. "You're becoming a pretty shifty guy lately. What kind of secret stuff are you up to?"

"I have my connections. Connections which include your school's principal, and Robert's teacher. Handy, isn't it?"

"Are you forming your own secret society? You're a wanna-be freemason, aren't you?"

Robert looked at Heisenberg and Mallory for some kind of follow-up explanation.

"Would one of you explain what a freemason is?"

"Freemasonry is an organization that used to be very secretive. They come together to share ideas and values, and work on self-improvement and better citizenship. Some people think the masons do much more than that, and that they use their connections to unfairly manipulate business, politics and anything else that they can control. They use construction and architecture metaphors in their teachings."

Kean piped up. "It's a mix between the boy scouts, a business meeting, and a debate club. That's what my uncle said, anyway."

"I'd say that's as good an explanation as any. And no, I am not trying to form my own club, or secret order, or cult. There are a lot of people who love to talk about the old mysteries of the ancient world, and the psychology behind them."

"Why do they listen to you?" Robert blurted out.

Heisenberg's face fell, and Mallory admonished Robert.

"That's rude, Robert. You just said no one should listen to him!"

"I didn't mean that."

"That's fine, Robert. I know that wasn't what you meant. I would point out that I have a master's degree in ancient history, so it's not entirely unreasonable that someone would listen to me."

Robert mumbled "sorry" and shrunk into the easy chair beside the counter.

"Don't feel bad, Robert. No harm done."

"Are you going to come with us to see the A.M.?"

"No Kean. I'll be here, working on the scar and trying to get a little more information about it. Some experimentation is in order."

"You're not going to try to close it by yourself, are you? Because that sounds dangerous."

"Our excursion today reminded me of the hidden aspects of the spellscar. With so much unknown about the scar, it would be foolish and dangerous to try and close it right now."

Mallory pointed her finger at Heisenberg "Good. Don't forget it. This is a team effort, bub."

"Yes ma'am. Now, we have another hour before you have to hop back onto to the subway and head home. Anyone have an experiment they'd like to try out?"

Robert spoke up from the easy chair. "I do. Remember how we talked about Mallory's deadhair?"

Mallory interrupted. "First, all hair is dead, dummy."

"Yours is more dead than normal."

"That isn't even possible! Something is either alive or dead. There are no degrees of dead."

Kean laughed. "She's right. Point to Mallory."

"And I told everyone that we call it my whisperlock. That's the name I decided on."

"I still think it sounds like something you find on a sandwich bag or something. 'Try plasto brand sandwich bags, now with patented whisperlock technology. Keeps your vegetables fresh and crisp!'"

The radio announcer voice that Robert used to do the pitch was ridiculously loud and pompous, and it only took a moment for it to send the room into fits of laughter. Even Mallory gave in and laughed along. After the laughter died off, Robert continued his point.

"We talked about her hair and how it grows back when it's cut, but we never investigated what happens to the cut hair. Have you ever seen what happens to it, Mallory?"

"No. It's just gone the next morning."

"So that's what I want to set up. I want to record the cut length of hair overnight so we can find out what happens to it. Does it turn into dust and blow away? Does it vanish with a pop?"

"Does an army of tiny magical mites come crawling out of the woodwork and eat the hair while Mallory sleeps inches away from it? Maybe they live in her hair?"

Kean pre-emptively backed away from Mallory. His instincts proved to be correct. Mallory brought her fist up in a rush and was swinging for Kean's shoulder. The swing brushed by his arm, and if he hadn't have moved, it would have struck him cleanly.

"I don't need to imagine thousands of bugs crawling through my hair, you jerk."

"I didn't say thousands. It might only be a dozen. Is that better?"

"No that is not better!" Mallory said as she stalked towards Kean. He ducked under her next attack, a finger flick aimed at his chest, and Kean danced back out of range.

"Okay okay, I apologize. Your hair is almost certainly 100% bug-free."

Robert muttered to Heisenberg. "That's probably not true. Don't we all have tiny skin mites living all over us?"

Heisenberg quietly answered back. "Not the time to bring that up, my boy."

Mallory grabbed the kitchen shears from the counter and snipped off a foot of her whisperlock.

"Here, catch!" she said as she threw the braided hair at Kean's head. Kean reflexively caught the hair, and a look of unhappiness crossed his face as soon as the braid was in his hand.

"Mal, that's not cool. I hate the feeling of your creepy deadhair. Feels like being cold and dark."

"Are you sure it's not the thousands of mites that creep you out?"

Robert stepped in between the two of them and took the hair from Kean.

"Here. I'll go put it in the observation room."

They watched Robert walk calmly down the hall and into the tiny closet that had been converted into their lab space. With a handful of cameras, microphones, and various other sensors, the observation room could record whatever events transpired in the room. They had all noticed that any kind of electronic surveillance intensified the effect and duration of backlash, and their experiments focused on quantifying how much of an effect each recording method had.

Robert placed the braided hair onto the small circular table in the middle of the room and retreated back into the hallway. He closed the door, and everyone moved back into the main room to watch the room on the monitor. Kean asked Robert a question as they stood watching the inactive room.

"Why doesn't touching her hair freak you out?"

"When I touch her deadhair, I feel some of the things you feel, but the memory of my grandmother keeps it from becoming uncomfortable. I think she protects me. Or maybe it's because she can talk to me in my dreams sometimes. Means ghosts and death aren't as scary as they should be, I guess."

"Has anybody else had any contact with ghosts since the big fight? Mal? You'd be the most likely."

Mal shook her head. "No. Not even a weird vibe or anything. I thought the hole into the realm of the dead slammed shut."

Heisenberg nodded. "I've never had any contact with a spirit, but I would assume that we would have bumped into another one by now, if the barrier between the living and the dead was still permeable."

"But what about Robert's dreams?"

"To be frank, I don't have an answer for that. It may have absolutely no connection to his magical gift at all. He might be the only person to ever receive a message from a ghost, other than your temporary contact with Whisper. Or, he may be from a long line of necromancers."

Robert frowned. "Necromancers would be magicians, at least according to the historical definition. If I am a necromancer, then it has to be tied in to my magic."

"Remember, my boy, that all recorded fact on any topic of magical gifts are, by their very nature, documents of a non-functional aspect."

Mal and Robert looked at each other in confusion, as they worked to puzzle out Heisenberg's complicated sentence. Kean translated.

"It's been written down, so whatever it describes probably doesn't work anymore. Don't believe everything you read."

Mal huffed. "Why didn't you just say that? You spent too much time spent in university, and it gave you an addiction to overly complex sentences."

Heisenberg blushed and then laughed loudly. "I wonder if I should seek treatment for that condition? Pendantics anonymous, perhaps."

As Mallory, Robert and Heisenberg watched the LCD screen for any sign of activity in the lab, Kean crept away down the hall. He stopped at the door to the lab and peeked through the plexiglass window. Chuckling softly to himself, he started to cast a spell. The sting of backlash came in almost immediately, accelerated by the cameras recording the room and his magical effect, but Kean persisted. The lock of hair sitting on the table was now covered by a mass of writhing, crawling bugs. Their mouths, surrounded by wicked-looking mandibles, clacked and clattered as their jaws worked ferociously to consume the hair. From the main room, a shriek of disgust and surprise came out of Mallory. "OH MY GOD!" she yelled, and she followed her exclamation with a rising shriek of panic and revulsion. Robert and Heisenberg were conferred with each other about the nature of what they were seeing, and what they should do to calm Mallory down. Mallory didn't wait for them to decide on a course of action: dashed back to the counter and grabbed up the scissors. She put the shears at the base of her whisperlock and chopped off the entire lock. As the hair fell to the ground, she kicked at it and sent it into the corner.

Heisenberg squinted at the screen, and noticed something.

"Uh oh" he muttered. "Mallory, dear, it's alright."

"IT IS NOT ALRIGHT THERE ARE BUGS IN MY HAIR!"

"Not really. Look."

On the screen, the bugs had lined up in a row and stood up on their hind legs. In unison, they waved at the camera, before springing into the air and hovering in place as they spelled out 'gotcha'. Mallory stared at the bugs for a moment with her mouth wide open. Slowly, her mouth closed and her surprise was replaced with complete and total fury. The bugs disappeared to the sound of Kean laughing maniacally.

"Who's creeped out now, Mal?"

Mallory glared at Kean, and for a moment it looked like she was about to jump at Kean and pound the smile off of his face. Somehow Mallory kept her composure and kept herself from attacking Kean. Instead, she grabbed her coat and stormed out of the building.

"She's really mad, Kean." Robert observed.

"I know. I kinda guessed that she would freak out if I did that."

"But you did it anyway?"

"It was pretty funny. Better than the time she glued my shoelaces so I couldn't take off my runners at the bowling alley a couple of weeks ago."

"Oh, I had forgotten about that."

"I didn't. I think this makes us even."

Heisenberg turned television off. "I wouldn't congratulate yourself just yet, my boy."

"Why not?"

"2 things: you're in danger of missing your train back home, and I believe Mallory took your train tickets with her when she left. Best catch her or you'll be hitchhiking home."

The triumphant smile on Kean's face fell. Kean and Robert grabbed their coats and ran out the door.

Chapter 3

"You had to pull a revenge prank, didn't you? You couldn't have just let her win? She hates to lose." Robert grumbled as they hustled through the downtown streets to the subway station.

"Totally worth it." Kean replied, even as he dug under his clothes to scratch at the backlash-induced rash that was driving him nuts. "Yikes, this is awful. The backlash from that spell hit me immediately, and it's way worse than normal. It feels like there are tiny barbed mandibles nibbling on every inch of my skin."

"If we miss the train because Mallory won't give us the tickets back, you'll have a lot of time to deal with that rash as we wait for our parents to pick us up. Unless you have money for another pair of tickets, because I sure don't."

Kean's eyes widened at the prospect of being stuck in downtown Toronto, and he broke into a run. He rushed to the turnstile inside of the subway station, and looked around desperately for Mallory.

"Oh no, oh no, oh no" he chanted in a forlorn voice.

From behind the ticket booth, on the other side of the turnstile, Mallory stepped out into view.

"Well, well, well. If it isn't the merry prankster and his accomplice."

Robert protested. "Mallory, I didn't have anything to do with it. I swear. Please let me have my ticket."

Mallory examined Robert and nodded.

"I buy your story, bub. Here."

She reached over the turnstile and gave Robert the ticket. Robert snatched it and hurried through the turnstile and down the stairs.

"I'll see you down there" he shouted. "Well, I'll see at least one of you, anyway".

Mallory crossed her arms and smirked at Kean. "Anything you'd like to say, funny guy?"

Kean squirmed slightly and looked around the room, as if he was looking for some kind of way to escape apologizing. His hands kept digging and scratching at each new flare-up of the backlash itch.

"Looks like you're a little itchy there, K. Maybe that's your conscience bothering you."

"Argh, dangit. You win. I'm sorry. It was a mean joke to play. I shouldn't have done it, but you hurt my feelings by teasing me about being creeped out by your hair. I'm sorry."

"Sorry enough to do a little apology dance?"

Kean gritted his teeth. "Oh come on" he protested.

"Just a couple of minutes before the train shows up, Kean. Time to hurry up."

Slowly, Kean started to do a pathetic shuffling dance while mumbling "sorry" over and over again.

Mallory laughed out loud. "I didn't think you'd actually do that. Wow! Here, let's go."

Mallory popped the subway ticket into the turnstile and pulled Kean through. They dashed down the stairs and made it onto the train just before the doors closed.

The trip home was quick and quiet, despite the throng of people pressed into the subway car with them. They switched to a Go train for the longest leg of their journey, riding from Union Station to the rail station near the edge of Antler Branch where their parents would be waiting for them. The sleepiness brought on by the rhythm of the train made their goodbyes brief and muted when they made it to the end of the journey. They would all see each other the next day anyway, so there wasn't much reason for a goodbye that was longer than a grunt or a 'see ya'. The three friends went their separate ways, into the cars waiting to take them home for the night.

Mallory arrived home and went straight to the kitchen to help with dinner. Her mom had the majority of the meal finished, like she did every time Mallory had her co-op, but there were still places to be set and condiments to be brought out.

"Mom, why do we have honey mustard?"

Mrs. Davidson paused in the middle of pulling a casserole dish from the oven to look at her daughter.

"Excuse me, what?"

"Honey mustard. It's on the table every night. Right beside the ketchup and the good old regular mustard. But it never gets used. I don't like honey mustard. You don't like honey mustard. Why do we own it?"

"It's an option, Mallory, a simple part of the dining experience. You never know when we might have a new meal that would go fantastically with honey mustard."

"The bottle isn't even open. And we eat the same 5 meals every week."

"Please Mallory, don't exaggerate. I cook a variety of main courses."

Mrs. Davidson finished plating their meal of vegetarian lasagna and garden salad, and brought the plates over to the kitchen table.

"Sure, mom. Totally different every day of the week. You're like a celebrity chef, making up new and exciting recipes every day. My mom, Gordon Ramsey."

Mallory's mom snorted, a rare response for her. "Oh please. I couldn't curse like that pig, even if I wanted to. He's just rude."

Mallory smiled up at her mom, and they started to eat dinner.

"Hey mom, I just found out about a school trip this weekend?"

"Seems a little last minute."

"I know. Like I said I just found out about it today. The teachers must have messed the schedule up or something. Anyway, I think it's the kind of trip I should go on. You'll definitely want me to go."

"Oh I will, will I?"

Mallory gulped down a fork full of gooey pasta, cleared her mouth and launched into a sales pitch for the trip.

"We keep talking about the future and my plans for post-secondary education. This trip will let me tour the campus of Western University and give me the opportunity to put some serious thought into what my educational direction will be. There's no cost to the trip, other than my own food and drinks, and I'll be back home around dinner time on Saturday."

"And you think that I would happily sign off on this kind of excursion?"

Mallory's mom punctuated her question by putting an intensely cross look on her face. Mallory tried to get into her moms' good books by grabbing the nearly empty salad bowl off of the table and taking it to the sink to wash.

"Aw, come on mom. You know it's a good idea. I swear it's not my fault that you didn't know before today."

"Mallory, please be quiet for a moment. My mind is made up."

Mallory slowly rinsed out the salad bowl and pouted down into the sink. She didn't know what to try next.

"Oh Mallory, could you bring that piece of paper sitting on the counter over to me, please?"

Mallory resisted the urge to refuse and storm off to her room. She normally avoided any kind of teenage histrionics, but being thwarted in her attempt to investigate a magic mystery was really upsetting her. Mallory picked up the sheet from the counter and walked it over to her mom.

"Hmm. Is that the right one, I wonder? Could you read the subject of that letter and tell me what it is, Mallory?"

"How would you forget? There isn't another letter anywhere in the kitchen. Much less a signed one like this."

Mallory's response trailed off as she finally read the title of letter. It was an official school trip permission form, signed and dated by her mom. Mallory looked up at her mother in confusion. He mom smiled and snickered at her.

"Gotcha."

"Mom, that's mean."

"Just having a little fun with you, dear."

"Good thing I didn't freak out and get really upset."

"You're right, that is a good thing. Keep that in mind next time you feel like flipping out."

"I don't flip out, mom. And thanks. I'm really looking forward to this trip."

"I am too. It will be nice to see the campus with you."

Mallory froze in her tracks. "With me?"

"I'm coming along as a parent chaperone. I haven't been to western in years, and I'd love to see what they've done with the campus. And then we can look at some of the facilities together."

"I'm going on a school trip with my mom."

"No need to say it like it's a terminal condition, dear. I won't embarrass you, I promise. And I'm going to drive up by myself, so you can have all of that quality bus time with your peers."

Mallory rolled her eyes and resigned herself to the situation. "Fine. You can come."

"Why thank you so much for your permission, madam. Now finish cleaning up and we'll head out for a sundae. That is, we can go out as long as you're not too ashamed of having ice cream with your mommy."

"Mom, quit it. You're a pest."

Mallory's mom smirked. "I learn from you, dear" she said, as she leaned in and gave her daughter a kiss on the cheek.

Cleaning the kitchen took Mallory another 10 minutes, the whole process accelerated by the promise of a sweet sundae reward.

She bolted out to the car with her mom right behind her, and jumped into the driver's seat.

"Not yet, young lady. You won't start driver's education until the summer, and you haven't even passed your beginner's driving test."

Mallory climbed over the center console and flopped into the passenger seat.

"Kean's mom lets him practice drive sometimes."

"That's all well and good for them. I prefer to follow the rules. You'll have plenty of time to drive, Mallory."

They buckled in and drove to the Dairy Queen. Mallory considered ordering something small and responsible, but the lure of chocolate, caramel and sheer excess broke her willpower. She ordered a large, waffle bowl sundae, smothered in caramel sauce. Even the normally reserved Mrs. Davidson went wild and ordered a brownie earthquake sundae.

As they sat and enjoyed their massive desserts, Mallory looked at her mom and caught a brief moment of sadness cross her face.

"You're missing dad, aren't you?"

"A little bit. It's silly."

"Why?"

"Because he'll be home next Friday night, and the week after that he's in constituency and at home for the whole week."

"So? Doesn't mean you can't miss him right now."

"I'm usually made of much sterner stuff than this. But today…"

Mallory saw the blush of embarrassment cross her mother's face as her sentence trailed off, and Mallory couldn't resist trying to find out more.

"What's so special about today?"

"Nothing. It's silly."

"You said that already."

"Well I'm not a teenage girl – no offense – so there is no good reason why the anniversary of our first date should still mean anything to me."

"First date? Wow. That must have been 50 years ago."

Mal's mom scowled. "Was that for the teenage girl shot?"

"Yeah."

"It's just that we've been able to make our schedules work and find a way to be together on this anniversary for the last 10 years."

"He couldn't make it this time, though."

"No. There's an emergency caucus meeting over the proposed budget amendments, and he can't miss it."

Mallory dug into her sundae and thought for a moment.

"Dad's career must be hard on you sometimes."

The tight smile that quickly crossed her mom's face answered Mallory's question.

"Oh, there have been some hard times, sure. Campaign time is awful. He vanishes for 30 days straight, and the only time I see him is when he's asleep or walking out of the front door. After the election it's better, but there are still some unpleasant times. I can't imagine how I would have dealt with it when you were very young."

"I'm pretty proud of dad" Mallory announced into the bottom of her dessert.

"I know honey. So am I."

"Does he realize that?"

"He does."

They finished their desserts and drove home, quietly enjoying the love they shared for each other.

Chapter 4

Mallory disappeared down the stairs to her bedroom and pulled out her laptop from beneath her bed. She burrowed into the center of her pile of thick warm blankets and sheets as the laptop started up and logged in. Mallory checked her email and then logged into Facebook to look and see if anything interesting had been posted. She was shocked to see her entire front page taken up with an electronic battle royale.

The fight was taking place in the comments on a seemingly innocent status update posted by one of her classmates, Claudia: "So good to have good friends, and super psyched to go 2 movies with special someone". The first response from some girl named Isis denied that "Josh" would have anything to do with Claudia, and Claudia had fanned the flames by trying to deny that she had been talking about Josh, and defend the idea that he could be into her. Several comments down, 2 other students had accused Claudia of being two-faced and complaining about some of her friends behind their back. Mallory barely knew the girl from sharing a couple of classes together over the last 2 years, and she had no idea why Claudia would be the target of such and angry tirade. As the emotion in the thread had escalated, the participants had added to the drama by posting their reactions to their own statuses, and now there were half a dozen raging electronic feuds going on. Scrolling down through the comments, caught up in the emotion of the conflict, Mallory found a comment from Kean's cousin, Damien, defending Claudia while trying to calm everyone down.

Mallory was surprised to see a response from Kean below it. As far as she knew, Kean stayed away from Facebook and Twitter and any other social media site. He seemed to be more comfortable with people in person than he ever was with digital correspondence. This post was evidence that he was still lurking and watching anyway. Kean had tried to get his cousin to leave the comment thread alone and avoid the exploding drama, but Damien rebuffed him and lost his temper when another kid took a pot shot at Damien's "slutty girlfriend". The rest of the comments devolved into an obscenity-laced screaming fit, complete with threats of physical violence.

Mallory sighed and navigated away from Facebook. The last few months at school had been filled with gossip and rivalries and messy romances. All of her friends at school were discovering love and hormonal lust for the first time, and it was getting a little out of hand. She understood what they were going through, and if things had turned out differently, then she might have been just as swept up in secret crushes and dreams of her first make-out session. But the bond she had formed with Sterling had short circuited the normal romantic life of a 15-year-old. In that one moment of connection, when Sterling had done the Sharing with her and Kean, she had experienced a closeness with him that should have taken years of experience and communication to create. They had joined together at a fundamental emotional level, and that closeness was still with her, even though Sterling had vanished into the sky.

She wasn't really sure what to call the bond. It didn't feel like love, at least not as it was normally described. And it didn't seem to have any physical component, but whatever it was, it overwhelmed the fleeting attractions she had to any of the other students. Mallory looked back at the screen of her computer and realized that she was languidly scrolling through images of the starry night sky as she thought about Sterling, as if she might recognize the glimmer of the star that his world orbited around. "Well that's a good use of your time, chick. How many stars could there be?" she muttered to herself. Mallory clicked away from the astronomical photos and put away the computer for the night.

The next morning the three friends gathered in the high school parking lot and waited for the school bus to arrive. The other students trickled in, until all 20 of them were standing and shivering. The bus barreled into the parking lot at an alarming speed, then screeched to a halt a few feet away from the waiting crowd.

"Well that doesn't make me feel safe" Robert muttered.

"You can ride with my mom if you want, but we'll probably talk about you if you do" Mallory teased.

Robert grumbled wordlessly and took his place in the line to enter the bus. The line moved quickly as the kids stormed up the steps into the bus and rushed down the aisles to get to the most valuable seats. The two benches at the back were left vacant. They were normally reserved for the punks and thugs, but there were no anti-social types on this trip. Those kids weren't interested in a tour of a university.

Robert, Kean and Mallory took over three benches in the middle of the bus. Robert sat across the aisle from the other two, and leaned over to stay in the conversation.

"Do you plan to sit perched like that for the whole trip?" asked Kean.

"No. I have a few books to read. But I thought we should figure out a strategy for our investigation."

"We won't be able to just roam around campus on our own."

Mallory frowned. "Why not?"

"Because there will be a tour guide with us. That's what Robert said."

"It's true. The group will get split up according to area of study interest, and each mini-group will have a guide to take them to the appropriate faculty."

"How do you know?"

"Read the website."

"So what are we going to do?" Kean asked.

"Dunno. Find the mysterious artifact, try to get a good look at it, and shut it off, I guess."

"Probably won't be that easy, Mal."

"I didn't say it was an easy plan. If you have a better idea, let's hear it."

"We don't really know where it is, do we?"

"Mister Website, do you have that info?"

Robert pulled out his smartphone. "I don't see anything on the website. Maybe it's not a big enough deal."

"It's a lost treasure from the bottom of the sea. How is it even possible that it's not being publicized?"

A new voice popped up in the middle of the conversation. "Publicity? For what? Is it something gossipy? I love to read up on celebrity gossip!"

Paula was standing in the aisle, between all three of the mages. She looked determined to join the conversation. Paula leaned towards Mallory, and Mallory moved back from the edge of the seat to get away from her. Paula swooped in and sat in the vacated seat.

"Thanks! So what are you guys talking about?"

Kean responded. "Uh, nothing much. Just the tour. Why is Damien all the way up at the front without you?"

"Oh, you know your cousin Damien. The moment the bus started, he pulled out his headphones and his iPad and started playing games. I tried to keep the conversation going but he was stuck in his video games. He's a great boyfriend but a lousy travelling companion. So, I thought I'd come back here and talk with you guys. Did you see the Bachelor last night?"

Mallory rolled her eyes. "I don't watch reality shows."

"Why not? They're awesome. So full of drama and emotion. And it's real people, you know? Not some stupid script telling them what to do."

Kean and Robert quickly looked away and dug through their backpacks to find some kind of excuse to leave the conversation. Mallory looked at them helplessly as Paula kept nattering on about her favourite shows.

"The ones with competitions are good, usually, but sometimes it gets boring if no one fights about it. I really like the ones that are all about romance. The last season of Big Brother had this couple who were so much like me and Damien. So Romeo and Juliet."

"Are you sure about that? You know Romeo and Juliet die in the end of the play, right?"

"Oh, why focus on the negative details. The love is the important part, Mallory."

Mallory silently cursed herself for responding to Paula's comments. She needed some way to politely tune Paula out, or the bus ride was going to drive her crazy. She looked over to Kean again, and shot him a dirty look for being blissfully involved in reading a book. The slight smile that crept over his face confirmed that he was letting her take the brunt of Paula's insatiable conversing, and he was laughing about it.

"You know, Paula, Kean was talking about Damien the other day. About the stuff they did on summer vacation last year. When they went on that camping trip. I bet they shared a lot of secret stuff. Feelings about life, and love. The really personal stuff that guys can only share with their close family members."

"Really? What kind of stuff?"

"Oh I couldn't break that confidence. Kean wouldn't even tell me the whole story, but there was a lot of talk of true love and future plans and the kind of girl Damien wants to marry. I better stop. I've said too much. Forget I said anything."

Paula took off like a shot, crossing the aisle and thumping down into the seat beside Kean. He tried to ignore her but the unstoppable stream of questions couldn't be avoided. Mallory chuckled, put in her earphones and closed her eyes as the music filled her ears. She gave Kean one last thumbs up in response to the scowl he was sending her way, and Mal slipped into a semi-conscious state of relaxation.

An hour later, the final track of the album faded out into silence, and Mallory opened her eyes. Up front, Paula was back in her seat and looked to be in the middle of a very heated argument with Damien. Even the teacher was looking over in alarm, perhaps debating whether or not she should step in and break the fight up. Paula gestured angrily and pointed right at Mallory. Mal pulled out her earphones to try and hear what Paula was shouting, but, even without the earphones impedance, she could only make out a fraction of the garbled words of the upset girl. Paula stopped shouting and stormed away from Damien, going as far away as she could from him without coming any closer to Mallory.

Mallory went over to Kean's seat and asked him to explain. From the look on Kean's face, it was apparent that he hadn't enjoyed his chat with Paula.

"Hey look Kean. Sorry about sending her over here, but she was driving me crazy. I owe you one."

"Look, I know she's a pain but that was a really terrible idea. You made her think that Damien was talking about some other girl to me, and I was keeping it a secret. I couldn't convince her that you made it all up and I didn't know anything. And when she got frustrated with my answers, she stormed up to the front and started yelling at Damien. For 20 minutes. And he just kept taking it and apologizing."

Mallory felt her jaw tighten up with embarrassment and guilt. Her pride tried to wire her mouth shut, but she forced it open and apologized to Kean.

"You know I didn't want that to happen. I didn't think Paula was that easily upset."

"Well she is. Damien has told me a few times that he has little fights with her all the time. I didn't know it was like this. I wish he'd just stop letting people hurt him."

"People?" Mallory asked.

Kean shook his head and slumped back into the seat. "Never mind. I think Paula's calmed down now. You probably shouldn't talk to her for a while. She was blaming you."

Mallory looked up at the front of the bus. Paula was staring out the bus window and frowning furiously, as if the farms passing by were her mortal enemies. Her dark brown bob haircut and oversized glasses gave her a cuteness that weakened her look of righteous anger. And her pastel cardigans, zany headbands, and scuffed up flats with a pink ribbon on each shoe only made the cute worse. Mallory just couldn't take her seriously.

"I thought she was just a boring motormouth, but who knew she was crazy too? I blame the reality television industry. It teaches girls to lose their mind without any caution or restraint. They've only been dating, what, a month?"

"Actually, 5."

"Wow, really? Still, not a reasonable reaction. Do you think I should go apologize to her? Would that make you feel better?"

"It's not about me, Mal. It's Damien I'm worried about. And you'll only make the fight start back up again if you try to fix it. Let it go."

Mallory went back to her seat dejectedly. Kean wasn't normally so glum. He could take almost any situation and find a way to look for the bright side, but this fight seemed to have overwhelmed his optimism. She watched Kean stare off into space for a while, until the bus intercom crackled to life. "Rest stop in 5 minutes" the disembodied electronic voice of the driver announced.

The bus pulled into the exit lane to the rest stop, still moving at a frightening rate of speed. Mallory and Kean exchanged worried looks as the bus barreled towards the sharp turn into the parking lot, and Robert squeezed his eyes shut and held on tight to the seat in front of him. Despite the feeling of certain doom, the bus safely negotiated the turn and lurched to a stop moments later. As they walked off of the bus, Mallory gave the dirtiest look she could to the grizzled old driver. The driver gave a gurgled burp as a response before shutting the bus door.

The herd of teens swarmed into the rest stop. A big chunk of the herd broke off and hurried to the washrooms. Most of the others dashed off towards the 4 different fast food stands, with a few sauntering over to the two pinball machines tucked away in the corner of the eating area. Mallory's mom stepped through the doors and stood with the three friends.

"How's the trip so far, guys?"

The three of them looked at each other and shrugged. "Good, I guess." Robert answered.

"Good to hear. I'm going to go grab a seat. Mallory, could you buy a coffee for me when you get yours, please?"

"What if I'm not getting a coffee?" she countered.

Mrs. Davidson's eyebrows rose up. "Then I would be very surprised. You lobbied quite energetically for the freedom to have coffee. It was the great 'Winter coffee protest'."

"Mom, quit it. You're so dramatic."

Mallory's mom laughed. "You would know, dear."

The three friends walked over to the line-up at the Time Horton's counter, and waited patiently for their turn to order. Stuck behind an old lady with a complaint about the heat of her coffee, they stood restlessly waiting for their turn. Mallory winced and loudly exhaled.

"Mal, are you okay?" Kean asked.

"Yeah. Ug." Mallory scowled as she replied.

"Are you sure? You look uncomfortable?"

"Trust me I'm fine."

Robert joined in. "He's right. It looks like you're in some kind of pain."

"What's going on, Mal?"

"I'm fine. It's just cramps."

A moment passed as Kean and Robert exchanged looks and tried to puzzle out what Mallory was talking about. Kean figured it out first and he blushed furiously. Robert caught on a second later and blurted out "GROSS!"

"It's not gross, it's nature you idiot."

"But why did you tell us?" Robert whined.

"Because you kept asking!"

"Still, you didn't have to say it. I didn't need to know THAT. You could have said you had an upset stomach or something."

"I don't see a point in lying. My period started this morning and now I have cramps."

"Oh man!" Robert said in disgust, while Kean turned an even deeper shade of pink and tried to disappear.

"The two of you need to grow up. If you're ever lucky enough to find a girl who will date you, she's going to have ovaries and she's going to go through the same thing, and I assure you she'll dump you on your butt if you react like this."

Mallory glowered at the two boys, with a stare that dared them to continue the argument. A moment of silence passed. Mallory released them from her stare, only to notice that the old lady in front of them had turned around and was watching them with a look of shocked indignation on her face. The old lady shook her head, picked up her coffee, and left in a hurry.

"Well, at least the sped the line up." Mallory muttered.

The three friends ordered their drinks. Kean and Robert tried to avoid eye contact with any other human being, while Mallory watched them in disbelief. "Boys" she grumbled. The cashier handed their drinks over to them, and they went over to an empty table in the middle of eating area.

"Are the two of you going to stare at your coffees like your life depends on it for the rest of the trip, or will you get over your embarrassment and start acting normally" Mallory said with a scowl on her face.

Kean pulled his eyes away from his obviously fascinating cup lid, to look Mallory directly in the eyes. "Sorry, Mal. I was being dumb."

"It's okay. I just can't have my best friends getting all wierded out because of my biology."

"We're your best friends?" Robert asked, still enraptured by his hot chocolate.

"Pretty much."

Robert smiled. "Huh. Cool."

Kean pointed discretely in the direction of the Burger King counter. "Did you guys notice that?"

Mallory and Robert looked over at the two people standing behind the counter. The cashier was an older woman, heavy-set and miserable while she muttered the current customer's order into the microphone. The other staff member was a young man with long brown hair tied back in a ponytail. He was standing at the soda dispenser, filling drinks and staring off into the distance. Mallory switched over to magesight and saw that the soda guy had the gift.

"He's a mage."

"Not yet. Look at his aura closely. It's got that muted colour to it, like his magic is beneath the surface. He's still asleep."

A sleeper was anyone who had magical potential but was still unaware of it. There had been many long conversations at the tea shop about sleepers: how many there might be, and how many of them would eventually wake up to their powers. It was always a shock to find another potential spellcaster. From day to day, the three friends felt like they were a part of a very special group that didn't have any members outside of the walls of the tea shop. Encountering a new mage in the wild ruined the illusion of being the only mages in the world.

"I wish we could go talk to him" Robert said. He still remembered how confused and frightened he had been when his magic had become active and he had been caught in the effects of his spell gone terribly wrong.

Kean shook his head. "You know that's a bad idea. Heisenberg said that we have to leave them alone. There's no safe way to push someone into discovering their gift."

"That's what he says, but it's not like he has proof. It's all guessing, right?" Mallory said.

"I think it's a good idea to play it safe. Besides, I wouldn't even know what to tell him. How would you react if a strange high school kid came up to you and told you that you could fly?"

"I'd think he was crazy. Hey, do you think we could fly?"

Robert shuddered. "The backlash would be incredibly bad."

"You're a spoilsport, Rob-o."

A bellowing voice from the entrance doorway startled the three friends. "All students to the bus now-bus leaves in 5 minutes" shouted the surly bus driver. As soon as the last word was past his lips, he turned and stormed out of the building.

"I guess we better get going. Lucky I already went to the bathroom" Kean said.

"Isn't there a bathroom at the back of the bus?" Robert asked.

Mallory warned him off with a shake of her head. "You don't want to go in there. Trust me. The smell convinced me to hold it until we got here."

"But what if we had driven straight through?"

"I was willing to risk the chance of bladder explosion."

The three friends polished off their drinks and rushed back out to the bus for the last leg of their journey.

Chapter 5

The last hour of the trip took them through the varied landscapes of Southwestern Ontario. Large swatches of farm land blended into quaint rural villages and then abruptly transitioned into the industrial monoliths of the automobile factories, before switching back to the countryside view. Faded hand-painted signs left over from last fall dotted the side of the highway, advertising the wide variety of produce grown throughout the fertile region. The diversity of biology was mirrored by the demographics and culture of the area. Entering the outskirts of London they could see the peaks of church steeples that were poking up into the sky, in the same neighbourhood as the top of the rounded roof of a mosque. Within a 5 block stretch, Mallory saw a handful of Polish, Vietnamese, and Colombian businesses and restaurants, all side by side.

As the bus moved through the city towards the university, the multicultural aspect became less obvious, and the distinct culture of the city faded into the vibrancy and temporary chaos of the student population. The throngs of students filled the sidewalks with a constant casual motion. None of the students seemed to be in a particular hurry, either to get to class, or to leave campus. The bus passed through the university gates and wound its way though campus. The massive residences flanking the road ended at the small steel bridge, a bridge that spanned over a vestigial creek bed. As the bus sat at the red light just on the other side of the bridge, Mallory studied the buildings rising up in the distance. She could just make out the sign in front of the building directly across the street: "Talbot College: Faculty of Music".

Talbot College sat at the bottom of a hill, with the majority of the campus buildings sitting on top of the hill. At the crest of the hill, the university's iconic tower rose up into the sky. The Canadian flag flying above the University College tower snapped erratically in the cold, gusting wind. The bus continued along the narrow campus road until it pulled into the parking lot behind the University Community Centre. As if on cue, fat raindrops started to splat against the windows of the bus.

The bus driver shouted out an order as he slammed opened the door.

"Everybody off!"

The kids all hesitated to leave the relative comfort and warmth of the bus for the blustery rain outside, but another shout from the driver jarred them into action. As she stepped off of the bus, Mallory saw her mother standing a few feet away, scowling underneath her umbrella as the rain blew in.

"Come on you three-follow me."

Mallory, Kean and Robert followed behind Mrs. Davidson as she shuffled quickly towards the grey building in front of them. The heavy, brown metal doors creaked loudly as she opened them up and stepped inside. The door closed behind them and they stood for a moment to gather their senses and wait for the shivering to pass.

"Would it be too much to ask to have a nice spring day for a trip like this?" Mrs. Davidson asked.

"Technically, it's still winter." Robert said.

Mrs. Davidson gave Robert a sour look, and then she led them off down the hallway.

"I haven't been here for quite a long time, but I believe I can still navigate us to the atrium. So many changes. I guess time has really moved on."

"You met dad here, right?"

"Technically, yes, but that was only in passing. We were both at the same international law seminar. He stole my coke."

"Why would you remember that?"

"Because I cussed him out for doing so. My, did he blush and stammer when I tore into him. He was very cute, which made me all the more angry at him. How dare he be so cute when he clearly has no respect for me and my beverage needs?"

"Mom, you're ridiculous." Mallory complained.

Kean and Robert snickered, and Mrs. Davidson joined in, turning the snickering into full-fledged laughter.

"My darling daughter, it's the ridiculous moments that you should treasure. There will be more than enough of the ordinary and unmemorable moments in your life. A life well led has a bounty of nonsense and wonder."

"What has gotten into you, mom?"

"Just feeling nostalgic, Mallory. It's what us old folks do."

After a few wrong turns and an unnecessary trip up and down the stairs, they finally arrived in the UCC atrium. The skylight 3 floors above provided almost no light, as the thick bank of storm clouds now filled the sky. All around them, the swirling detritus of student life tucked in to every corner and across the floor. Flyers advertising a seemingly limitless number of events, concerts, lectures, and pub nights covered the designated poster boards, as well as every inch of the support pillars that ringed the room. Off to the right, the Spoke tavern had its large barn door entrance closed. To their left, the food court was sparsely occupied by the students unlucky enough to have a full Saturday on campus. The rest of the field trip group was already seated in the food court. The three friends sat down amongst their classmates. Mallory made sure to sit as far away as she could from Paula. From what she could see, the fight between Paula and Damien was cooling off, and they were approaching reconciliation. Mallory hoped that they would make up and things would stay calm for the rest of the day.

An energetic blond girl in purple and grey sweats bounced up to their tables and announced herself.

"Hi everyone! My name is Kim, and I'm the lead tour guide for today. Since there are a lot of you, we'll be breaking you into groups of 4 or 5, and each group will have their own guide. All of the guides, including me, are current students, and we'll be able to give you a really honest look into campus life. We're going to split you up according to your faculties of interest, so think about which faculty you'd like to tour and we'll get the process underway."

Kean muttered to Mallory and Robert. "Any clue on which faculty is holding the artifact?"

"History? That's a faculty right?" Mallory responded.

"I'm not sure. Hold on." Robert answered before hurrying out of the group. He walked over to the counter of the student union service desk, and grabbed a course guide. Robert tried to sneak back into the group unnoticed, but Kim dashed that plan.

"Just as a reminder for everyone-please stay with your group at all times, and let your guide know if you need anything. I'd be happy to answer any questions you have, but I can't move things along if I'm chasing after strays."

Kim had a bright smile on her face, but the angry glint in her eye sent Robert into a fit of embarrassment. He slouched down behind Kean and Mallory, hoping to disappear.

"She's not somebody to mess with, is she?" Mallory said.

"Nope. Hope she's not our guide."

From behind Kean and Mallory, Robert's voice peeped up. "History isn't a faculty all by itself. It's a part of social studies."

"What else is in social studies, mysterious voice?"

"A number of programs that I'm not going to tell you, Ms. Funnypants."

"Okay, but if we end up in Paula's group and she gets upset again, I'm going to tell her you have something to tell her."

"Please leave Paula alone, Mal" Kean pleaded.

"Okay, okay. Just kidding. So we're going to social science, then?"

"I think so."

As Kim droned on about the student's council, the two restaurants in the UCC and the exercise facilities, Kean looked around the room and wondered about life after high school. He didn't have a direction in mind. Maybe he'd go to university or college, but he wondered if it might be a good idea to take a year off from school and get some experience living a normal life.

And knowing that there wasn't going to be a course on applied magic use meant he wouldn't be studying the one topic that really fascinated him.

"Time to divide into faculty groups and get going. Sid here will be leading the science group, Amy will lead Arts and Humanities, and I'll be in charge of the Social Science group. Line-up by your tour guide, everyone!"

All three of the friends groaned at the discovery that Kim would be their tour guide. They groaned even more loudly when Paula and Damien moved over to stand behind Kim.

"We'll never get a chance to investigate anything with this bunch watching us" Mallory whined.

"Not much choice, Mal" Kean responded.

The three friends shuffled over slowly towards the Social science group. Mallory focused on looking off into the distance and not at Paula. Robert was the last to approach the group, and his attention was drawn by a colourful poster on a nearby pillar. He stopped and read the event announcement. As he realized what he was reading, he shouted out to the guides.

"What about Information and Media Studies? That's the faculty I want to find out about."

Kim frowned. "FIMS isn't a part of the tour. It's a smaller faculty and it doesn't have a lot of general appeal. We only go to the most popular faculties. We don't have time or the volunteers to go to every building on campus."

"But I'm considering enrolling in the technoculture program, and I'd really like to see the building."

Mallory muttered to Kean. "Is that a real program?"

Kean muttered back. "I guess so. We should back Robert up on this."

Mallory stepped forward and spoke up. "That's the one I want to tour too."

Kim looked suspiciously from Robert to Mallory and back. "Oh really? And what program are you interested in?"

Mallory looked at Robert, silently pleading for a hint. Robert quickly gathered a ball of spell energy and cast a spell to control the scrolling electronic text board that was hung above the entrance behind him. The spell looked like a stream of neon numbers flickering and twisting around itself, still adhering to a linear path but moving organically at the same time. It met the junction point between the Ethernet cable and the port and the spell slipped inside the device. The other end of the spell stayed anchored to Robert's fingers, like the string of a marionette, and his fingers twitched and moved as he took control of the board. He tipped his head back at the sign to signal Mallory to look at it. The message stream flickered and changed from an announcement about academic counseling, to "Come see the magic of Journalism! Media and Information Sciences!" the word "journalism" flashed repeatedly, until Mallory nodded and blurted out "Journalism!"

Kim paused to consider the situation, before giving up the fight. "Fine by me!" she said with a forced smile on her face. "We can just move things around and do a little reconfiguring here. Amy, you're taking classes down at the FIMS building-can you take these two and anyone else who wants to go?"

Amy bounced up to the front of the group. "Sure! Glad to!"

"Are they all overly cheery? Is that a job requirement?" Mallory wondered out loud. Kean shushed her in response.

After gathering together the 2 other students who also wanted to see the faculty of Media and Information sciences, Amy made the final preparations for the tour.

"Now, our tour should take about an hour and a half, and that's going to include a short break about halfway through. We're going to be doing a fair bit of walking, so I hope you brought some comfy shoes. And Ms. Davidson, are you planning to come with us on the tour? Some parents like to join the tour, while others prefer to go do a little shopping while we're having our hike and talk."

Mallory's mom answered. "I think I'll amuse myself."

"Great! Here's a card with my cell phone number on it, just in case you need to get a hold of us while we're walking about. And Mallory, do you have a cellphone?"

"Yup."

"Okay, so we'll give you a call when the tour is almost done and we'll meet you back here. Sound good, Ms. Davidson?"

"That's fine, Amy. Have fun, everyone."

The kids fell in line behind Amy. The first surprise of the tour was a sudden change in direction. Instead of walking out the front doors of the UCC, they went down a nearby set of stairs.

"Come on, guys. We're going to go on an underground adventure!"

"We're right behind her-why is she yelling?" Kean muttered to Mallory.

"Too much school spirit? Maybe she gets paid more for volume?"

They rushed to keep up with Amy as she disappeared down the stairs and through a double set of brown metal doors. The tunnel on the other side of the doors was only semi-submerged, dark on the left side but weakly illuminated on the right hand side by a series of short windows at the top of the wall. The dim light gave the amber colour of the walls a sickly yellowish tint, and the florescent lighting flickering above injected a faint blue into the colour palette.

The tunnel took them from the UCC to the basement of the Social Sciences building. They emerged from the tunnel into a milling crowd of people waiting for their turn to buy coffee and food from the 2 tiny, competing coffee shops in the room.

Mallory asked why there were 2 coffee shops here when there was one back in the UCC.

"The students love coffee! And there are a lot of us here, so the rush to get a coffee before class starts is pretty impressive.

There's some kind of coffee shop or cafeteria in almost every building on campus. They're not all open all the time, but chances are pretty good that you can get a cup when you need one."

After weaving their way through the line, Amy led them into another tunnel. This one was narrow, with barely enough room to allow all three kids to walk beside each other.

Robert let out a noisy sigh."You know, I don't like tunnels. Not at all."

"I know. Bad memories. Are you going to be okay?' Kean asked.

"Yes. But if we end up in an abandoned unfinished area, I'm running for the nearest door."

Kean, Mallory and Robert sank into a grim silence as they all relived the fearful trips through the subway tunnels on their way to the confrontation with Herlech. The look that passed between the three friends confirmed that Robert wouldn't be the only one to freak out.

Amy resumed her tour guide narration as they left the smaller tunnel.

"And now we're in one of the oldest buildings on campus-University College. It was one of the first 4 buildings that were constructed back in 1867, as the arts building. English, French, Drama, are all taught here. There's a large performance space that's used by the Drama students to stage our award-winning productions. And no, there isn't a Tim Hortons in this one. Here's the performance space."

The massive room with giant floor to ceiling windows in the east wall was so much more impressive than a simple performance space. It was like stepping foot into a cathedral of polished wood and glorious light. Having just left the dim artificial lights of the underground paths, the kids were dazzled by the intensity of the sunlight that was breaking through the cloud cover to illuminate the room.

Robert walked into the center of the room and slowly rotated around to view the full panorama. Mallory dashed up onto the stage at the south end of the room, and she marched up and down the stage floor with deliberate footsteps that echoed throughout the space. Kean smiled as he watched his two friends interact with this new and awe-inspiring venue. Amy gave them a few minutes to enjoy the room, while she checked her iPhone for new messages. After that pause, she clapped her hands and announced their next destination.

"Off we go to Natural Science!"

Dropping back into the subterranean tunnels after being bathed in sunlight was a bit of a shock. They squinted and blinked their eyes to adjust to the light level in the new tunnel. The tunnel on the way to University College had been marked with posters, graffiti and other signs of human life, but this tunnel was strangely clean and sterile. Halfway through the tunnel, a massive gust of warm air buffeted the group.

"I love that feeling" Amy exclaimed. "We're passing right by the physical plant. It generates high pressure steam and chilled water for the entire campus, and when the ventilation system kicks in, the warm air comes blasting through here. It's like standing in front of a giant hairdryer. Fantastic on a rainy day."

The next stop on their tour was a quick one. Amy walked them though a geology classroom and pointed out the racks of mineral samples that filled the back third of the room.

"Some of that stuff's radioactive too, but don't worry, we won't be here that long."

The last one out of the room was Robert, who hung at the doorway and looked back at the racks with longing in his eyes. "Can't we spend a little time looking at the samples?"

"Well, we could, but that would mean we'd have to skip the trip to the media studies building."

"Robert, come on. That's what we came here to see-remember?" Mallory said, giving Robert a stern look.

"Okay, but if we have time, I want to come back here."

"Fine, Robert. Whatever."

"So it's decided? Great! Let's Go!" Amy said.

Chapter 6

A short tunnel took them from Natural science to the Chemistry building, and then on to Middlesex college.

"Mostly math classes here. Some English too." Amy explained as they transitioned into yet another tunnel. "Almost there-this is the last one before our destination"

The final tunnel sloped downwards, and twisted back and forth in a zig-zag unlike any of the other tunnels. It ended in a wide open space and a set of large double doors that opened slowly when Amy pressed the button. When they stepped through the doors and into the media building, all three of them could see the reason for the tunnels strange construction. They had travelled down a steep hill, from the top of the hill at Middlesex College, down underneath the road and across, and now they were standing in another giant edifice. Unlike the natural and historic feeling of the University College hall, this building spoke of modern design and new ideas. Geometric designs and glass and steel building materials gave the shape to the multistory open atrium. A constant thrum of moving air filled the background noise.

"This is officially named the North Campus Building, which is very uncreative for a university, if you ask me. Within this building, the FIMS faculty has programs for journalism, media studies, and information sciences. This is where you come to learn to be a librarian, but that's a graduate program."

"That's really interesting. Is there a pop music program-"

"How about the new exhibit?" Mallory interjected.

Amy turned and looked at Mallory. "I'm not sure that there is an exhibit here. It's not normally a place where anything is put on public display. But I can find out!"

Amy stepped away from the group and made a phone call. Robert complained to Mallory.

"You didn't have to interrupt me. I was going to get her to take us to the artifact."

"We only have a little bit of time left before we have to head back, Robert. We don't have time to take the long way."

"It would be nice if once and a while I could be in charge of how we do things, you know."

Mallory glared at Robert, before noticing that Kean was nodding in agreement with Robert. She took in a deep breath of air and apologized.

"Sorry Robert. I can be a little bossy when I'm trying to get something done."

"I've noticed."

Mallory gave him another glare, this time playfully, and she punched him in the shoulder. Amy stepped back into the group and clapped her hands.

"You are totally right, Mallory. There is a new exhibit on the third floor. It's some kind of artifact on loan from the National Archaeological Museum of Athens, and it's being studied by the physics department."

"Why is in the media building, then?" asked Kean.

"Don't know for sure. They have it in the satellite broadcasting room, so maybe it's being monitored by some other far away university. Anyway, it's all the way up at the top of the stairs. We have just enough time to go up and see it before we need to head back to your mom."

"Hey Robert, how'd you know the exhibit was here?" Kean quietly asked.

"Poster in the UCC. There was some kind of multimedia presentation happening here, and one of the topics was the device. There was a low resolution picture of the Antikythera device, but I recognized it immediately. It was lucky that I noticed it before we went off with the wrong group."

"Good work, buddy."

They stepped onto the grey concrete staircase that dominated the right-hand wall of the interior space. The echoes of noise from all over the building rose up with them, and the thrum of air and water being forcefully pumped through unseen mechanisms.

"What is that noise, Amy?" Mallory asked.

"It's the heating and cooling system. The passive water-based system keeps the building at a constant temperature and saves an enormous amount of energy. It's a little loud, and it doesn't change temperature quickly, so most people here bring a sweater with them when the weather changes suddenly."

"It's like standing near a waterfall that's just out of sight. It must get pretty annoying if you're trying to study."

"They probably just tune it out" Kean said.

The noise surrounded them when they reached the top of the staircase, and they hurried out of the open space to leave the sound on the other side of the doors to the hallway. Robert sighed in relief as the doors closed and blocked the noise.

"Hey Robert, are you okay? Looking a little pale." Mallory asked.

"I am. Things were a little too noisy out there. A lot of interference." He answered purposefully, making eye contact with Mallory and showing her the digitized glow of his eyes for a moment before blinking them away.

Mallory frowned with a look of confusion on her face. "I thought sound didn't bother you that way."

"It doesn't, but that noise was making it more difficult to focus while I was looking around."

"What are you talking about, guys?" Amy asked. Mallory and Robert had forgotten that Amy was listening to them, and both of them were at a loss to explain what they were talking about.

"Migraines!" Kean blurted out. "Robert gets migraines occasionally, and sometimes bright light or loud noise can trigger one, I think. Right Robert?"

"Umm, yeah. Migraines" Robert mumbled.

"So where's the exhibit, Amy?"

Amy took a moment to consider the explanation given to her. "Do you need to have a rest, Robert?"

"Uh, no no. I'm fine, just fine. Can we see the exhibit now, please?"

The long red hallway branched off at regular intervals to lead to small classrooms and offices, and near the end of the hall they turned down one of the offshoots. The room at the end was different from the other classrooms. Thick blue fabric was draped on 3 of the walls, and a small wide door closed off a cage full of electronic equipment on the remaining wall. Neatly bundled black cables ran from the electronics to a control console near the door, and from there the wires spread out to the cameras and microphones placed throughout the room. A massive LED screen hung suspended from the ceiling, and it displayed the image of small pedestal with the artifact sitting on top of it. The three friends stopped and stared at the artifact.

"It's beautiful" Mallory whispered, and Robert and Kean both nodded in agreement. All three saw the artifact surrounded by dazzling display of magelight that moved around in a pattern that was somehow geometric and organic, designed and chaotic. The Antikythera device was magically powered and pulsing with potential energy. Despite what they had believed before, that magical artifacts could not exist, there was proof in front of them that you could bind a spell within a machine.

"Can we see it in person? This isn't the only part of the display, is it Amy?" Robert asked anxiously.

From the depths of the equipment cage an older male voice responded. "Hey you kids keep yer hands off my project!"

Robert jumped back from the video screen and looked around the room. Mallory and Kean looked to Amy for some kind of explanation, but she was silent and unhelpful. The grumbling voice from within the cage came closer and the man behind the voice stepped into the room. He was tall and thin, with a greying ponytail and a set of wireless rimmed glasses slipping halfway down his nose. He walked towards them, jabbing his index finger at Robert as he advanced.

"Do you think we let any runny-nosed smart-alec kid come in here and get their hands on a historical artifact like that? You'd probably try to steal it, or cover it in graffiti. Lousy kids!"

The distance between the grumpy academic hippie and Robert narrowed, and Robert started to lean back in fear of what was going to happen. The hippie stopped his advance just before his finger poked the tip of Robert's nose, and the man let out a cackling giggle.

"Hoo-eee! You are one gullible dude. You should see your face, man. Professor Dondallo, at your service."

The sudden shift in Professor Dondallo's behaviour caught all of them off-guard. Even Amy the ever-cheery tour guide looked uncertain and uneasy. Kean looked at everyone else in the room and decided to take the lead. He stepped forward and shook the professor's extended hand.

"Hi Professor. Nice to meet you. We're touring the university and we noticed a poster mentioning a new artifact being displayed here. We're just starting a project on ancient Greek engineering, which is why it would be great to see the Antikythera mechanism."

"Really? Gotta give you kids bonus points for being informed. Old Greek gizmos are pretty obscure- wouldn't expect someone of your age to know anything about it. I wish I could show it to you in person, but it's a no-go. Safety issues."

"Safety? What could be unsafe about a rusty old gearbox?" Mallory questioned.

"First off, it's not rusty. Second of all, it's generating some kind of radiation. And radiation means hands off for the general public."

"Some kind of radiation? You don't know what kind? How is that possible?"

Kean winced at Mallory's question: she was very close to the line between inquisitive and rude. He prepared himself to step in and do some damage control, but Professor Dondallo laughed as he answered her.

"I know, right? It's crazy. The radiation changes intermittently, switching intensity and type without any warning. And get this-it stops radiating if someone walks into the room and can see it. So the only way we can study it is remotely."

"That's astounding." Robert exclaimed. "It reacts to direct observation?"

"Yep. It would be a world-changing discovery, if it emitted anything stronger than a tiny flux. Even when it goes into overdrive, the output is barely measurable. There's a chance that it might do more than that, and maybe by studying it for a long enough period of time, we'll get some insight into what it's doing any why it acts that way."

"So it doesn't really do anything, and it stops doing whatever it does do when a person sees it, but we can't see it because it's not safe?" Mallory asked. Her arms were crossed and she was tapping her foot impatiently.

The professor shrugged. "That's about it. Safety regulations. And there's the added bonus of you being underage non-students. Way too risky to let you get near it. But trust me, anything you could learn from it you can learn by watching the webcast."

Professor Dondallo turned away from the kids and went back to the equipment cage. Amy clapped her hands, startling the group.

"Well, that was really interesting, but we should keep moving."

Mallory and Kean looked at each other and silently decided who would take the lead. They needed to stay behind and ask the professor some questions. Robert was staring at the lcd screen, too enraptured by the broadcast to help in the subterfuge. Mallory kept her eyes locked on Kean and nodded her head at Amy. Kean shook his head to refuse the direction a couple of times, but the insistent gleam in Mal's eyes forced him to relent. He gave a shrug and exhaled noisily before walking over to Amy.

He put his hand gently on Amy's forearm and talked softly to her. "Amy, is there any way we can spend a few more minutes in here?"

Amy pulled her arm away reflexively and stepped back from Kean.

"We'll take a 10 minute break now, and then we can continue with the tour. And I think it might be a good idea to review the university's harassment policies at that time."

Kean blushed and tried to stammer out an apology as Amy quickly left the room with the other students following her out. Mallory waited until they were gone.

"Not the smoothest technique, Cassanova, but it'll do the trick."

"Mallory, that was terrible. I wasn't trying to flirt with her I swear! I just wanted to connect with her."

"Oh I'd say you connected alright."

The professor piped up from his unseen spot in the cage. "I've been there, dude. Touching is a no go here, unless you get clear permission beforehand. And try to get it in writing just in case."

"Are you kidding?" Mallory asked.

"Kinda."

"Can we ask you a few questions about the artifact, professor?"

The professor stepped back out into the room and brushed the wispy stray hairs from his eyes. "Sure thing."

"Why is the artifact here? Shouldn't it be in a science lab or something?"

"Originally it was coming here to be studying by the engineering meatheads, and get displayed for the high school kids like you guys. But that was before we knew what we were actually getting. The mechanism was supposed to be broken and severely corroded, but when it arrived on campus, it was perfectly intact. Turns out there were two copies: one that was ruined and this one that was fine. Must have been a real language barrier issue between the museum in Athens and the engineers. So when they opened up the packing crate, they found this gleaming creature inside of it, and they rushed it off to the secure vault in the library of all places."

"Why?"

"When the faculty heads got a look at the thing, they all wanted to have it in their building. Natural sciences, chemistry, engineering, even the business school tried to get their hands on it. They settled on the natural sciences building, because they already have an impressive display area and they need more public visibility. It was there for 1 night, and then they discovered that it was putting out random radiation."

Robert still stood transfixed by the video image, absorbing the information trickling through from the device. "How did they notice the radiation?"

"The display area is in the middle of a lab space, and one of the radiation monitors was left running by accident. When they saw the recorded output the next morning, the lab rats descended and started testing the thing. That's when they discovered that it goes inert under direct observation. That had them tearing their hair out for a few hours-those folks do not like irregular behaviour. One of them finally pieced it together and left the device unattended with an EMF meter. Voila! Strange EM waves."

Mallory interrupted. "Didn't you say it was emitting radiation?"

"Yeah, but that's a pretty big category. Radiation is the process of energetic particles or waves travelling through space. It can be the nasty kind from plutonium or x-rays, or it can be harmless radio waves. Even body heat is technically a type of radiation. So this thing emits electromagnetic waves, low-frequency, infrared, you name it. And it's always in tiny bursts of varying durations. The science guys are both thrilled and freaking out."

"So you're not a science guy?"

"Not really. I'm devoted to chasing information in many different directions at the same time. Started off with a dual undergrad degree in psychology and English, and then got a Masters in Library and Information sciences. Still wasn't done being a student, so I did my PhD in LIS and took a few journalism courses to follow it up. Now I teach in the Library and Information Services graduate program. I have some sciency stuff in my brain, but mostly I just like recording and tracking information."

"And how did you get the device moved to this building?"

"I just pointed out that they needed to observe it without interacting with it, so a remote lab site made sense. And since this building has the fastest, most kick butt internet connection, we could host the lab webcast for anyone across the world to see. That makes the other research facilities happy, which makes it easier to get international funding. Now I'm the keeper of the radiating mystery box."

Robert watched the video screen intently, this time looking for the EM waves that Professor Dondallo had mentioned. As his eyes refocused, and the pale glow of magic covered them, Robert scanned the screen but found nothing. Though the EM meter displayed in the corner of the screen denoted an EM wave output, the broadcast couldn't repeat them along to the viewer.

Robert turned his scan to the room itself. He searched each wall and doorway until he caught the faint hint of unusual electromagnetic radiation that was distinct from the normal background radiation. He started to meander towards the unseen wave source while trying to block out the strain from ignoring the other spectrum noise. He stopped at the doorway leading back into the hall and asked the professor for directions to the bathroom. Kean and Mallory moved over to Robert as the professor directed them into the hall and around the corner to the bathrooms, and all three of them moved off quickly to the bathrooms.

"Do you know where you're going, Robert?"

"There's an unusual EM signal coming from that direction. It keeps fluctuating in time with the magical aura so I'm pretty sure that's where the device is."

"Great. Let's get over to it and find out what we're dealing with."

Chapter 7

Robert stepped into the lead as they walked down the white hallway. After following the trail for a few minutes, and finding their way back from a mistaken dead-end trip to the journalism library, they arrived at the end of a narrow side hallway. An unmarked wooden door stood in front of them.

"This is it-whatever is pumping out the weird EM waves is behind this door. We're lucky I have this new gift for seeing the invisible spectrum" Robert announced with pride.

Mallory pointed up to a narrow bundle of cables fastened at the spot where the wall met the ceiling.

"Not trying to ruin your moment, big guy, but we could've just followed those wires to here. Pretty sure they run from the professor's equipment cage to this room."

Robert deflated and pouted a bit. "I guess."

Kean examined the doorframe and the wires. The top of the door itself had been notched out to allow the cable bundle to enter the room with the door closed. Kean stood up on his tip toes and tried to look through the notch and into the room, but the space was just large enough for the wires. They all switched over to magesight and confirmed the source of the magical aura was behind that door.

"That's it. The Antikythera mechanism is on the other side of the door."

Mallory stooped down and examined the door handle. "The lock is a pretty simple one. And there's no electronic card swipe, which is good."

Kean stooped down beside Mallory and asked "why is that good?"

"Electronic locks could mean alarm systems. This way, maybe no one would know if we popped it open and took a quick look."

Robert checked his watch. "We're almost out of time. Amy's coming back in a minute or two."

Malory stood up and sighed. "That sucks. We haven't finished investigating the scene or interviewing anyone who might have been affected by the A.M."

"We don't have any reason to think it's affecting anyone yet. Let's get back to the broadcast room."

The three friends walked back into the broadcast room just as Amy returned with the rest of the tour group. Kean made sure to avoid eye contact and stay as far away from her as he could, and the sight of the 6 foot tall athlete cowering behind his friends made Mallory laugh. Amy shot a glare over at the three of them, before regaining her composure and over-wide smile.

"Okay, everyone refreshed? Let's keep the tour going. Next we'll go through the radio and print journalism area, then back downstairs and off to the visual arts building."

"That's the end of our investigating. Did we even learn anything of value?"Mallory quietly said.

"No, but I'm going to fix that. Cover for me when we get out into the hall." Robert responded.

"What? What are you going to do?"

"Nothing. Almost nothing. Just cover me."

The group marched out into the hall under Amy's instructions. Robert hung back until he was the last person leaving the room. As the group made its way towards the radio rooms, Robert fell further and further back. When they reached the t-junction at the end of the hall, Robert slipped down the opposite direction of the group and walked quietly towards the room housing the Antikythera Mechanism.

"I hope he knows what he's doing." Mallory muttered. "He's never the impulsive one."

"Yeah. It's usually you, running off into the arms of danger without a plan."

"At least I'm used to it by now."

Robert moved as quickly as he could without breaking into a full run. The slapping sound of his hard-soled boots hitting the tile floor was already too loud for his liking, and the continual effort it was requiring to read EM emissions from the mechanism without getting overwhelmed by the background noise was taking its toll. The temperature of the air around him felt too warm for his liking, and a bead of sweat ran down his face. Robert wiped the sweat off and kept moving forward.

Finally at the end of the hall he stopped at the door and prepared himself for the next step. He was going to test the door lock to see what happened. If sirens and lights went off, then he'd pretend to be lost and looking for the bathroom. He wasn't sure what he'd do if the door opened. Robert steadied his nerves and took one more look down the hall. He shook his head in amazement at his rash actions. Running off and trying something like this wasn't his normal behaviour. He was breaking rules and taking risks, and only a 6 months ago the very idea of doing any anti-authority activity would have given him a terrible bout of nausea and crying. Robert wondered just how far he could push himself now. The courage to skirt the rules would probably dry up if he got caught and punished for something, he reckoned.

He took a deep breath and pushed down on the door handle while squinting his eyes shut, in anticipation of a blinding floodlight and a blaring siren. Instead of a cacophony of noise and light, the same silence perpetuated in the hall. Robert held his breath and waited another minute for some kind of reaction. Finally he opened up his eyes and prepared to head back to the group, until he noticed that the door in front of him had gently swung open. He was looking directly at the Antikythera Mechanism.

Mallory and Kean lurked at the back of the group as a bored teacher's assistant explained the functionality of the audio recording booth they were all crammed into. Kean tried to listen to the monotonous description of the microphone settings and different audio qualities, but eventually he gave up and focused on the monitor in the corner of the room. Suspended from the top of the wall by a mechanical mounting arm, the lcd screen was displaying the makeshift lab housing the A.M. The meter readings were illegible on this small screen, but the line graphs in the bottom corner were still visibly fluctuating. Suddenly the image of the A.M. was obscured by something moving between the camera and it, and when the device came back into view, Kean was startled to see Robert standing beside it.

Kean gasped and then faked a cough to cover the sound. He jabbed an elbow into Mallory's arm and tipped his head in the direction of the monitor. After the fifth jab, Mallory turned her head to glare at Kean. She went to hit him back in response, but as she saw what he had been trying to show her, her fist uncurled and dropped to her side. They both watched, stunned, as Robert crept towards the Antikythera Mechanism and crouched down right in front of it. He tilted his head as he examined the face of the device, looking at the energies as they swirled in and out of folds and crevices. Mallory and Kean switched to magesight to get a better idea of what Robert was interacting with. The aura of the machine was calm but bright, and it moved slightly towards Robert as he approached it. Robert extended the fingers of his right hand until they were fully outstretched, and he brushed his flattened hand gently through the energy stream. The sinuous ripples that shuddered through the aura made the energy seem alive. In reaction, Robert flinched. As his hand jerked away from the energy, he accidentally brushed the face of the device, moving the configuration levers and activating the device. The aura flared and spiked towards Robert as it expanded outwards, while the meters and monitors all went silent.

Kean tugged on Mallory's sleeve. "We should go get him, Mal."

"If we do he's definitely going to get caught. Hopefully he'll realize he's gone way too far and he'll hightail it out of there."

It looked for a moment as if Robert was about to show some sense and slip out of the room, but he only made it as far as turning towards the door. Kean and Mallory could see his eyes were frighteningly wide, and his body went rigid as he tried to move away. He pitched forward off-balance and the rigid stiffness in his body gave way as he crumpled into a pile on the floor. Mallory and Kean ran out of the radio room and down the hallway. Halfway to the lab room, Professor Dondallo joined with them in the race to the boy in the lab.

"What the heck is your friend doing in there?"

"Right now, being unconscious." Mallory snapped as she sped up and ran down the hall.

Robert was lying facedown, halfway out of the lab room. Mallory shouted his name and crouched beside him. A twitch went through his body, followed by another. A long, low moan rose out his mouth.

"Well at least he's not dead" Kean said.

Mallory pounded Kean in the calf, hitting him hard enough with her knuckle extended that she triggered a charlie horse. "Stupid thing to say, Kean."

Kean hopped around, stifling the cry of pain that his calf muscle was trying to force out of him. Robert rolled over onto his shoulder and blinked his eyes repeatedly.

"Wow, what happened?"

"You passed out or something. You were in the lab by accident, and you fainted."

"I..what? Hold on." Robert pulled his legs up into a ninety degree bend at the knees and started to sit up.

"Hey don't sit up so fast, man" Professor Dondallo warned him. "You might pass out again."

"I'm okay, I think. It's just a migraine that I ignored too long."

Both Mallory and Professor Dondallo replied "really?"

"I have migraines occasionally, and usually I just rest in a darkened room and take some extra-strength pain reliever, but I didn't want to miss the trip, so I took the tylenol and came on the trip. It was okay until just a few minutes ago, when the bright lights in the broadcast room made my symptoms worse. I was going to splash some cool water on my face in the bathroom, but the headache made me a little confused and I ended up here."

Amy came barreling up to the small group gathered around Robert. "Oh my gosh what happened here? Is everyone okay?"

Robert sat fully up and looked at the crowd around him. "I feel fine now. Honestly. I just got overwhelmed by all of the bright colourful lights."

"I have to call your parental supervisor and campus security to see what they need us to do next. Let's make him comfortable and we'll wait to find out what to do next."

Slowly they helped Robert over to a padded bench seat in one of the small student lounges. Kean folded up his coat as a pillow, and Mallory draped her coat over Robert to keep him warm. 10 minutes later, Mallory's mom came hurrying up to them, accompanied by a campus security officer and an EMS worker. Mallory and Kean had to step back out of the way as the new group of adults descended onto Robert and examined him. They decided that Robert was in no immediate danger, but it would be safer to take him the hospital to be seen by a doctor. Amy rounded up the rest of the class and cleared her throat to get Kean and Mallory's attention.

"They have it under control guys, so let's keep the tour going."

"But he's our friend. We can't leave him."

Mrs. Davidson replied. "Yes you can, Mallory. I'll stay with him at the hospital. When the tour is finished, give me a call. The four of us will drive back home together."

"But mom" Mallory complained, disappointed at the whine in her own voice.

"He'll be fine, sweetheart. Go on."

Reluctantly, Mallory joined the tour group and left Robert in the care of her mom and the medical staff. Kean gave her a squeeze on the shoulder as she pulled up beside him.

"Pretty scary stuff. He just toppled over."

"Can you remember Robert talking about migraines before? Was that a complete fabrication, or have I missed something?"

Kean thought about it for a moment. "He hasn't called them migraines before, but yeah, I think he's been getting headaches. Usually he gets them when he uses his spectrum viewing ability."

"That's right-he said trying to read radio waves as he skipped from channel to channel made his head hurt. So was that what knocked him out? Did the A.M. shoot out a big dose of radiation?"

"No, the monitors went dead as soon as Robert touched the device, so it wasn't radiation. At least, it wasn't normal radiation. The magical aura flared out when he moved the device, but I didn't really see how powerful that was."

The tour group left the North Campus Building and went next door to the John Labatt Visual Arts Centre. Amy listed off the various art techniques that were taught in the workshops inside, but Mallory couldn't focus on the tour guide.

"We didn't really learn anything from this trip, and now poor Robert is stuck in the waiting room at the hospital for who knows how long?"

"We know one very important thing-the A.M. is still functional after hundreds of years."

"Unless it isn't the real one. Since the records are all being changed and no one really remembers it, maybe this one is brand new. Heck, maybe the old one wasn't even real. And the burst of whatever that came out of it doesn't mean it's working. "

"It's working well enough to be stable. It only shot out the magical energy burst when Robert changed the configuration. I think he turned it on."

"If he did, what did it do? Other than knock him out?"

"I don't know. Nothing really noticeable or quick, I'd guess. Did you see anything happen in the hall while we were waiting for the security guy to show up?"

Mallory frowned. "No. Everything looked normal. But I wasn't watching anything other than Robert."

The group looped back to the front entrance of the building and walked out into the gloomy afternoon. The threatening rain held off as the tour group marched back up the center hill and into the small building in the center of campus.

"This is the McIntosh Art Gallery. " Amy announced. "It was built in 1942 and it's Ontario's oldest university art gallery. It doesn't look very big, but it has over 3000 square feet of gallery space inside, and administration offices and its own library in the basement. The artists who hone their craft here at Western come back to display their works at the Mac. Let's take a quick look through the current exhibits before we end the tour."

The entrance space of the gallery was small and constricted. The tour group quickly filled the foyer and blocked the last few students from entering, as the first in line tried to figure out which way to go. Almost immediately in front of them, a spiral staircase led into the basement and the administrative offices. Amy faced the kids and started directing them towards the large arched opening to the left of the bright red front door.

"Into the northern gallery, everyone. Keep moving ahead so everyone else can come in."

Kean and Mallory waited for the group to move out of their way. The foyer was cleared and they both stepped into the building to look around. The rooms were awash with diffuse, coloured lights. The dim natural light that was able to sneak past the cloud cover was tinted and warmed by the vibrant stain-glass window tops of the large gallery windows. The overhead lights were colour-neutral and they added illumination without changing the artists intended colour. They turned towards the north gallery and moved to stand behind the rest of the group.

The featured piece of the current exhibit, "Dancing glass", stood in the very center of the large gallery room. The statue of steel and stained glass reached up into the air, towering above the head of the older woman who stood in front of it. The tips of the wings of this massive eagle sculpture extended out so far that it was almost as wide as it was tall, and the animal's half-open beak tilted skyward in a pose that suggested a primal cry of triumph escaping into the air itself. The sculpture caught the light in the room and reflected pools of coloured shadow into every corner. A shift in the light occurred and the rays of dim sunlight coming through the windows seemed to focus and intensify as they converged on the statue.

Mallory felt the magical itch creep up her spine, and she looked over to Kean. Kean's surprised face told her that he was feeling the magic use too. Neither of them were the source of the spell. They both switched their vision to magesight. The spell was diffused throughout the room, pulling the light to the statue and illuminating it in a break taking display. The roots of the spell led back to the calm lady smiling serenely as she stared up at the eagle sculpture and gently tugged and pulled the spell with her fingers to make the colours dance throughout the panes.

"Kean, she's-"

"I know. I know."

Chapter 8

The new mage continued to make the light dance with her artistic spell for another minute. Everyone in the room stood silent and in awe of the beauty in front of them. The dazzling display slowly came to an end, and the light in the room went back to a natural speckling of shade and brightness. Kean and Mallory kept their eyes trained on the woman. When her spell ended, they both could see a small pocket of magical backlash force coalesce and dart towards the woman. Mallory instinctively and sympathetically flinched and braced herself for the impact, but the older mage didn't mirror her response. The woman relaxed her body and stretched out her fingers to welcome the karma as it slammed into her. Her smile stayed fixed to her face, even though a trace of pain joined her expression. The woman turned her gaze towards the group. She scanned the crowd in front of her, stopping when Mallory and Kean became the object of her attention. The woman's smile widened to a joyous exultation, and she clapped her hands together in excitement. She took a moment to contain herself, and then she gave a quick introduction.

"Hello everyone, and welcome to the Mcintosh gallery. My name is Mary-Anne Medestin and I am the gallery's curator. I'm standing in front of the centerpiece of our newest exhibit, "Dancing glass". This particular sculpture is simply called "flight" and it is a composition of welded steel framework and thousands of pieces of stained glass. It took the artist, Keith Davis, over 4 years of devoted work to complete this statue. And it almost didn't make it to the gallery. On its way to the gallery, the truck containing the sculpture was driven off the road as the driver swerved to avoid a deer bolting across the road. This is the peril of travelling on the rural Ontario back roads. Luckily, the packing around the sculpture kept it from receiving any real damage, and after a brief delay for the tow truck, the statue arrived here. You might have noticed that the statue appears to change colour as the sunlight moves across it. Through careful use of refraction and colour theory, the artist has created this illusion, and when the sunlight cooperates and strikes the statue at the correct angle the effects are, well, quite magical."

Mary-Anne smiled and looked directly at Mallory and Kean as she said the last line. Mallory and Kean both went white as a sheet. "She knows" hissed Mallory. Kean elbowed her.

"Shh. It might just be a coincidence."

Mary-Anne finished her presentation. "If any of you are interested in taking a photograph of the statue, please avoiding using a flash. Not because it will harm anything, but because you'll get quite a dazzling blur in your photo. If there are any questions at all, please feel free to come over to me and ask. I'm sure some of you are brimming with curiosity."

Amy took over and issued her instructions to the tour group. "We'll take 10 minutes to browse through the gallery, and then we'll meet back outside the front doors. Have fun, everyone!"

The crowd thinned out as the kids meandered from artwork to artwork. Mallory and Kean slowly walked up to Mary-Anne and waited until everyone else was out of earshot.

"Uh…hi." Kean said, suddenly aware of having no idea of what to say.

"Hello to you. Did you like the display?"

"Yes. It was very different."

"Oh I guess you could say that. It was a little costly, but a flare-up of my old arthritis is a small price to pay for a moment of wonder."

Mallory stepped in. "You know what we are? Or what we can do, I guess?"

Mary-Anne cocked her head to the side, chuckled and responded. "I know that you're something, alright. Both of you. I can see there's something profoundly special about the two of you. And I think you know that. I would guess that you also know that some things, once described, lose their mystery, so I'll keep from going on about it."

Kean and Mallory exchanged a look. Mallory turned her head back to Mary-Anne and watched her aura again. The presence of magical attunement washed through her aura and gave her an overall glow.

"How long have you been aware of what you can do?"

"Many years, my dear. Though, I don't know the half of what I could actually do if I put my mind to it. It doesn't really lend itself to thorough testing, does it? Much more of an art than a science. And of course, the more you push, the more the world pushes back, and that can sting a little bit."

Mallory started to ask a rapid-fire string of questions.

"Have you met others? Is there a club? We sort of have a club. It's only 4 of us, and 3 of us are still in high school, but the fourth guy is older. Not as old as you are, but older than us. Oh crap I just called you old. I'm sorry."

Mary-Anne pretended to scowl at Mallory, before breaking into a laugh.

"You are very excitable, and I don't blame you. Meeting another…artist is quite a surprising occurrence. There are very few of us with the capacity, and even fewer who have discovered how to use it."

"It's probably safer that way" Kean said.

"You're probably right. So where are you from?"

"We both live in Antler Branch, north of Toronto."

"I'm so glad I chose to work the gallery shift today. I like to watch the prospective students as they come through the gallery. I hope to see a glimpse of one of the sleeping artists, and occasionally I see one. This is the very first time that I've seen an active one, and two of them at the same time is a momentous occasion to celebrate."

"Well, we came for the tour and to-"

Kean was interrupted by Mallory's sharp elbow jutting into his ribs as she exclaimed "Oh no, Amy's looking for us. She's going to freak out if she thinks we're lost."

Mallory started to drag Kean off towards the rest of the group as she finished talking to Mary-Anne.

"Our other friend wandered away from the tour and passed out in the NCB, so the tour guide is really uptight and panicky now, so we better find her. Here's the number of the club where we hang out and talk 'art'. Call us and we'll figure out a good time for another visit. Nice meeting you."

They hurried off into a small side room filled with postcard-sized canvasses. Kean pulled his arm out of Mallory's grasp and questioned her.

"Why did you drag me off like that? She's a mage like us!"

"She's a mage, but we don't know what her motives are. You're assuming she's a good witch of the west, but what if she isn't?"

"Why would she lie?"

"Maybe she's crazy, maybe she thinks her power comes from the blood of other mages, maybe she's a burglar in her spare time and she was setting us up for a robbery."

The image of kindly old Mary-Anne sneaking through a window wearing a burglar's mask made Kean laugh.

"She's not a thief."

"We don't know that for sure. And we have no reason to believe that she isn't trying to get her hands on the A.M. Imagine what Herlech would have done to have an actual artifact in his possession. I just think we have to be careful around strangers, especially magic-users."

"You should a little paranoid, Mal."

"Better safe than sorry, Kean. Let's get back to the group and see if we can go off to the hospital. I want to head home."

Mallory snuck over to Amy and spun an elaborate cover story to talk their way out of the gallery and into freedom. Amy gave in and called Mallory's mom to make sure it was okay to release Kean and Mallory from the group. Mallory stood nervously shifting her weight from foot to foot as the phone call took place. Amy finished the call and waited for what felt like an eternity to Mallory. Amy finally spoke.

"Your mom says it's okay, so you two can go. You have to go directly to the hospital, though. If you're not there in 10 minutes, your mom is going to call the police, and I don't think she was kidding about that."

"No, mom usually doesn't kid when she's stressed out or worried."

"Do you know how to get to the hospital from here?"

Kean stepped up and unfolded the campus map he was carrying. "We head down to Middlesex College, down the stairs, and turn left. We should see the hospital when we go around the curve in the road."

"That's right. Give me a call if you get lost. I hope you enjoyed the tour, and please let your friend know that I hope he feels better."

Kean and Mallory waved goodbye to Amy and gave her their thanks as they hustled out of the gallery. The clouds condensed above them and released a grey drizzle down onto them. By the time they arrived at the hospital, Kean's hair was plastered to his forehead, and Mallory's natural curls were frizzing up and expanding.

"Great, I'll have a semi-fro for the rest of the day."

"You look fine. Hey, there's your mom."

Mrs. Davidson was standing at the back of the admitting area, watching the front doors for Kean and Mallory's arrival. She waved them over to her.

"I take it by the look of you both that it's raining again?"

"Yeah, and it's a cold, windy rain. This day is starting to suck."

"I'd like to remind you, Kean, that you've maintained consciousness all day, which is one achievement your compatriot Robert has failed to earn. Now let's get back to him and see if he's ready to come home."

They followed Mallory's mom through a set of double doors that soundlessly opened and closed as they passed through them. The only indicator that the doors were open was a rushing of air from one room to the other, a breeze caused by the air pressure difference in each zone of the hospital. To contain the spread of any airborne illness, each set of doors functioned like an airlock between sealed compartments, and the hiss and breeze added to the creepy feeling of being there. Mallory shivered and followed closely behind her mother. Kean shoved his hands deep down into his pockets and tried to keep his mind off of the memories of his previous trips to the hospital.

They walked along a bright blue line painted on the floor that led them to the examination area. Robert was lying on a stretcher, with a stack of pillows under his head, and his eyes closed. A thin hospital blanket was pulled over his legs, but he was still dressed in his own clothes. Mallory and Kean rushed up to the side of the bed and peered down at Robert.

"Should we wake him up?" Kean wondered.

"What if he's supposed to be asleep? But isn't it a bad thing for someone who passed out to fall asleep?"

"I think that's only for someone with a concussion."

"I'm not asleep" Robert said, causing Mallory and Kean to jump with fright.

"You jerk! Don't scare me like that!"

"Hey, I scared Mallory. That's funny." Robert said dreamily.

"So are you okay?"

"Feelin' just fine."

Mrs. Davidson spoke up. "He's feeling a little too good right now, because of the migraine medication they gave him. He's going to be a little…relaxed for the next while."

"Whee!"

"So he's goofy on pain meds, but other than that he's okay?" Kean asked.

"According to the doctor, yes. It was a combination of fatigue, migraine, and poor eating habits today that caused Robert to pass out. The doctor recommended that Robert have a blood sugar test done with his family physician, to rule out any other factors, but as soon as the doctor says okay, we can leave. I'm going to go get the all-clear: stay here and make sure he doesn't fall out of the bed."

Mallory waited until her mom was out of earshot and asked Robert to describe what had really happened with the Antikythera Mechanism.

"It was weird. Really, really weird. I was watching the waves emanating from the inside of it, and the waves kind of hypnotized me a little bit. It's such a complex pattern, and I've never seen natural and magical waves mixed together like that. Some little imperfection caught my attention, some kind of erratic flicker that didn't match the rest of the pattern, and then I accidentally knocked the switches. All of a sudden, ZAP!"

"Shh, Robert. Don't shout!"

"Oops. Sorry. Didn't notice that my voice was getting loud. Is it loud now?"

"No Robert. Keep going."

"I'm going somewhere?"

Kean sighed. "No, Robert. She meant 'keep telling your story."

"Oh yeah. So the switched got moved, and the machine turned on. It shot out a giant burst of magical energy, and that energy was still tied together with the waves."

"Wait a minute-all of the meters were showing no radiation after you touched the A.M."

Robert shrugged. "Don't know what to tell you, but the EM waves were still there, with a bunch of other radiation thrown in.

I was looking so closely at the machine that the huge burst of energy blinded me and made me feel really funny. Next thing I knew, I was waking up on the floor."

Kean looked worried. "If it can randomly shoot out that much energy whenever anyone bumps it, then it's really unsafe."

"Oh it wasn't random."

Mallory and Kean were both surprised. "What?"

"That was exactly what the thing was supposed to do. The switch I bumped moved smoothly around the face of the mechanism and clicked into place when it reached its destination. I turned it on, and it did what it was designed to do."

"Any guess on what it was doing?" Mallory asked.

"Nope, but it would be a really good idea to keep an eye on the lab and anyone who had contact with it, cause that burst of energy was looking for people to affect. It was a spell in search of a target."

"Or victim." Kean replied grimly.

"How do we know Robert wasn't the target, and it's all done now?" Mallory countered.

Robert shook his head. "It smashed into me but it kept going. I had the feeling that it couldn't affect me the way it wanted to, so it just used brute force to knock me down."

"How can a spell want something? What are you trying to say? It's alive?"

"It wasn't alive. But it was a very complicated spell with a lot of instructions built into it. Most of the time, a spell serves a single purpose-"

"Uh, guys, it might be a good idea to stop talking about this here. My mom is coming back and there are a lot of people just walking around. "

Suddenly aware of the very public nature of their conversation on magic, the three friends looked around in a fit of nervous paranoia. Mrs. Davidson approached them while watching their odd reaction.

"I don't what the three of you were contemplating, but stop it. You already look incredibly guilty. "

"We're not doing anything." Mallory protested.

"That's what they all say. Robert, put on your shoes and coat-the doctor has given you permission to head home."

"Can we stop for ice cream?"

"No, I don't think so. We need to head straight back home. Your mother is quite concerned and would like to see you as soon as possible."

Robert groaned. "You told my mom? She's going to be so over-protective."

"She's just worried about you. Don't discount a mother's love."

Mrs. Davidson wrapped her arms around Mallory and hugged her tightly, too tightly for Mallory to escape from the embarrassing embrace.

"Come on, mom, let me go."

"Never, my baby girl. I am your mummy and I wuv you."

Mallory twisted her body and slipped out of the embrace, as her mother chuckled.

"Really mom-sometimes you are a wierdo."

Chapter 9

The car ride home was spent in quiet conversation. The three kids used the pretense of discussing a video game to talk openly about the spell Robert had been knocked out by and their future course of action. Mallory crossed her figners and hoped that her mother wouldn't catch on to the strange nature of their chat.

"So on this new level you're playing, the problem is that the magic spell that was cast by the mysterious artifat is going to affect something or someone, but your character isn't there to watch it."

"Whatever is happening might be unnoticeable to normal people. Hey, you could call that May-Anne lady and ask her to check things out."

"No way! Were you not listening before? She could be crazy or evil!"

"Who is Mary-Anne?" Robert asked.

"The last level of the game took me to the art gallery on campus, and the curator there was a lady named Mary-Anne. " Kean took a quick look at Mallory's mom before continuing. "And Mary-Anne reminded me of that nice old lady mentor in the game, you know the one who already has her magical powers and she offers to help the hero with his own quest?"

"And I thought she was a little bit like the evil mage character, and the hero would be dumb to trust her."

"Maybe the hero is just paranoid."

"Maybe her sidekick is really gullible and easily tricked."

Robert squinted at the other two kids and tried to follow along with the conversation.

"This is a little too complicated for my head right now. If that lady can go look for something going magically wrong, then what's the harm?"

Mallory sighed. "Because she might be power-hungry and eager to steal the artifact the hero is trying to keep out of dangerous hands."

"Did she really seem that evil?"

Kean shook his head. "Not at all. She used her gift to make something beautiful. She spoke calmly and kindly to the hero and his highly excitable sidekick. The nice old lady did absolutely nothing to raise their suspicions."

"You're confused over who the hero is in this story and who is the big lunk of a sidekick there, pally." Mallory muttered.

"Well, there is a risk in pointing the witch towards the artifact, but the hero, who is still tired and confused from his battle with the artifact, needs to know what the device is doing, and his sidekicks are just bickering between each other and making his headache worse. The nice old witch should be contacted." Robert said in a pained tone of voice.

Robert leaned his head back onto the seat and closed his eyes to rest.Mallory pulled out her smartphone and searched for Mary-Anne's contact info on the art gallery's website. She found the number, and looked at Kean.

"Are you sure this is a good idea?"

"Calling her right now is defintely not." Kean said in a low voice.

"We need to know what's happening over there, and she can tell us."

"Then send an email."

"That'll take forever. Who knows how often she checks it."

"Send a message now, and follow up with a call later." Mallory grumbled but couldn't argue with Kean's logic. Calling the Art Gallery lady right now would catch her mom's attention. Mallory could already feel a vague uneasiness from her magical instinct. They were too close to openly discussing magic in front of a normal person. Mallory typed out a brief email message and clicked 'send'.

"Okay I sent her an email with my phone number and a promise to call her later. Hopefully she's not a weird technophobe who can't open her email."

Mallory's phone rang and she looked at it with surprise. On the third ring, Kean prodded her.

"You should probably answer it."

"Hello?"

"Hi this Mary-Anne. Is this Mallory I'm speaking to?"

"Uh, yeah. Hi.That was quick."

"I just received your message. How may I help you?"

"I was on the tour earlier, and we talked about artists creating art and stuff." Mallory winced at her own words.

"I certainly remember talking about stuff like that. You left quite quickly after our chat."

"Well, we had to go get our friend at the hospital. Anyway, we need some help, and you're the only one there that can do it."

"I see. And what do you need help with? I hope that it's all very legal and ethical."

"Definitely! We never do anything illegal. We're just trying to keep things from getting out of hand. There was some kind of artistic display at the NCB today, an unexpected event. We're wondering if the art is still there and active, and if it's having any kind of effect on the people there."

"Well, I can take a look for you. Is there anything else you'd like to tell me about it? Did you see the artist?"

"I can't really say right now, sorry. "

"That's not very much to go on. I'll head over there in a bit and I'll phone you back."

"Thank you very much, Mary-Anne. I'm sorry to be so secretive, but we have to be cautious. Bye."

Mallory hung up and turned back to Kean.

"Well that made me feel like a jerk."

"Secrets usually do. I think it was the right thing to do, though."

They drove in silence for another 30 minutes, passing through the tiny village of Norwich and the sparse farmland that surrounded it. On the edge of Norwich, Mallory's phone rang again.

"Hello?"

"Hi there, this is Mary-Anne from the art gallery again."

"Hi Mary-Anne. I'm Mallory."

"Yes dear, I know that. You mentioned it in the first call."

"Sorry, I 'nervous, so I forgot. . My friend's name is Kean, and our other friend Robert was at the hospital when we were at the gallery. He's also an artist, I guess."

". My, what an interesting group. Is your friend okay?"

"It looks like it. He was overwhelmed by a migraine. Too much visual art does that to him."

Mallory hoped she didn't sound too ridiculous. Talking in code was turning out to be much more complicated than she would have ever imagined.

"I'm glad he's recovering. I wanted you to know that I took a walk down to the north campus building, and there is something going on down there."

"Is the, um, art still there?"

"It is, and it's affecting the people in the building. The nice guard at the door of the building explained to me that there has been an outbreak of illness. Food poisoning is what they suspect, and there had also been an argument that turned into a physical confrontation in one of the classrooms on the third floor. And of course you know about the small explosion that damaged one of the rooms."

"Um, yeah. I heard about that."

"They've put a guard at the door to make sure that everyone can safely get to their classes, but the area around the media lab is off-limits for the time being. The guard suspects that there could be radiation up there. Does that sound ridiculous?"

"Not really. And you could see the aura of the effect?"

"It was very faint from the first floor, but I did see it. Whoever is creating it must be spending a lot of effort to keep it going."

"Can you do me another favour, and ask the guard to tell you if anything changes? If it gets worse, we need to know and maybe we can come back and stop it."

"How could it keep going, dear? The spellcaster will have to rest at some point."

Mallory paused. "I hope so."

"Hmm. I think you have even more you could tell me about this, but I won't press you right now. If anything changes here, I'll give you a call."

"Thanks."

Mallory hung up and gave Robert and Kean a quick summary of the conversation.

"And I'm stumped on what to do next."

"We should tell Heisenberg about the trip. I'll call him when I get home." Kean said.

Robert sighed. "I have a bad feeling that I'm going to spend the rest of the day confined to bed rest as my mother watches me for signs of concussion or brain damage. I'd be surprised if I'm allowed to leave the house tomorrow."

"Are you feeling back to normal now?" Mallory asked.

"Somewhat, but the pain reliever is still making me very tired. I think I'm going to nap for the rest of the trip."

By the time the car pulled into the driveway in front of Robert's apartment building, he was snoring loudly from the back seat. Mallory and Kean had to shake him awake. In his groggy state, he flailed around as he tried to figure out where he was, much to the amusement of his two friends. Kean walked Robert up to the elevator, where Robert's mother met them. She draped a blanket over his shoulders and started quizzing him in detail about his trip to the hospital, and Robert shot a forlorn look of regret at Kean as the elevator doors closed. Kean laughed and went back to the car to finish the long trip home.

The update phone call to Heisenberg was brief, interrupted by the impending start of family game night, so Kean promised that they'd come down to the tea shop the next morning for a full debriefing. Kean put aside his adventure-filled day and lost himself in the fun of board games with his parents and his cousins.

The sun blazing through his window the next morning made Kean want to stay in bed and bask in the heat while accomplishing nothing. He gave himself another 15 minutes of idleness before getting out of bed and starting his day.

Kean barreled through a long list of chores and homework, moving from one to the next without any delay, and by lunch time he was free of his household obligations. Kean called Mallory and made plans to meet at the bus stop.

15 minutes later, Mallory was at the stop waiting for him to arrive, but Robert was nowhere in sight.

"Huh, did you talk to Robert?" Kean asked.

"Indeed I did, and he is not getting out of the house today. His mom is keeping a very close eye on him. I also had the delightful experience of talking to her and convincing her that Robert hadn't taken some kind of sinister drug during the trip."

"Drugs? She thought he was on drugs?"

"Not really. I got the impression that she was just being thorough. So, it's just you and me today. How much did you tell Heisenberg last night?"

"Just the basics. I had a buttload of stuff to do last night, and this morning too."

"You're always busy. I get tired just watching you, Keaner. Why do you push yourself so hard? Swimming practice, your part-time job at the grocery store, tutoring at the library, volunteering with your mom and dad, on top of all of your normal homework. Don't you just want to relax and enjoy your life?"

Kean kicked at the dirt and thought about the question.

"I don't like being still. My mom always said that I had more energy than good sense. And now I feel like there is so much more that I can do, but I have to learn how to do it, and that will take a lot of time and practice. But there are still times where I sit on the couch and watch movie marathons too."

The bus pulled up and they took their seats near the back. Mallory threw back her head and groaned.

"I am sick of riding on the bus. I cannot wait until I have my own car."

"How are the driving lessons going?"

"Poorly, in that they barely ever happen. My mom is dragging this out as long as is humanly possible to keep me 'safe' from road accidents. By the time she lets me drive the car alone, I'll be in an old age home."

"It would be pretty sweet to drive anywhere we wanted to go."

"Who said I would take you with me, dingus?" Mallory smirked.

In response, Kean popped in his earphones and turned up the music.

An hour later, after a switch to a subway car and back to a bus to get around a detour, they arrived downtown. Mallory pulled out her phone and called Heisenberg.

"Hey there, old man. We're downtown and we should be there in about 15 minutes. Do you need us to pick up anything?"

"No, nothing except your capacity for being intrigued. I've been tinkering with a theory, and I'm ready to test it out. It should be ready for the three of you to see."

"Robert didn't come with us-his mom wanted him to stay home."

"Oh well. More excitement for the two of you, then. If I'm correct, this could become intensely interesting in a matter of moments."

"I thought we agreed that you wouldn't try anything without planning it out and making sure it was safe."

"Oh, it's fine. I've been very cautious, I assure you. I'll explain it all to you before proceeding. Deal?"

"Fine. Deal."

Mallory hung up the phone and marched with Kean in the direction of the tea shop. They crossed the busy and crowded streets that were still full of traffic even though it was Sunday afternoon, and continued along down the small side-streets. They were standing at the intersection of Queen Street and St. Patricks, 2 blocks away from the tea shop when an unpleasant sensation overcame them. The feeling of primal magic intensified quickly, building into a terrifying force that made their nervous system scream, and filled their vision with blinding magical light. Kean and Mallory started to scream in concert with the force assaulting them, but the sound of their voices was drowned out by the crash and boom of a massive explosion that sent a pillar of smoke and fire into the sky directly above the tea shops location.

As suddenly as the event had begun, it ended. Mallory's knees buckled and she had to grab onto a streetlight post to keep from falling down. Kean bent at the waist and took a deep breath to steady himself before turning to Mallory. She nodded to him to signal that she was alright, and they took off running towards the shop. They cut through the seating area beside the Queen Street market, and when they crossed Renfrew Place, the sight in front of them froze them in place. Halfway down St. Patrick Square, where the tea shop had been standing moments ago, there was a smoking crater of rubble and burning debris. Mallory's foot brushed against something lying in the street, and she bent down to discover the pair of thick glasses that Heisenberg wore when his eyes were too tired for contacts. Mallory gently picked up the partially melted and twisted pair of glasses, and started sobbing.

Chapter 10

(5 minutes earlier)

Heisenberg looked over his notes one more time. Scrawled across the whiteboard and spilling onto several addendum sheets, he had a working theory on how to collapse the spellscar and render it inert. He stepped back from the board and rubbed his tired eyes. He was almost certain that his theory would work, but that missing last five percent of assuredness gave him reason to pause. By tracking the line of effect from the scar to the locations of the events of last year, he could see the anchor points of spell energy: one at the halfway point between the scar and the university in London, one on the roof of the Old Alex theatre, and the spellscar itself.

Heisenberg went back to his hastily assembled model of the scar and the anchor points. On the café countertop, he had set up coffee cups connected by lengths of yarn that met in a lattice in the middle, all tied to an elastic band in the center. The elastic was pulled equally in three different directions, leaving it stretched out in a rounded triangular shape. He plucked at the strings with his left hand and watched the coffee cups jitter in response. He took his hand away and cast a spell on the model. Now the cups moved again, pulled by the strings towards each other, and pulled back into place by an unseen reciprocal force representing the universes' desire for consistent reality.

Heisenberg shaped another spell while maintaining the first one, crafting a thin magical scalpel to gently detach the anchor thread from the farthest cup. As he coaxed the thread from the handle, the opposing forces tugged the string towards the center and the elastic band snapped into a thin slit. The two coffee cups still tied to the elastic shuddered in the redistribution of resistance, but they stayed in place. After waiting a moment for any other consequences to arise, Heisenberg nodded in satisfaction and dropped both spells. He winced and hissed through his teeth as the universe repaid his magical tinkering with a dose of backlash. It covered his hands in mild rope burn, like his hands had been wrapped in yarn that had been yanked away suddenly. He sullenly wished the universe would appreciate that he was trying to fix things, and give him some leeway on the repercussions of his investigations.

The phone call from Mallory replayed through his mind as he felt the urge to tinker with the spell scar. He knew that he had promised her to leave it alone until they had arrived, but the temptation was maddening. The question Heisenberg grappled with as he stood and stared at the counter, was how much of Mallory's wrath was he willing to endure? Over the last few months he had seen that her temper can boil over and explode when provoked, and it took a stronger man than him to withstand her fury. On the other hand, he thought, there was room for a little experimentation. A non-invasive test that left the scar intact should be easily brush under the carpet and left unnoticed.

Heisenberg decided that he would test the elasticity of the lines of energy that kept the scar intact, the tethers that anchored it in place. He gathered up his magical energy and closed his eyes as he directed the spell energy outwards. The shapeless proto-spell wove through the streets, undefined in size and form until it reached the nearest tether line. When it came up to the tether line, Heisenberg shaped it into a grasping hand, and cupped it around the line. A jolt of energy jumped from the line to Heisenberg's spell and raced all the way back to Heisenberg himself. An electrical ache overcame his entire body, and he tried to drop the spell. The spell hand tried to let go of the tether line and pull back, but the line refused to let go of the embrace. What was worse, Heisenberg couldn't dismiss the spell. The entanglement with the tether line was forcing his spell to continue to exist despite his intense desire for it to vanish. Heisenberg pulled back again, hoping to yank the spell free and break the connection. The tension on the tether line increased as he tried to disengage from it, until he crossed the threshold of what it could resist. In the distance, the far terminus of the line became unseated and started moving towards Heisenberg at a terrifying speed. He could feel the energy building as it approached him. From the opposite direction, he felt the second tether line also unbound and it started rushing towards him. He hoped for a moment that the two energy lines would change course as they approach the spellscar and pass by him harmlessly, but the third line stayed immovable and unaffected, and it forced the balls of energy to continue on their crash course. They slammed into Heisenberg, and the world around him disappeared in a blinding flash of white light and heat.

Chapter 11

Robert was deep asleep and dreaming. The migraine medicine that the emergency room doctor had prescribed to him yesterday had kept him in drowsy for the last 24 hours. Robert was hoping that one more long nap would clear the last effects out of his system. The transition from awake to the dream world had been so fluid that he was surprised to find his grandmother's spirit in front of him. The background of the room around them washed away and was replaced by, of all things, a Laundromat.

"What are we doing here, Wai Po?"

"This was the first place your grandfather and me went to, after we moved to the city. We didn't know anyone. We didn't speak English. Our apartment was just upstairs. Tiny, tiny. We lived in two tiny rooms for 2 years, saving up enough money to buy the variety store."

"But why are we here?"

"They have laundry machines, but they can also fix clothes. Not many Laundromats still have a tailor, but this one does."

Robert looked around the ghostly room for any other people, but they were alone. The sound of all the washers and dryers running simultaneously was strangely ominous to Robert. It was a wall of white noise that pressed in from all sides. Robert noticed that his pockets were turned inside out and his left pocket had a large tear running parallel to the seam.

"That is the same rip that your grandfather had, the reason why we came down to find a tailor. He had been walking around all afternoon, with coins falling out of the hole in his pocket. We did not have so much money that we could just throw it away. He blamed me for losing the money. He thought I had spent it on shoes, but where would I put new shoes? Foolish man, sometimes.. Then he found the hole in his pocket, and your grandfather turned as red as a beet from embarrassment. When he didn't know he had the hole, he was sure somebody else was to blame. He created a story to explain it. Story was stupid, but he still believed it. Most people create an explanation for something they don't understand, especially if they don't want to understand."

Robert thought about his grandmother's apartment and if he had ever seen her sew, but he was pretty sure that she never did. Wai Po nodded.

"He wanted me to fix the hole but I told him that I was no good with a needle and thread. I refused. So we came down here and looked for the owner. But no one was down here, so your grandfather marched up to the counter and started fixing his own problem."

Wai Po gestured towards the counter and a sewing kit appeared on it. Robert walked over to it and looked questioningly at his grandmother.

"Go ahead. Fix the rip."

"But I can't sew."

"If you don't believe, of course you will fail. But why worry about such a small task? Just fix it."

Robert plucked out a needle and threaded it. He was surprised that he was able to do it on the first try, but then he remembered that this was still a dream, no matter how real it felt. He took the needle and thread and sewed up the hole.

"I like these visits from you, Wai Po, but it would be more helpful if you could just tell me what I needed to know, instead of giving me these very strange visions and metaphors. What does the sewing represent?"

Wai Po shook her head and patted Robert on the cheek. "If I could tell you, I would. I am in a place that is much different than life. There is no time here. I see pictures and I hear sounds from the living world, but they float in without explanations. What I see from the living world makes me think of my own memories, and I get a feeling that I need to share those memories with you. I don't know what they mean, only that you need to know them."

"Can you connect to anyone else?"

"Not like this, not the way I can talk to you. You can see me. You know who I am, and you know that I am dead. Other people I was close to, like your mother, I can visit them but they don't think I'm real. And that makes me disappear a little bit."

Robert tied off the thread and went over to his grandmother to give her a hug. He could feel a cold sensation seep from her to him, a chill that would stay with him for hours after he woke up. He ended the embrace and showed her the repaired pocket.

"See, Wai Po? I finished, but I don't know how well it will hold."

"Good enough. But ripped cloth is never as strong as it was before. Even with the fix, it is still weaker and it could rip again. Only takes a sharp poke and cut, and the rip is wide open again."

"Is that bad?"

"Maybe. If it tears open and somebody keeps pulling on it, maybe the tear gets too big to fix. Maybe hole is so big that there's nothing stopping things from going through it. So keep it closed up. But, before you fix a hole, check the other side for something you lost. Like all that money grandfather lost. 10 dollars was stuck in the lining of those pants, and we didn't find it for 2 months. He should have looked before sewing the hole closed, but he always rush rush rush."

"But what did I lose? What am I looking for?"

The dream ended suddenly as the ringing of the telephone cut through Robert's nap and woke him up. He rolled over and grabbed the phone.

"Hullo?"

"Robert, there's been an accident." Mallory sobbed.

"What? What are you talking about? A car accident?"

"No. Kean and I were on the way to the tea shop and we were a block away when something went wrong. There was a big rush of really bad magical energy and then…it exploded. The shop exploded and Heisenberg was…"

Mallory's sentence dissolved into incoherent weeping. Robert tried to shake the last bits of sleep out of his mind and focus on what Mallory was trying to tell him. He rolled onto his back and sat up on the couch. Robert clicked on the tv and turned to cable 24, the 24 Toronto news station. The news confirmed that an explosion had taken place in downtown Toronto, and the picture of a plume of smoke rising up into the air made Robert's heart sink. The news anchor gave the few details available: they were suspecting a gas leak caused the explosion, and there's no word on any injuries. The building was referred to as 'vacant', and Robert thought that was strange.

"Mallory, the news is reporting the explosion, but they aren't mentioning any casualties. He might be okay."

"It's gone. The whole building is gone, and we talked to him right before it blew up" Mallory yelled at Robert. In the background, Robert could hear sirens from the approaching emergency vehicles.

"Mallory, were you close enough to get hurt by the blast? Are you and Kean okay?"

"I'm fine. We were far enough away that the explosion didn't touch us."

"What about the magical effects?"

"What?"

"If the explosion was caused by a spell, then it could have damaged you, even from a distance. Check Kean for any sign of spell effect, and have him check you."

After a moment, Mallory responded. "No, we're fine."

"So what did the magical part of the explosion look like?"

"It was a massive pillar of spell energy that was intertwined with the actual fire and smoke. I wasn't even using magesight, but I could see it clearly. Before the explosion, we felt the energy building up, and it was incredibly painful. I remember screaming from the pain and pressure. Kean was screaming too. I thought I was going to pass out, but I managed to stay conscious."

"Okay. Are the emergency vehicles there?"

"They are. They went right past us."

"I want you and Kean to go get checked out by a paramedic. Please?"

Mallory huffed out a deep breath that still had the traces of her sobbing in it. "Fine. We'll go over there now."

"As long as you're not hurt, why don't you guys come over to my house and we'll talk about it."

"I just want to go home and see my mom."

"Oh, okay. But call me if you need anything, okay?"

"I will Robert."

"Can you put Kean on the phone?"

"He's heading over to the ambulance already. I'll tell him to call you later."

Robert started to reply, but Mallory hung up abruptly. Robert put the phone down and turned up the volume of the television. As the reporting of the explosion continued, they kept downgrading the severity. 30 minutes after the first report, they were calling the building an abandoned and derelict row house that was slated to be demolished. And they were pretty insistent that the building had been completely empty at the time of the blow-up. It was as if Heisenberg had never existed in the first place.

Chapter 12

As soon as Mrs. Davidson stepped out of her car, Mallory collapsed into her mother's arms, sobbing once again. Mrs. Davidson looked at Kean for some kind of explanation of her grief.

"It's okay honey. I know it's frightening to be near any kind of accident. Were you hurt?"

Mallory kept crying, so Kean answered.

"No, we're both fine. The paramedics checked us out."

"Well that's a relief. I'm so glad that you're fine."

"But, but, Heisenberg was in there, and no one can find him."

Mrs. Davidson leaned back and looked down at her daughter.

"Who are you talking about, sweetheart?"

Mallory stopped crying in mid-sob and stepped back from her mom. "What?"

"I said that everyone's fine so we can go home."

"No you didn't-you asked who I was talking about, like you've never even heard of Heisenberg."

"Well, there's no point in arguing. Let's just get in the car and head home."

Mallory's mom abruptly turned and got back into the car, leaving Mallory and Kean at a loss for words. They looked at each other, then piled into the car and settled in for the ride home. Halfway through the trip, Mallory spoke up again.

"Mom, I don't know why you're being weird, but you know Heisenberg. The tea shop owner who we've been doing our co-op placement with. We come down here once a week, every week. Sometimes twice."

"You're always out of the house; I can barely keep track of where you've been and where you're going."

"That is not true, mom. You make me call you if I'm even 10 minutes late, and I write down my entire schedule on the calendar in the kitchen so you can find me whenever you want to. That's your rule. You know where I am at all times, so you know that I've been here over and over again."

"Mallory, I'm in no mood for your complaining. It's bad enough that I had to come down here to pick you up, after you've spent all afternoon wandering around downtown Toronto and happen to get too close to a building demolition. I'm sorry that it frightened you but there are people in the world with real problems and I suggest you stop being so overly dramatic and move on with your life."

Kean felt uneasy being stuck in the car and witnessing the strange argument between Mallory and her mother. Mrs. Davidson was on the verge of shouting at her daughter, simply for asking questions.He noticed that his shoulder had started to itch as well, intensifying as the argument heated up. He thought about what that could mean for a moment and decided to test out his theory.

"Mrs. Davidson, the building that blew up wasn't supposed to be demolished. It was an accident, and the building was owned by our friend Heisenberg. You have met Heisenberg several times, and he's even been over to your house."

"Don't you start joining in, mister. If I tell your mother that you've been running around all day and lying about what you've been doing, you'll be grounded for months."

As Mrs. Davidson became more agitated and angry, Kean watched her with his magesight and confirmed that a swirling cloud of magical backlash was thickening around her head. Somehow, talking about Heisenberg or the explosion was triggering a backlash. The reaction was causing her memory to change. Kean spoke up and interrupted as the darting cloud of magical energy pushed Mallory's mom into a state of rage.

"Uh, that was a very confusing and scary event, Mal. I think you're just remembering things wrong. "

"What?!? Are you nuts?"

"Mal, it's the backlash from the explosion playing tricks on your memory." Kean said, stressing the word 'backlash'.

Mallory stared at Kean, and when she understood what he was hinting at, her eyes widened. Mallory turned her head and watched her mother intently for a second. When she saw the karmic backlash flickering through the air, Mallory blurted out an apology.

"I'm sorry mom. The whole thing had me messed up and confused, and I was mistaken. You're right."

Mrs. Davidson still looked angry, but a few more minutes of driving in silence gave her the time to calm down. As the anger left her face, the wisps of backlash disappeared.

"Oh, I sometimes forget how wildly emotional you teenagers are. So many hormones whipping through your circulatory system, muddying up your thinking. Someday you'll look back at this time in your life and you'll be very grateful for the sane people in your life."

"You're right mom."

"Hey, Mrs. Davidson, could you drop us off at Robert's apartment building? We'd like to go up and check on him. He sounded like he was recovering pretty well, but it would still be nice to see him."

"Alright. But I'm not waiting around for the two of you. You'll have to walk home, and I expect you home for dinner, Mallory."

Mallory nodded and slumped back into her seat.

The music from the radio filled the air for the rest of the drive. Mallory and Kean were too hurt and confused by the disater downtown to fake casual conversation. The car pulled up in front of Robert's apartment building. Kean and Mallory got out of the car and thanked Mrs. Davidson for the ride before heading inside. They buzzed up to Robert's apartment, and rode the slow elevator all the way up to his floor. Robert answered the door almost at the same time that Kean's hand was knocking on it.

"Come on in, guys. Do you need a drink?"

Kean looked at Mallory. She was staring vacantly at the window and the grey clouds outside.

"Yeah, a drink for both of us would be a good idea. I don't remember when we had one last."

Robert brought back 3 cans of pop from the kitchen: a diet rootbeer for him, a cream soda for Kean, and a coke for Mallory. They followed Robert back into the living room.

"Is your mom around, Robert?" Kean asked.

"No. she's at the grocery store. She's pretty sure that I'm not going to die from the headache now, so she's trying to catch up on all the weekend tasks she had piling up."

"Hope you're helping her out."

"Of course I am, Kean. I always do my chores, unlike you and Mallory."

"What?" Mallory had been tuned out of the conversation, but the mention of her name caught her attention.

"Of all of us, I'm the best kid. I do my chores, I finish my homework early, and I am over all a pleasure to be around."

Kean squinted at Robert. "I think the medication is still making you goofy."

"Can't handle the truth, huh?"

Mallory interrupted with an angry tone in her voice.

"Guys! Cut it out. You can't just joke around and pretend things are normal."

Robert ignored Mallory's anger and sat down on the couch to watch the television. The news channel was still showing the smoky ruins of the tea shop, but the image was only on screen for another 30 seconds before it cut away to other news.

"There's less and less coverage of the explosion. I bet that they'll stop mentioning it by the 11 o'clock news. The whole event is being erased."

Robert flipped up the screen on his laptop and placed it on the low, wooden coffee table in front of the couch. He clicked through several local news websites and showed the declining interest in the explosion and its effects. The final site that he surfs to is hard to read and ugly. It was nothing like the other professional sites. It claimed to be the site that will publish "facts THEY don't want you to know" and the word conspiracy was featured prominently on the front page.

"I found this after digging around a bit. It's not even showing up in the search results normally: I had to use an anonymizer and a VPN tunnel to find it in the search results."

Kean responded. "A) I don't understand what you just explained and B) why did you think to do that?"

"I had a hunch. Kind of an itch behind my eyes. There was more to see but it wasn't being shown. So this guy, and I think it's a guy because of the macho way he writes, is talking about the explosion and the cover-up that is keeping people from knowing the truth. He hints that it's secret government demolition, possibly alien-related, but check it out with magesight."

Mallory and Kean both took a look and saw the faint bit of magic embedded in the text. It seemed to flare occasionally as they watched.

"See that? I think the universe keeps trying to correct this page somehow, and this guy's spell energy is keeping it from happening."

"Wonder if he's aware of his power?"

"No, not likely. If he was, he'd realize that the minor shocks and stings he's repeatedly getting are karma, and he'd stop pushing. I don't think anybody who isn't attuned to magic could even find this site, so he's not achieving anything."

Mallory examined the screen full of rambling text. "Do you think he was involved in the explosion?"

Robert shook his head. "No. He's clueless. We should keep an eye on his site in the future, but right now he knows less than we do."

Robert saved the site "c0deX0fSecretz" in his bookmarks. "Spelling is not his strong suit."

"Probably the right spelling was already used as a title by somebody else's site."

"Naw, Robert's right. There are a bunch of spelling and grammatical mistakes all over the page. Might have a little bit more luck convincing people to believe him if he fixed that."

Robert closed the laptop and sat back.

"I guess I'll ask the question we need to answer: what do we do now? Without Heisenberg, should we keep investigating the artifact?"

Mallory folded her arms tightly around herself and pulled her knees up to her chest as she shook her head slowly. Robert waited for her to give a verbal answer, but Mallory didn't say a word.

Kean moved over to the spot right beside Mallory and put his arm awkwardly around her shoulders. Mallory didn't react at all to Kean's attempt at comforting, and he sheepishly withdrew his arm. The three kids sat in silence, searching for the answer but finding only sadness. Minutes ticked by. Kean absent-mindedly pushed around the stack of magazines on the coffee table, and Robert scratched marks onto the pad of paper in his hands. Finally, Mallory spoke up.

"I feel lost."

Kean nodded. Robert said "me too."

"I can't deal with this right now. Thinking about spells and auras and backlash only makes my heart hurt."

"Maybe the artifact will stop working, now that it's been triggered. Like it had one last charge stored up, and now its drained of energy."

"I hope so, Kean."

Robert kept doodling while he added in his own opinion. "At least we won't forget, the way your mom and everyone else is forgetting. We're immune to that spell effect."

"I wish I could forget."

Kean turned to face Mallory directly. "No, you don't want to forget. You'd lose all of the good things we shared with him if you did."

"This memory backlash is really strange. It's weird that we've seen it twice in a few days. Everyone has forgotten about the artifact being a wrecked piece of ocean salvage up until last week. I wonder how far the effect can go. Across the city? Across the whole world?"

"Enough, Robert! No more questions. I just want to go to school tomorrow and be a normal kid. Do homework, eat lunch, and let the adults solve the world's problems. "

"Okay Mallory. Sorry."

"It's just, I mean…"

Mallory tried to finish her thought, but the emotion of the day choked of the last bit of her sentence. She stood up and walked to the front door. Kean followed.

"I guess we're leaving, Robert."

Chapter 13

4 days of school blurred by. Mallory walked around feeling invisible. The grief that sat inside of her chest was so strong that she expected people to acknowledge it and say something, but no one said a word. As the days passed by, it became clear that no one in the world remembered Heisenberg, at least no one that the kids had contact with. Kean tried to talk about the accident, and how it was keeping him from sleeping well at night, but Mallory would just shake her head and walk away each time. Robert comforted himself with puzzling over the occurrence and trying to find out how the explosion had happened. For Robert, the grief was detached and he had a hard time really believing that Heisenberg was gone.

"It's just not the same feeling I had when I talked to my grandma. I know she's gone. When I think about H, it's different."

Kean finished chewing his mouthful of unappetizing baloney sandwich and replied. "I don't know what to tell you, Robert, but Heisenberg is definitely as gone as gone can be. I stood at the crater and I saw the empty spot where the tea shop used to be. I want him to be okay, somehow, but there's no reason to believe he escaped the explosion."

"But my grandmother…" Robert trailed off.

"Maybe Heisenberg was totally erased from reality by the effects of the magic energy he was messing with. Not killed by it, just made to never have existed in the first place. Which makes me feel a little bit worse, if that's possible."

Robert and Kean stopped their lunchtime conversation as Mallory sat down at the table. She looked exhausted. They made a feeble effort to talk about the day's events at school, but eventually they slipped into silence, and they stayed quiet until the bell rang to summon them back to class.

After the first class in the afternoon, Mallory turned the corner in the hallway to find Kean and his cousin Damien in the middle of an angry argument. They didn't notice Mallory entering earshot, so she slipped back around the corner and out of sight. She started to leave, but Kean's shouted words kept her in the same spot.

"You're being stupid, Damien! You don't owe her anything!"

"Shut your goddamned mouth, Kean!"

"If you don't stand up for yourself, she's going to keep kicking you around and hurting you. No matter what she does, you have to be true to yourself. Stop doing what she tells you to do."

"That's so easy for you to say. Why don't you just stay out of my business and go bother someone else. You nosy little brat."

The sound of a scuffle breaking out pulled Mallory forward so she could see what was happening. Kean and Damien were shoving each other, grabbing onto each other's clothes and pulling back and forth. For a second, it looked like Damien was about to throw a punch at Kean, but instead he let go of Kean and stormed off. Mallory pulled back and waited to see what would happen next. Mallory heard Kean breathing heavily, from exertion and from the stress of the confrontation. She took a step towards him before hearing him say 'hello'. As she went to answer, he kept talking. It took Mallory a few moments of being confused before she realized that Kean was on his cell phone.

"I just don't know how to handle him now. He knows I'm trying to help him. I think he does, but he just gets angry when I say anything. Yeah, I know. I know. I am trying to stay calm and listen to him. I just want things to get better. Okay. Thanks mom. Love you. Bye."

Embarrassment washed over Mallory as she stood lurking in the hallway, listening in to private family conversations. Kean came around the corner and stood face to face with Mallory.

"Hey, I didn't see you there."

"I wasn't here…I mean…I just got here. I'm going to class. Sorry! Sorry!"

"Sorry for what?"

Mallory squirmed as she tried to find the right way to say it. "I heard everything."

"Everything?"

"The argument, the phone call, everything. Well, not the start of the argument, I guess, because I have no idea what Damien did to piss you off, but I got here when the shouting started. I didn't want to listen in, Kean, I really mean it. It was an accident and I'm really really sorry."

Kean shot an angry look at Mallory and stormed off down the hall. Mallory chased him.

"Come on Kean. Just stop for a second and we can talk about this. Don't be angry."

Kean stopped. "There's nothing to talk about, and I can be as angry as I want."

"But-"

"But nothing, Mal. You're not in charge of how I feel. There are some things that you have no say in, things you can't fix. You'd probably make things worse if you tried."

"What is that supposed to mean? Are you calling me a meddler?"

"Huh? No. I mean, what's a meddler?"

From out of nowhere, Robert stepped in between Kean and Mallory and answered Kean's question. "Somebody who interferes in the affairs of other people without invitation, that's a meddler. But that doesn't matter right now. You two need to come with me."

Mallory and Kean stared at each other, still angry and hurt but not really sure on what to do next. Robert forced the issue by grabbing them both by the hand and dragging them down the hall to the computer lab. He directed Kean and Mallory into adjoining computer stations.

"Go to the livestream for CP24-it's bookmarked in the 'news' folder."

They both followed Robert's instructions and navigated to the website. In the live video stream on the site, they watched the blond morning news anchor talk about an outbreak of civil unrest taking place at Western University. Behind the anchor, the scene of the unrest was being shown. The North Campus Building, current home to the Antikythera Device, was locked down with security guards stationed at the doors. An ambulance and several police vehicles parked across the driveway to block entrance. The Anchor went into the details.

"Police are reporting that, roughly around noon today, there was a spontaneous student protest that started on the second floor and spread, seemingly to all parts of the building. The protest escalated to violence and vandalism, and campus security had to move in and subdue the protestors with the help of the London Police. The cause of the protest is still unknown, and all suspects have so far refused to explain why they chose to disturb the peace today. There have also been scattered reports of a mysterious illness in the building, though currently they are treating those reports as a hoax. Until the building is confirmed safe, however, all classes are cancelled and the building will be on quarantine. When we have further details, we'll let you know."

The news anchor moved on to a teaser for a new story, before cutting to a commercial. Mallory turned around and looked at Kean and Robert.

"What are the chances that it had nothing to do with the AD?"

"Approximately zero. It seems that I'm now perpetually connected to the device. I felt it activate."

"What did it feel like?" Kean asked.

"Robert, you don't look so good. Are you feeling okay? You should sit down."

"I don't feel particularly well. As soon as I started to watch the live stream of the building, my migraine came back."

Robert sat down in an empty chair off to the side of the long table covered in computers. Kean made sure that his browser and Mallory's browser were both closed.

"Is it any better now that the video is off?"

"Somewhat. The sensation has lessened to a pressure behind my eyes, which is the way it felt when I was first aware of it."

"So does that mean the AD is still functional and doing whatever it was doing?"

"It's very difficult for me to tell. I'm very far away from it, and the signal is fuzzy and hard to tune it to. And I'm afraid that approaching it would cause me considerable pain and possible injury."

"So…you're not sure?" Mallory pressed the issue.

Robert sighed. "If I have to guess, and I'd really prefer not to, I'd say that it's on, but waiting to be triggered. It's in stand-by mode."

Mallory put her head down on top of her folded arms. "I quit. There's no avoiding this, is there?"

"Not unless we want to let that magical box keep messing with people's lives."

"So let someone else figure it out!"

"Who?"

"I don't know, Robert. Maybe the magical art lady. Maybe some ultra-secret team of super-wizards. Just not us. Not now. Not without Heisenberg. This sucks."

Kean nodded. "I know, Mal. But even if we pretend that everything is fine, the AD will continue to hurt people."

"You have no proof it will."

"The problem is, we don't have any proof that it won't. Mom always says that if you see a fault, you have to try and fix it."

"Your mom is a pain in the butt."

"Agreed."

Mallory growled in frustration before standing up and pacing around the room as she planned.

"There's no way we can get there today. And cutting class tomorrow will get me in a world of trouble with my mom, so that leaves Saturday. And of course, we're all broke, so we have to bum a ride to London."

"Would your mom drive us again, on the pretense of a follow-up visit to finish the tour?" Robert suggested.

"Mom has a pottery class pretty much all Saturday, and she's already warned me that nothing short of medical emergency will get her to cancel that."

"She seems very dedicated to her crafting. I'm a little surprised."

"Yeah she took it up a while ago, and it does make her chill out and relax. She's not a lot of fun when she's tense. So, no ride from her."

Kean spoke up. "I think Damien has to go down to London in the next few weeks anyway. Maybe I can convince him to go this Saturday?"

"Really? You'd still ask him, even after that fight?"

"What fight are you talking about?"

"Nothing, Robert. It's none of anyone else's business. Not even really nosy friends who lurk in hallways."

Mallory blushed. "I already said 'sorry'. I can't apologize any harder."

"Just forget it. I'll talk to Damien and get things set up for Saturday."

"And what, we'll figure out what to do on the ride up?"

"Unless you have a better idea."

The kids finished off the week and made sure they were fully prepared for their weekend mission. At 9:30am on Saturday, Damien pulled into Mallory's driveway and honked the horn. Mallory came running out of the house, and she jumped into the back seat of the battered 2001 Corolla.

"I saw you pull up, pal. You didn't need to honk. My mother is going to have a field day warning me about 'gentlemen callers who honk their horns at ladies'."

"Who talks like that? Is your mom from a 1800s cotton plantation or something?"

Mallory flicked Damien's ear with her finger. "Shut up. You don't even know what a plantation is."

"For a chick who needs a ride to a town 2 hours away, you sure are bitchy."

"Excuse me? Did you just call me a bitch?"

Kean interrupted from the passenger seat. "As much as I would love to spend the whole day with you two fighting, how about you both shut up and be nice to each other? Mallory, you remember my cousin Damien, the nice guy who is going to drive us to London, for free, and wait for us to tour the campus building, AND give us a ride back?"

"But, he, oh fine. Perhaps I was a little nasty. Sorry Damien."

"And Damien, you know my best friend Mallory, the girl who kept you from flunking French class last year? She tutored you for 3 weeks straight, every night, and the only reward she got out of it was a tray of cookies you made for her. Which were burnt."

"Kean, you don't gotta be so heavy handed. I get it. We're cool. Right, Mal?"

"Oui. Nous Sommes tres fantastique."

"So where's the other kid, the new guy? Don't you travel together all the time?"

"Oh, Robert? He's staying home. He's allergic to something in that building. Gives him a migraine."

"Alright. You guys ready to roll?"

Kean and Mallory both answered "yup" and with that, Damien put the car into reverse and pulled out of the driveway.

Chapter 14

They drove out to the edge of town and struck out for their destination. Damien followed the back road route towards the northern outskirts of London. There was something relaxing and interesting about the patchwork of farmland and houses surrounded by trees that all of the kids enjoyed. It was so different from their suburban home surroundings.The fighting that had started the day was quickly forgotten, and the car was filled with laughing and singing for the duration of the trip. They arrived at the University and Damien pulled the car into the massive parking garage across the street from the University Hospital. He explained what he was going to do.

"I have to go find the record department here and pick up my mom's file. They said it would only take a few minutes, but that's never true. Hospitals move slow. When I'm done, I'll call Kean."

"Right. And if we are finished early, we'll give you a call and check if you need anything."

"Can I ask why you had to drive all the way down here to get your mom's file? They could have easily sent it by certified mail or courier or something. It would have been cheaper too." Mallory hoped that her question wasn't too nosy, but it had been bothering her the whole trip.

Damien kicked at the ground and sighed. "Mom doesn't trust them. She says that they'd try to protect their ass by intentionally losing the file, or they might even send a fake file."

"Really? That sounds a bit crazy. Paranoid."

"Mallory!" Kean said, shooting her a warning look.

Damien shrugged. The profoundly sad look on his face told Mallory that he didn't have a good answer for his mother's demands.

"Sorry, Damien. I was just rambling. Ignore my foolish mouth."

"Come on, Mallory. Let's go. Damien, we'll talk to you later, okay buddy?"

"Yeah. Sure."

Mallory and Kean headed south, following the sidewalk towards the NCB. Kean watched Damien over his shoulder, as Damien slouched across the road and into the hospital.

"Poor guy."

"So, can you tell me about what's going on, or is it a secret?"

"Mal, it's not my place to tell you. Just leave it alone, okay?"

"Okay. Hey, did you tell Robert that we made it?"

"Yeah, I sent him a text when we pulled up. It's so weird that his magic doesn't work like ours anymore. It's all waves and radiation now. Did you know he's trying to listen to radio waves without a radio?"

"Is that useful?"

"Who knows? But it would be cool if he could."

Mallory and Kean tried their best to look casual and cool as they approached the NCB. They were expecting flashing lights and a retinue of armed security guards, but luckily their expectations were overblown. In front of the main entrance there was a tired-looking security guard sitting in a chair, reading a paperback novel. They kept walking and passed by the front of the building at a leisurely pace. On the other side they left the sidewalk and walked down the grassy hill towards the neighbouring building until they were out of sight.

The building in front of them was a long and squat structure that looked like an industrial storage facility. The sign beside the entrance door unhelpfully identified the building as "Staging".

"Wonder what that means? Maybe this is where all of the forbidden experiments happen."

"They probably keep all of the extra furniture in here, or something."

"You have a distinct lack of imagination sometimes, Kean."

Mallory switched over to magesight and scanned the area for signs of any magical activity. She could see the faint traces of the AD's effect permeating the NCB, but the energy was passive and steady.

"Looks like the AD is asleep again, and nothing else is magically active in there."

"That's a relief. I can see a side entrance, through those bushes over there. I can't see it clearly though."

"I'll fix that, my man. I need to stretch out my spell legs."

"Spell legs?"

"You know what I mean-like stretching out your legs after a long car trip. I need to exercise my magical ability to keep it limber."

Kean was confused. "Your spell casting is stiff? How can you tell? Do I need to warm up with practice spells before I cast?"

"OH NEVER MIND! I honestly don't understand why you are so very literal, Kean."

Kean snickered under his breath. "Because it gets you so riled up, that's why."

"Listen, I'm going to cram a spell up your nose if you don't cut it out."

"Gotcha."

Mallory glared at Kean for a moment, daring him to cross her again. He put his hands up in a gesture of surrender, and she accepted it and turned to face the NCB side entrance. She snuck one more glance at Kean and cracked a slight smile accompanied by a head shake.

Mallory focused on the brush that was obscuring their line of sight. She threw out a handful of thin, twisting lines of spell energy. As always, her spell took on the look of chalk drawings traced onto the air in front of her. Her imagination loved the look of those powdered lines as they came together to create a colourful and childlike picture that had come to life. The lines extended from her fingers and shot into the shrub, entangling the branches. Mallory gently tugged on the lines to part the branches and leave a clear view of the door itself.

Kean peered through the newly created path and examined the door. Perched above and slightly to the right of the door was a surveillance camera that quietly scanned the space in front of the door. One of the maintenance staff stepped out of the door and the camera whirred and tracked his motion until he was on the sidewalk. Kean quickly scanned the rest of the building looking for additional cameras, but the one over the door seemed to be the only one. He nodded to Mallory.

"Got it. One camera over the door. You can drop the spell now."

Mallory flicked her fingers to untangle the lines from the scrub brush. The chalk lines obediently disengaged and snaked their way back to Mallory's hands. As the lines reached the tips of her fingers, backlash transformed them from the thin lines she had designed, to vines covered in thorns that snapped around her hands and pricked her skin. She sucked in air as the stinging pain covered her hands.

"Cripes. That sucked. I was hoping that carefully ending the spell would lessen the backlash."

"Doesn't look like that helped at all." Kean said, as the red thorn welts rose up on Mallory's hands.

"Guess not. Well, off we go."

They walked from the front of the staging building and pushed through the bushes to reach the side door of the NCB. As soon as the camera moved to track their position, Kean cast his spell. He summoned a small bundle of spell energy and shaped it into the form of a jittery and nervous squirrel. The spell squirrel ran up the doorframe and directly under the camera. The surveillance camera dutifully followed the motion of the squirrel, giving Mallory and Kean a chance to close the distance to the door without being seen. Mallory yanked on the door, only to discover it was locked from the inside.

"Must be a pushbar" she muttered, as she looked around for a way to open it up.

"Just use a spell."

"Still a little sore here, Kean. Give me a second."

"There's only so long a squirrel under the camera is plausible, Mal. Hurry."

Mallory hunched over and looked between the door and the doorframe for a clue on how to open the door. She could just see the latch holding the door closed through the thin crack. She dug around in her satchel for a moment, and pulled out her multitool. She slipped the long, thin blade of the tool underneath the latch and pulled up quickly. As the knife moved the latch to the slide, she yanked on the door handle and was rewarded with the door flying open.

"Sweet!"

Kean pushed Mallory forward into the building and followed in after her. As the door closed behind them, Kean stopped walking. A strange look crossed his face. Kean started wiggling his limbs and butt while pulling randomly at his clothing. A strangled squeak escaped his lips during this weird dance. Mallory was alarmed.

"What's wrong, Kean? Are you having a seizure?"

"No. Eep. I'm…fine" he managed to say through gritted teeth.

Mallory watched him gyrate and suddenly realized what was happening. She fought the urge to laugh, but a stream of giggles crept out of her anyway.

"Kean, can I ask a sensitive question? Is there a squirrel in your pants?"

Kean refused to answer, but his shimmying and grimacing confirmed the particular karmic punishment he was experiencing. Kean dashed down the hall and found a bathroom. "Wait here" he ordered Mallory. He reemerged a minute later, looking considerably calmer.

"I had to check if there were any scratches in…places."

"Do I want to know the results?"

"Everything is fine down there. But that was not a pleasant experience."

They crept down the hallway on the lookout for a staircase, signs of spell activity and any additional security. The building appeared to be deserted and quiet. At the end of the hall they found the stairs and moments later they found themselves in an unknown part of the second floor.

"I have no idea where we are."

"Who needs a map when you have the gift of...magique!" Mallory said, finishing her statement with a dramatic twirl. Kean just rolled his eyes in response as Mallory waved her arms in a flourish and dramatically looked around.

"My uncanny gift of magical sight has shown me that the direction we need to travel is....this way!" she said as she dashed off down the hall.

"I can do exactly the same thing, you know" grumbled Kean as he followed her.

They snaked down the branched corridors, getting lost in dead ends a few times, before finally finding the right branch that took them to the Device's holding room. Before Mallory could dash down the hall to the door, Kean threw his arm out to stop her.

"Another camera above the door."

"Huh. Was that here last time?"

"Nope. Just the one inside."

"They must have beefed up security on the door after Robert broke in."

"So will you do the magical honours, or should I?"

"Couldn't we just put a mirror in front of it or something?"

"Take a sec and think about that idea, Kean."

"What?"

"If you put a mirror in front of the camera, then the guard watching would suddenly see a picture of the camera itself, which would probably raise his suspicions a bit."

"Well you come up with a better idea. I'm still itchy and creeped out by the squirrel backlash."

"That's a heck of a sentence to hear."

"It's wierder to say it, trust me."

"I guess I can take this one, even though my hands a raw with thorn scrapes."

"Hey, I have a better idea. What if we take a picture of the hall from the same angle with one of our phones, and then hold the picture up to the lens?"

"That's better than your first one, but how do we get up to it to take the picture, without being seen by the camera in the first place? If we can avoid the camera, we don't even need the distracting picture."

Kean shrugged. "Guess that's true. There has to be a better way in though. The less magic we use around the device, the better."

"Why's that?"

"Take a look at it again. The magic that's coming off of it right now, even when it's inactive, is a little strange. It's kind of wrong."

Mallory focused her magesight on the room in front of them and the energy being emitted by the device. Sure enough, looking closely at the aura revealed a jagged and unpleasant aspect to it. It was different and opposed to the normal energies the two friends had used before.

"See? When you look really closely, you start to feel resistance from the device itself, like it's magic is causing feedback with ours. If we cast spells when we're right beside it, the two energies would collide."

"And it could be a nasty collision, is that what you're thinking? Like matter and anti-matter smashing together?"

"Anti-matter? Probably not but-hey hold on a sec."

Kean blinked his eyes repeatedly to readjust to using his normal sight, and then he jogged down the hallway and around the corner out of sight. Mallory was frozen for a moment, unsure if she should follow Kean.

"Kean! Kean! Where are you going?" she hissed. "First time we come here, Robert takes off. Now Kean does it this time. And they call me the impetuous one."

Chapter 15

Mallory paced the short corridor for a couple of minutes while she considered her options. When she heard footsteps coming back down the hall, she jumped into the corner of the tiny alcove and scrunched down in hopes of being less visible.

"Hey, where'd you go, Mal?"

"I'm here, hiding from what I thought was a security guard. Didn't we all have a serious talk about running off without explanation, buddy?"

"Oh. Oh yeah, sorry. I was kind of caught up. Follow me-I figured something out."

Kean grabbed Mallory's hand and led her off down the hallway. They turned left at the cross and then turned left again into an assistant professor's office. Kean got down on all fours and crawled into a small ventilation shaft in the back wall. Mallory was sure they would both get stuck in the tiny space if she went in.

"Mal, come on. Keep following."

Kean crawled out of sight and Mallory reluctantly followed. 5 feet down, the shaft intersected with another larger maintenance shaft. this larger space had large water pipes and bundles of multicoloured cables lining the walls. Kean partially stood up and pointed at a grate in the wall at eye height.

"Take a look through there, Mal."

Mallory crept up to the grate and looked through to see a small, dark room.

"Great, a dark room."

"How about you look with your magical sight. Jeez. I have to explain everything."

Mallory stifled a return volley and instead looked into the room using magesight. The Anithikythera Device shimmered with it's strange magical aura.

"You found a back door."

"Well, back vent, to be accurate, but yeah. And everything is turned off in there. They must have shut down the monitoring setup when the building was locked down."

"Are you sure the cameras are off in there too?"

"I know how to check, I think."

Kean pulled out his phone and called Robert. The crackling noise that accompanied the ringing sound worried Kean. He wondered if being in the heart of a building, surrounded by industrial materials, would end up blocking the phone signal. After 3 rings, Robert answered. Kean told him to check on the live stream of the device.

"Alright, but why are you whispering? Are you in trouble?"

"No. We're in the walls of the NCB and if we're too loud, a security guard might hear us."

"You're in the walls?"

"I'll explain later."

"The research website is showing a dark screen, and there's a notice. 'Due to unforeseen circumstances, the live monitoring will be suspended until further notice. We apologize for the inconvenience."

"Great, that's what I needed to know. Thanks, Robert."

Kean hung up and gave Mallory the thumbs up.

"It's all off. We can go in."

Mallory dug around in her satchel and pulled out a small maglite flashlight.

"You have a flashlight and a mutli-tool in your bag? What else is in there, Survival Annie?"

"Remember when I was stuck in the abandoned elevator shaft with a ghost for company? I decided that it would be nice to be a little bit more prepared for strange situations."

"...Fair enough."

Mallory scrambled over the pipes on the wall and popped the grate off of the opening. She snagged the metal cover on its way down to keep it from clattering onto the floor. She handed the grate back to Kean and hauled herself through the opening, with her flashlight clenched between her teeth. The difficulty of gracefully landing on the other side became obvious to her as she dangled half-way between the two rooms. "I shouldn't have gone head-first" she muttered to herself, the flashlight garbling her words into a unintelligible growl. Mallory contorted herself and managed to reach one arm back to the lip of the opening while bringing her left leg through. She hissed in pain as her shin scraped an exposed piece of metal flashing. After a moment of silent cursing and panic, she brought both of her legs through the opening and she landed on the ground of the observation lab with a dull thud. Mallory stood motionless and waited for some kind of reaction to her presence, but the room stayed quiet.

"Okay Kean, I'm in. There's room for you too, but don't come in head first: it's a pain in the butt."

Kean slithered through the vent with amazing ease and ended up standing beside Mallory. Mallory went back to looking into her bag.

"You're a bit of a showoff, aren't you?"

"I crawled through a hole-how is that showing off?"

Mallory found the small pack of bandaids and tended to the scratch on her shin. Kean crouched down to check out the wound.

"It's not too bad, but it did break the skin. Here, let me put the bandaid on."

Kean took the bandages from Mallory and gently applied them to the scrape. He used the edge of his t-shirt to wipe away the tiny trace of blood left on her leg.

"There you go."

"Thanks Kean. You'll make a great mom someday."

Kean snorted and laughed. "Let's get down to business."

They left the lights turned off in the tiny room and used Mallory's flashlight to illuminate the device. Though neither of them had been able to take a close look at the Antikythera device durng their first visit, it looked virtually unchanged since then.. Kean examined the face of the device and tried to puzzle out the meaning of the position of the control levers.

"I think the levers have been moved."

"Of course they have. Robert moved them" Mallory retorted as she peered at the back of the device.

"I know that. I meant that the levers have been moved again. The long one with the crooked scrollwork on it was pointed upwards before, and now it's at 9'0'clock."

"Changing the settings might be the reason the thing activated again. What are the other two levers pointed at?"

"Um, a cluster of stars, I think, and another engraved icon. Maybe a sigil, or a word."

"Can you get a better look at it?"

"Not really."

"Use your phone and take pics. I'll do the same."

A barrage of picture taking commenced, filling the room with flashes of light. By the 4th picture, Mallory noticed something.

"There's a latch back here. It's tiny and it blends into the ornamental metalwork, but it looks like a functional latch."

"Why would anyone need to get inside of the box? Do you think it has moving parts?"

"Dunno. Let's find out, shall we?"

"GEEZ MALLORY NO!" Kean shouted, but her hand was already extended to flick the tiny gossamer hook out of its eyelet. The back of the device swung open on a previously invisible hinge.

"See? It was perfectly safe." Mallory tried to hide the nervous shaking in her hand as she pretended to be calm and cool.

"You didn't know that! The stupid box sent Robert to the hospital when he brushed against it, but you decide it's safe to mess with it?"

"Granted, not one of my finest decisions, but hear me out. If there's a latch, it means the makers of the device wanted people to get inside of it."

"But what if it was boobytrapped?"

"Now you're just being paranoid, Kean. Oh my god. Look!"

Kean hurried around to Mallory's side and peered into the inner workings of the device. Tiny spell clouds, alternating between rigid geometric shapes and organic forms, orbited around the center of the device. The orbits of the spell clouds were described by silver-white beams of light as thin as thread. The spells were in perpetual motion, brushing within a millimeter of each other but never colliding.

"Mallory, this is a real artifact. These spells are existing and functional without any mage directing it."

"Wait, what?"

"There's no signature. If a mage was currently fueling these spells, they would have his or her colour, but they don't have any colour. And even with spells this small and low-powered, shouldn't we see some trail leading off towards the caster?"

"So you're trying to tell me that these spells were cast by a mage-"

"Or mages" Kean interjected.

"Or Mages, and the spells became permanent and independent?"

"There might be better explanations than that. But I can't think of them."

Mallory watched the spell constellation twirl and dance in the tiny space.

"I don't have a better theory. I wish…I wish Heisenberg was here."

Kean sniffed back a tear as the sadness of their lost mentor struck him again. "I know. But we have to do our best, the way he would want us to."

Mallory nodded. "Agreed. So, we have an ancient device that is fueled by about a dozen permanent magical spells. The device can accidentally be triggered, and every effect that it's caused so far has been harmful to the people who interact with it."

"And the magic is almost completely hidden by the outer casing when its closed. We couldn't see any of the specific spell traces before you opened up the box."

"Do we know for sure that this thing will only hurt people? What if it also has really helpful settings, like curing cancer or solving crime?"

"We don't have any proof it can be helpful, but we have two very real events where the thing hurt people. Trying to use it for good would be way too dangerous, and we're not ready to try to do that."

"You're probably right. We can maybe figure out more about the device after it's safely disabled."

"Hopefully."

"We should call Robert and tell him about this."

Kean went to make the call but stopped. "No signal."

"That's a bit weird. We had signal in here earlier. Yup, mine is cut off too. Wonder if the device is blocking the signal now."

"If so, that might mean it's generating higher levels of radiation, which means we should hurry up."

They stayed stationary for a full five minutes, crouched in front of the Antikythera Device and watching the inner workings for a sign of how to disable it.

Okay, how does this sound? Each spell is weak and very small, so it must be the interaction of all of the spells that give it the power to affect anything."

Mallory weighed the idea. "Sounds plausible."

"Good. And, since it depends on the whole group of spells to work, then dispersing one spell should disable the whole device. Countering just one of the spells should be pretty easy and safe. Does that make sense?"

"As much as it can, Kean. At least that doesn't sound like it has much potential for a nasty surprise: at the very worst, our counter-spell fizzles and leaves the thing intact."

"That's my guess too."

"Right. So, paper rock scissors, loser casts the counter-spell?"

Mallory held up her clenched fist and waited for Kean to do the same. They counted to three and extended their hands. Mallory threw paper that was cut up into shreds by Kean's scissors.

"It's all yours, Mal."

"Gee, thanks. You know, there might not even be any backlash. Think about it-this box full of spells is clearly disobeying the universe's suggestion that magic doesn't exist, so disabling it is actually returning the universe to the expected order."

"Don't know if I'd bet the farm on that, Mal."

"Let a girl hope, buddy."

Mallory summoned a handful of her own magical energy and shaped it into a clasping pair of tongs. She directed the energy into the spell constellation, and slowly began to close the tongs onto one of the tiny spell clouds. When the spell cloud was within her counterspell's bubble, she started to shrink the bubble until it pressed upon the cloud itself.

The two spells intermingled and began fighting each other. Mallory could feel the tension between her spell and the devices spell pushing back against her will. Suddenly, the conflict reached a tipping point, and Mallory's counter spell began to erase the device spell. As the device spell dissolved into ethereal nothingness, Mallory felt a build-up of resistance forming around her. The build-up accelerated quickly and filled the air with painful electricity. The counter-spell made one final push to destroy the old device's spell, and the collision slammed the device spell into an unseen barrier. The energy in the air condensed into a single point and ripped a hole in the reality in front of them. A tiny, micro-rift formed in the air between Mallory and the device, a perfect simulation of the rift above the battle site back in Toronto. Through the micro-rift, a burst of uncontrolled spell energy came barreling into the room. It smashed Mallory's counter-spell into oblivion, and it continued towards Mallory and slammed into her hand as she tried to jerk it out of the way. Kean reflexively grabbed at Mallory's arm and helped her get out of the path of the rift's explosive output. The energy from the rift hurtled into the cinderblock wall behind them and disintegrated the mortar holding the wall in place.

Chapter 16

The destruction of the wall had absorbed the remainder of the energy expelled from the micro-rift. The tiny tear in the fabric of reality winked out of existence, leaving the target of the counter-spell moving unharmed around its prescribed orbit. Mallory warily brought her hand up towards her face to survey the damage. She let out a huge sigh of relief.

"Thank god I still have fingers. They went numb when the rift energy hit them."

Kean looked at the partially collapsed wall behind them with wide eyes and then turned back to Mallory.

"Are you okay, Mal? Oh jeez, that could have been terrible!"

The sound of the fire alarm going off drowned out Mallory's answer..

"I'm fine but we gotta get out of here" she shouted

"Close the device! They'll know we messed with it."

"The hole in the wall might clue them in to our messing with things."

Mallory closed up the device carefully, slipping the latch back into place when the two pieces were joined again. A slight tension pushed back against her until the latch was secured. Mallory looked around the room as the fire alarm rang and echoed all around them. She saw a study, industrial shipping box on the ground, and guessed its purpose.

"Kean, grab that box and get it open!"

"What are you planning?" Kean asked while opening the box.

Mallory gently picked up the Antikythera Device and took it over to the open shipping box.

"Good, I was right. This is the box the thing came in."

"What? Whoa, hold on. Are you stealing the device?"

"Technically we are. And it's safer that way. Look, it fits in perfectly. And the box will keep the levers from being accidentally moved, so we won't have any magical misfires."

Mallory closed the box up and picked it up. It was heavier than she anticipated. She had unthinkingly grabbed it with her numb hand and the weight quickly overwhelmed her injured fingers. The box slipped out of her grasp for a second and jerked towards the ground. Both Mallory and Kean gave out a shriek of terror and surprise as they tried to catch the box before it hit the ground. Mallory managed to regain her grip on the box and avoid the impact. She handed the box over to Kean.

"That was close. I don't want to find out what happens if this thing smashes to the ground."

"Yup. I think I hear something down the hall-We gotta go now!"

Mallory followed Kean out through the hole in the wall and listened for the new sound. Between the ringing of the alarm she heard the crackle and squawk of walkie-talkies. The two friends bolted through the nearest stairwell and ran down the steps until they found an exit door.

"Spell for the camera?' Mallory asked.

Kean shook his head. "Just hold your coat up to cover us. They know someone is here.We just don't want to be identified."

Mallory pulled off her jacket and held it above the two of them as they pushed open the door and rushed outside. As they stepped outside, Mallory's phone started to ring. She looked around in a panic, dreading the chance of being discovered. The small crowd of security and emergency crews at the front entrance of the building didn't seem to notice the sound of her ringing phone. Kean and Mallory ran off before anyone did notice anddecided to investigate the sound. Mallory turned the ringer off on her phone as they dashed over the patchy grass, and they didn't stop running until they reached the scraggly forest of scrub and trees behind the NCB. They stopped running when they were out of sight from the building and took stock of the situation.

"This is close to the worst case scenario."

"At least we didn't blow up. Much. How's your hand?"

"Feeling is coming back."

"Was it karma?"

"Not really, more like raw energy shooting out of the reaction. Backlash usually feels directed, you know? Aimed at you. But this was just a blast."

"Did you see the same thing inside the rift that I did?"

Mallory looked surprised. "No-you could see inside? I was watching the collision of the spells and then I was trying to shield myself from what was happening. I guess I stopped watching."

"When the tear happened, right before the blast, I got a peek through the rift to something. Or somewhere. Whatever it was that I was looking at, whatever I saw, it froze me in place for a second. It was like my brain needed the world to pause for a moment so it could understand what it was looking at. And then I saw the energy blast about to knock into you and I moved."

"I wish any of that made sense to me right now. Well, whatever this stupid device is meant to do, it won't help us get the hell out of here. Can you give Damien a call and convince him to leave as soon as possible?"

Kean pulled out his phone and had a terse conversation with Damien. Kean hung up the phone and repeated the information to Mallory.

"Damien says that he's going to be another half hour, and if we want to wait in the car, it's on the 3rd floor of the parking garage. And he thinks I should quit being such a pain in the ass."

"Words to live by. Think we can get to the car unseen?"

Kean examined the side and back edges of the parking garage.

"We can hop over the edge there, and then go up the staircases. There might be cameras, though."

"I'll take care of them. Let's go."

Mallory and Kean moved slowly through the scrub forest, trying in vain to be completely silent. The noise from the NCB behind them was diminishing and no additional emergency vehicles had shown up after the first fire truck, ambulance and police cars. Mallory watched the ambulance drive away with its lights off and at regular speed.

"I hope that means no one was hurt."

"Probably. The building was pretty much empty. The odds are really high that no one was near the blast."

"I'd be more comforted by the odds being on our side if my twinkly special powers didn't go against the odds every time they're used."

Above each of the doors of the parking garage stairwell, a camera sat perched and immobile. When they approached the door, Mallory drew the simplest spell she could imagine. She drew a square of blackout cloth that sprung into existence directly under the camera's view and lasted until they had closed the door behind them. By the time they reached the 3rd floor, the spell backlash had dimmed the light entering Mallory's eyes.

"Kean, make sure I'm following behind you. The backlash has partially blinded me. It's like I'm wearing 3 pairs of sunglasses at the same time."

"Okay, here's the car, and here's the back seat door."

"Are you proposing something inappropriate, Mister Kean? A little back seat dalliance, perhaps?"

Mallory couldn't see Kean's embarrassed blushing, but she could tell from his voice that her jibe had worked.

"Mallory, just get in and don't be dumb. It's easier to hide in the back."

"Kean, you gotta relax. Chicks don't dig guys who are that uptight."

Mallory climbed into the back bench seat of the car while Kean put the device box in the trunk. He covered the box in the old, scratchy wool blanket that was perpetually left in the car for emergency picnics and campouts and he closed the trunk. A flicker of motion from the ramp caught Kean's eyeHe realized that someone was walking up the ramp and towards their car. Kean hurried around the side of the car and slipped into the back seat beside Mallory. They both scrunched down and hid. Kean contorted his head so that he could get a partial glimpse of the threat in the reflection from the driver side mirror.

"It's a security guard" Kean whispered.

"Does he look aggressive?"

"How should I know? I'm barely able to see half of his body. I can't tell what his mood is. He's walking down the row of cars."

"Fast or slow?"

"He's not running, but he's not going super-slow either. I've lost sight of him. Shh!"

The two kids pressed themselves as low and as far back into the seat as they could. Minutes ticked by in silence. Kean counted to 100 in his head and decided that he needed to take another look. He slowly brought his head up and looked over the seat and out the back window. The security guard was at the far end of the row of cars, standing by the stairwell door. The dim light of the garage, coupled with the thin wedge of weak sunlight at the opposite end of the building made the whole space gloomy and hard to see.The guard had a large flashlight in his hand and he flicked it on. The guard's flashlight beam swept down the row of cars and towards Damien's car. Kean dropped his head quickly and flattened out his body to avoid the light hitting him. Kean's fear of getting caught was quite evident to Mallory, who could see the panic in Kean's eyes as he lay on top of her, braced on his elbows and knees, separated from her by mere centimeters. The urge to giggle at the situation took hold of Mallory and she fought to stay still and not burst out laughing. The mad look that crossed Kean's face only made the urge to laugh stronger. Kean popped his head back up for a split second to confirm that the guard was finished his inspection. The guard had turned off the light and stepped through the stairwell door. As the door closed behind the guard, Kean sighed in relief and Mallory let out the ferocious giggling fit.

"Well howdy there, fella. Oh, if the girls in grade nine could see me now-how jealous they'd be."

Kean scowled at Mallory and tried to move away from her without inadvertently touching her inappropriately. His contortions fueled more laughter from Mallory. Kean finally made his way clear of her and he sat down on his side of the seat.

"Why do you keep teasing me like that, Mal? The 'girls in grade nine' don't even know I exist."

"Good grief you're oblivious. You really don't know, do you? You are one of their favourite discussion topics. I've wandered into a few conversations about you in the last few months, and there's usually some giggling and squealing that happens. You're one of the most desirable boys in the school, and considering that you're the same age as these girls that normally tend to swoon over the senior boys, you're pretty hot stuff. To them."

"I...uh...I'm just gonna pretend you didn't tell me all of that."

"Play it your way, chief. I –EEK!" Mallory gave a tiny yelp as a buzzing vibration went off in her pocket.

"Are you okay?"

Mallory looked sheepish.

"Just my phone. I forgot I had it on 'vibrate'. Hello?"

"WHAT DID YOU DO?" Robert shouted from the other end of the phone conversation. It was loud enough that Kean could hear it. Mallory held the phone away from her ear.

"Hey, hey now. No yelling, Robert."

"There was a giant EM burst that originated from the university about 15 minutes ago, and it nearly knocked me on my butt."

"How did you know to look for it?"

"I had a feeling that something was about to happen. It was an itchy feeling, like when magic is being used. It must be that the

EM burst was associated with a magical effect. Did the device activate again?"

"…in a manner of speaking. See, we went into the building and snuck past the guards and cameras to find the device and we had to crawl through the vent to get into the room. I found a latch at the back of the device and I opened it, and we found spells inside. Kean suggested that we disable the device by nullifying one of the tiny spells inside and I went along with the idea, even though it asounded dangerous-"

"Hey, that's not true!" Kean protested.

"I'm on the phone, Kean. Shh. Anyway, a counter-spell was cast and it almost worked but then something went a little wrong, and a tiny little rift formed, like the one back at the collapsed subway site but much much smaller. The tiny rift closed, but before it did, it kind of blew a hole in the wall. But I'm fine, even though it almost blasted me. And the device is safe and sound…with us."

"Mallory, I don't want to be rude, but please be quiet for a second. I need to tell you something."

The tone of Robert's voice made Mallory stop her rambling explanation completely and listen.

"Go ahead, Robert."

"When that burst happened, I heard something inside of it. A radio transmission. It was garbled up and incomprehensible, but there's a message in there. I recorded it, and I'm not going to stop until I decipher it. Mallory, I recognized the speaker in the transmission. The words were gibberish, but I know that voice. It was Heisenberg, Mallory."

Mallory tried to reply to Robert, but all she could manage was a string of stuttered syllables. The words refused to coalesce into completion. She managed to spit out "you're wrong. It's a mistake."

"It's not, Mallory. I don't know how the message was created, or where it came from. Maybe it was a recording that was triggered by the rift formation, but I'm sure it was him."

"You could be delusional, Robert. You've been on pain pills recently for your migraines. Maybe the device made you bonkers. Or maybe it was a ghost pretending to be Heisenberg."

"Does that seem reasonable?" Robert asked.

"None of this is reasonable!" Mallory shouted.

"I don't believe it was a ghost, either Heisenberg's or an imposter. There's a different feeling that comes along with a communication from the dead world, a distance and loneliness that I always feel when I have my dream talks with my grandma. That feeling wasn't there."

"I know that feeling. So it's not a ghost. Oh my god. Hold on, Robert, I have to explain to Kean."

Mallory put the phone to the side and excitedly repeated the story that Robert had just told her. Kean grabbed the phone from her and asked Robert "Are you sure? Really sure?"

"Kean, I'm certain. It was Heisenberg."

Kean whooped loudly in celebration, shouting, "Yes!" at a volume that made the word echo through the entire garage. Mallory grabbed the phone from Kean and shushed him.

"We'll get caught, dummy. Remember the stolen property in the trunk?"

"Stolen? What did you do? Was there an explosion? The news is reporting an explosion." Robert asked, alarmed.

"Just a little one. Barely knocked out the wall of the lab. And it was totally an accident."

"The police don't think it was an accident. The news is reporting it as an explosion that may be terror-related."

"What? That is very bad news. And an immense overreaction, if you ask me."

"I doubt they'd let you clarify and explain. It might be best to leave the area quickly."

"As fast as we can, but we have to wait for our ride. I'll call you when we get back home. Bye Robert."

As if on cue, the driver's side door opened and Damien flopped down into the seat.

"Alright, let's get going."

He turned around to see why no one was in the passenger seat beside him, and he smirked when he saw Mallory and Kean in the back seat, with their hair mussed up and clothing disheveled.

"Oh, I see what's been going on back here. Hope you didn't make a mess, buddy."

"What? Oh that's gross dude. Don't be gross."

"I assure you there was no fooling around back here, Damien. Your ccousin has been a perfect gentleman."

"Whatever, that's not my business. You ready to go or what?"

"We're ready. Oh, the news is reporting some kind of incident on campus, near the art building down the road. Better go the other way off campus so that we avoid the traffic." Mallory proposed, trying to be nonchalant about the route change. Damien shrugged and started up the car. Both Mallory and Kean watched out the back window as they drove off campus, watching the flashing lights of the emergency vehicles which had been joined by an explosives disposal unit and a couple of ominous looking black cars. They held their breath as they drove away, but there was no sign of pursuit as they left the city and headed back home.

Chapter 17

The fog in front of his eyes slowly started to clear. Heisenberg looked around the room he was in to get some sense of where he might be. A dull, constant throbbing pain filled his head. He went to brush the sweat off of his forehead, only to discover that he was restrained and shackled to the hospital bed he was laying in. Heisenberg tested the restraints to see if he could just slip out of them, but his only reward for his effort was an increase in his headache pain.

"Don't strain yourself, sir. You've been sedated, and you're bound to hurt yourself by thrashing around."

Heisenberg's mouth was dry and pasty, but he managed to croak out a comeback.

"I'm 'bound' to hurt myself? What did I do to deserve a pun?"

The woman at his side moved closer, and Heisenberg could now see that she was a nurse. She listed off his rule violations.

"First off, you snuck out of your bed, despite being in no shape to gallivant around the hospital. And then you made your way into the communications room and you started to fiddle with the ambulance dispatcher's radio. All the while, you were mumbling and shouting utter nonsense, most likely caused by your affected mental state. When we discovered you, the security guard had to wrestle you away from the radio and back into the bed. With the help of another shot of sedative."

"I don't really remember any of that. Could I have a drink please?"

The nurse brought a cool glass of ice water over to Heisenberg and she placed the straw tip in his mouth. That first sip of water was the most delicious taste he had ever experienced.

"Why am I so thirsty?"

"You've been in a comatose state for the better part of a week. I have to say, we were all surprised to find you suddenly up and about after that. Some of us had assumed you would be in a comatose state for the rest of your life."

Heisenberg blinked the last bit of fog out of his eyes, and tried to bring his hand up to his face to wipe away the sleep from the corner of his eyes. The handcuffs kept his hand immobile.

"Now that I'm awake and clearly alert, could you do me the favour of releasing the security restraints, please? I have a dozen itchy spots that need a week's worth of scratching."

"I'm afraid that won't happen."

"Why? Was I that disruptive when I took over the radio? Did I play some awful music or tell some terrible jokes?"

The nurse looked at Heisenberg like he had two heads.

"Have you really forgotten how you ended up here in the first place?"

Heisenberg took another long sip of water. "I suppose I must have. But I assure you that I wasn't doing anything out of the ordinary immediately before that mysterious event."

"I'll let you sort that out with the detectives when they arrive."

The nurse urged him to take one more drink and then she stood up and went to leave."

"Hold on, miss. Detectives? Police officers?"

"Yes. They'll be here momentarily to take you into custody."

Heisenberg watched the nurse leave and afterwards he turned his gaze to the room around him. For the first time, he noticed the guard standing in the corner of the room glowering at him. The guard kept his arms folded tightly across his chest as he stared down his nose at Heisenberg. In response, Heisenberg gave him a little wave with his shackled hand. Heisenberg briefly considered unlocking the restraints with a spell and trying to escape, but the number of people watching him, combined with the pounding headache and his residual injuries convinced him to wait it out.

He watched the television in the corner of the room until two sweaty men in cheap suits came hurrying into the room. Right behind the two men, the nurse followed in and pointed Heisenberg out.

"There he is, gentlemen. I'll undo his restraints now."

The taller man pushed his glasses back up his nose and cleared his throat. "Ah, thank you, nurse. Has he been much trouble?"

"Not since we strapped him down and sedated him."

The shorter fellow was as wide as his partner was skinny. His face was covered in sweat, but despite this, he had a woolen tartan scarf draped around his neck. The sweat and the flush of his face made the shorter man look angry and on the verge of exploding into curse words and shouting.

"He still doped up now?"

"Oh, no, it's worn off. He's been chatting and fairly pleasant, to tell the truth."

"Well don't get to close to this one. He's heading to a cell to rot for a very long time."

"Um, excuse me? I'm going where? What did I do?"

The skinny detective stepped forward and snapped a pair of handcuffs around Heisenberg's momentarily freed right wrist.

"You are charged with armed robbery, arson, and attempted murder."

"What?" Heisenberg shouted. He was answered by the short detective grabbing him by the collar and cutting off his airway with the cloth.

"You stay calm and cooperate or this is going to be a rough ride, hear me?"

Heisenberg nodded and the detective let go of his arm. Heisenberg followed their instructions and slowly stood up. A quick bout of dizziness passed through Heisenberg's head, but the skinny arm pushing him forward kept him from waiting for the dizziness to pass.

"Are you in a hurry or something, detective? I have to warn you, that pushing me along too quickly could lead to some very messy, nausea-related consequences."

To emphasize his point, Heisenberg crossed his eyes, grimaced, and puffed out his cheeks while making a quiet retching noise. The short one jabbed Heisenberg in the lower back with his fist.

"You vomit on me and I'll make you piss blood" he hissed.

Heisenberg noticed that the skinny cop was alarmed at the stout cop's threats, and he shot a warning look at his partner. The skinny cop signed the stack of papers handed to him by the nurse, and led Heisenberg out of the hospital and into the parking lot.

"Warren, open the car."

The stout cop scooted off towards the row of cars. The skinny cop steered Heisenberg to an older blue Ford Focus sedan. The back door on the passenger side was held open by Warren, who jabbed a finger in the skinny cop's direction.

"I'm not riding in the back with him, Boris. You cram in there with him."

"But my legs are longer than yours. I'll be folded over like a lawn chair."

Heisenberg spoke up. "If it helps, I could just catch a cab or something like that, how about that?"

Officer Warren responded with an open-handed slap across Heisenberg's cheek, hard enough that Heisenberg's eyes watered.

"Guess that's a no."

Officer Boris pushed Heisenberg into the back seat and folded himself into the spot beside, making pained faces and sighing unhappily as he did so. Warren got into the driver's seat and drove the car out of the parking lot and into the street.

"So fellows, could either of you do me a favour and tell me why I'm under arrest? The nurse wasn't terribly helpful on this subject."

"You know full well-you blew up a train."

"No I did not."

"Give him a punch in the mouth when he gets smartass like that" growled Warren over his shoulder.

"I'm not attempting to be difficult, gentlemen, but I really can't believe that I'm responsible for an explosion, whether it included a train or didn't."

"They found you by the wrecked train and tracks, covered in soot and rubble from the explosion. And they didn't find the train's cargo, which means you had accomplices" Boris explained.

"I'm still not admitting that I did any such thing, but perhaps the missing cargo was simply obliterated."

"The explosion only destroyed the engine of the train. The follow-up crash demolished the freight cars, but it didn't vaporize the cars or their contents. The rest of the freight was found surrounding the wreck site, but there was no trace at all of one particular crate. That was the target of you and your allies."

"Interesting. How many people are involved in my secret cabal?"

Boris narrowed his eyes and leaned in towards Heisenberg. The anger and accusation in his voice surprised Heisenberg.

"Don't mock us, you wretch. We know of you and your cowardly allies, as you know full well about our organization."

"Who-the police?"

Heisenberg saw Warren's gaze flick up to the rear view mirror and meet with Boris's. Heisenberg re-evaluated his situation.

"It occurs to me that I should have asked earlier. May I see your police identification, please?"

Both of the other men in the car ignored Heisenberg's request. He sighed and continued.

"Ah. I see. You're not police at all. I should have realized this was the case, based on the quality of your vehicle if nothing else. Who brings a dented, late-model sedan with patches of rust on it to transfer a prisoner? It should have been either a secure transit van with uniformed officers, or a much nicer car for high-ranking but more discrete law enforcement. The choice of vehicle would have depended on how I was criminally classified. As a simple thief, it would have been the van, but as a dastardly terror suspect, it would have been the elite treatment."

Boris reached into the leather backpack on the floor of the car and pulled out a cloth and a small bottle. He took the lid off of the bottle and tipped the contents onto the cloth. A sickly sweet odour rose up from the rag and bottle and Boris hurried to close the bottle up. Heisenberg started to ask what Boris was doing, but his words were stopped by the cloth now pressed over his mouth. Despite his struggling, Heisenberg was unable to dislodge the hand of the fake cop from his mouth, and the fumes from the ether on the rag sent Heisenberg speedily into unconsciousness.

When Heisenberg returned to consciousness, he was in a new and unfamiliar location. A second set of handcuffs had been added to him while he was unaware, and the cuffs bound his wrists to the arms of the ornate antique chair he was now sitting in. The upholstery of the chair perfectly matched the gilded wallpaper that covered the 3 walls that Heisenberg could see. The sideboard table, china cabinet, and massive dining room table directly beside him were all pieces made to complement each other, and had been made some time before the turn of the century. He was in a very expensive home filled with history and taste, and the man sitting across from him reflected that same elegance.

"Ah, my mysterious friend. I'm very glad to see you returning to the world of the living. I have a great many questions for you."

Heisenberg studied the seemingly dapper gentleman who lounged in front of him. His clothes were well made and hand-tailored to fit him, but the wear on the knees and elbows revealed that the clothes had been worn more than they were meant to be.

The pale band of skin around his left pinky finger betrayed a removed ring of considerable size, one that had been worn frequently enough to leave the patch of un-tanned skin, but was now missing. The man had taken care to comb and gel his hair, but the wisps of a shaggy unmaintained hairdo still poked out around his ears and at the back of his neck. The thin moustache on his upper lip blurred into the scruff covering the rest of his jaw. Heisenberg opened his mouth to make the first of a series of witty insults about the man's appearance, but he could only manage a slurred "what?"

"Don't stress yourself, old man. The after-effects of being knocked out by drugs will leave you incoherent for a while longer. And that's fine for me, because it gives me time to explain your situation and how important it is that you do what I say. We're far from any nosy neighbours or passer-by, so there's no use in calling for help, by the way. And if you think that you can just run out the door and escape when my back is turned, the armed guards patrolling the grounds will change your mind. Before I keep going, where are my manners? I should make you more comfortable."

The gentleman walked over to Heisenberg's chair and undid the handcuffs. Heisenberg gently rubbed the chafed skin on his wrists and flexed his hands to return full blood circulation to them. The gentleman stepped back from Heisenberg, appraised him for a moment, and then began to pace the room while talking.

"You and your associates made a very daring plan to retrieve the item, I must say. Property destruction and dangerous illegal activities aren't your usual mode of operating. You're all such goody goodies about things like that normally. You must have known, somehow, that we were going to finally capture our device and in your desperation, you found a willingness to break your own 'rules'. Bravo. I will need to know how you found out about our plan, but that can come later. We have all the time in the world to find the weak link in our organization. What we do not have time for, is to wait around for the location of the device. I need to know where you put it, or where your friends have hidden it."

The power of speech had finally fully returned to Heisenberg.

"Don't know what you're talking about, buddy."

"The name, sir, is Stewart Worksley, not 'buddy'. And you're delusional if you think I'll buy your claims of ignorance."

"I was just a passenger on the train."

"First strike, Michael. It was a freight train."

"Maybe I'm a hobo. Or maybe I was on a casual stroll near the train tracks, looking for interesting floral specimens when the train hurtled by and had it's unfortunate accident."

"The police reports are quite clear that you were seen near the engine mere moments before the explosion. The 3 crew members who witnessed the accident identified you as the saboteur. I might be willing to accept that you were just an innocent victim who stumbled on the scene without knowing what was going on, if this piece of paper had not been in your pocket."

Worksley held out a sheet of paper in front of Heisenberg's face. It was a printout of the article about the Antikythera device that Heisenberg had been using as a reference.

"You recognize the Kingmaker, don't you? More importantly, where is it?"

Heisenberg was genuinely confused now, trying to understand where he was and how the device tied in to all of this. He had never heard the Antikythera Device referred to as the Kingmaker, not once in any of the references or history of the device.

"I don't know where it is. I've been in a coma for days, maybe weeks. For all I know it's been destroyed."

The piece of paper was replaced by Worksley's face, pressed in so closely to Heisenberg's that their noses were almost touching. A waft of Worksley's foul breath snuck up Heisenberg's nose and made him wince.

"I will give your people some credit, Michael. They understand how significant the Kingmaker is, even if they're too cowardly to use it for its intended purpose. My advice to you, good sir, is to remember how to contact your people, and help me get the artifact back before our relationship turns unpleasant."

Heisenberg pulled his head back as far as he could, in a vain attempt to avoid the smelly and abrasive man.

"Speaking of unpleasant, your breath is practically murderous."

Worksley took a step back and straightened his dinner jacket, ignoring Heisenberg's insult.

"We shall eat dinner in a half hour. You may walk around and use the rest room until that time. And if you don't find the Kingmaker for me before sunset tomorrow, you will die."

Chapter 18

Kean was starting to doze in the front seat. He kept thinking about everything that had happened since Heisenberg had brought them back to the spellscar. There was some connection between all of the strangeness, but the answer was still out of his reach. It hovered at the edges of his understanding and hinted at a revelation. The key was the similarity between the tiny rift that formed when Mallory had tried to shut down the antikythera spell, and the giant spellscar caused by the battle with Herlech. After a half-hour of puzzling over it, Kean had a hunch he wanted to look into. He asked Damien to change his route home to pass by the battle site.

"What are you, nuts? That'll take us right through downtown. It'll add at least a half-hour to the trip."

"Would you do it for a double cheeseburger combo, scooby?"

"Hey screw you, Kean."

"But you're not allowed to eat fast food at home anymore, are you?"

Damien frowned. "No. We're on a strict, nothing-delicious diet at home."

"And you do enjoy a nice, hot, greasy cheeseburger. Especially with dill pickle fries on the side, and a cold strawberry milkshake as a drink" Kean said, waggling his eyebrows and licking his lips.

Damien cracked a smile and agreed. "Fine, but I need the combo up front."

"What if you double-cross me?"

"I'll just drink the shake first, and you can keep the burger until we're back on track."

They shook hands and, after a quick stop at the burger shack, they were driving towards the heart of Toronto. The mid-afternoon traffic was steady. It wasless hectic on a Saturday than during a normal, crazy work day but it was still a bustling stream of vehicles and people moving around the downtown core. They had to divert from their intended route twice to dodge the seemingly random street closures from construction, and a lucky last minute observation from Mallory kept them from getting stuck in the middle of a sudden parade celebrating Greek independence.

"With the smell of that cheeseburger filling the car for the last 20 minutes, I'm sorely tempted to hop out here and go get souvlaki."

"We're already way too close to being late, and your mom will flip out if you're not home when she gets there."

"You're right. The next time we make a plan that involves bribing anyone with food, make sure I order something for myself too. Unless you're willing to share, Damien."

Damien grabbed a handful of fries from the bag and shoved them into his mouth, "No way" he mumbled.

They drove around the parade route, and passed within a block of the ruins of the teashop. Kean turned around to watch Mallory's reaction.

"You okay?"

"I guess so. It's difficult to tell how I feel. I want to believe what Robert told us so very much, but then I remember that giant hole in the ground."

"I don't think Robert is lying or anything."

"Of course not. I trust him, but I don't exactly trust his perception. Who knows how accurate his new version of his abilities is."

"What are you guys talking about?"

Kean and Mallory looked at each other in surprise. They had both relaxed and forgotten that Damien was listening to their conversation. Mallory took the lead in trying to explain.

"Robert's been studying electromagnetic imaging and radiation, and he's got a new meter that reads the EM waves around him and displays information about them. He thinks he's discovered some weird new source of EM waves in the neighbourhood, but I have a feeling that he's just reading the machine wrong."

"And there's a giant hole in the ground?"

"Uh, yeah. Off in the ravine behind the subdivision. Robert took the reading there, so he believes some kind of event took place there. A little too sci-fi for my liking."

The explanation seemed to satisfy Damien's curiosity. A few minutes later, they pulled up to the curb across the street from the battle site. Kean studied the area intently with his magesight.

"Nothing. Thought so. Take a look Mallory."

Mallory scanned the site for herself, and confirmed what Kean had said: the spell scar from the battle had now vanished. The only remainder of it was a faint magical trail leading southwest, the direction that they had come from.

Damien had dug out the cheeseburger from its wrapper and was diving into the burger with gusto. In between bites, he asked what they were looking for.

"The old subway station here collapsed back in September, remember?" Kean said. "During the clean-up, they found all sorts of historically significant items, and there was supposed to be a plaque set up to commemorate the workers who built the station and the history of the site. I was going to use a picture of the new plaque in a class report, but I can't use a picture of an empty dirt lot. Anyway, we can get going, as soon as you can get the grease off of your fingers."

Damien popped the last bit of cheeseburger into his mouth, and finished his meal by noisily licking his fingers.

"Delicious."

"That's a little gross, dude."

They arrived back in Antler Branch half an hour later. Damien pulled up to Robert's apartment building and dropped Kean and Mallory off.

"Sure you don't want a ride back to your house, Mallory?"

"No, I'll walk home after we talk to Robert. Thanks for the ride, though."

"No problem. Hey, what's that?"

Damien pointed through the window to the metallic case in Mallory's hand. He hadn't noticed the device's travel case during the trip.

"Oh this? It's my camera case. Well, it's the school's case, really. I just borrowed it for the weekend to take pictures."

Kean joined in. "Yeah, pictures of the plaque, and other historical stuff."

"Yup, that's right. So, yeah, thanks again Damien. See ya."

Mallory waved and ran into the lobby of Robert's apartment building, hoping to avoid any follow-up questions. Kean gave his cousin a quick 'thank you' accompanied by an apologetic shrug before following in behind Mallory. They buzzed up and walked to the elevator. The doors to the elevator opened, but Kean held back from going in.

"Hold on, remember the AD messed Robert up. We better check and see if he's already being affected by it."

Kean called Robert and asked him if he could feel any effect from the device.

"No, I'm fine. I can't even 'see' it's radiation right now."

"Okay, we're coming up. If you start to feel anything wrong, go back inside your apartment and we'll take the device away."

The ride up to Robert's floor was a nervous one. They stepped out onto his floor and saw Robert standing there waiting for them. There didn't seem to be any sign of pain or distress coming from Robert.

"It's still okay. Is it in that box?"

"It is. And this thing is heavy." Mallory complained.

"Perhaps the box is designed to impede the functionality of the device. Let's go inside."

Inside Robert's apartment, they placed the box on the dining room table and examined it closely. Robert couldn't find any trace of radiation, natural or magical.

"I want to try an experiment."

"No way! Experimenting almost got us blown up today." Kean said emphatically.

"But I'd like to know if the device will resume emitting energy once the box is opened."

"If it does and it blows a hole through the wall into your kitchen, do you have a plan to explain the mess to your mom?"

"Or if it fries your brain?"

"That's a terrible thought, Mallory."

"Terrible but totally possible."

"Okay, I'll delay my investigations until a time where we can do it in a safer fashion. Are you taking the device with you?"

"I don't know. Kean and I didn't exactly have a lot of time to plan what to do with it."

"You should leave it here."

"And let you fiddle with it when we're not here to save you from yourself? Not going to happen."

"I have to go with Mallory on this one, Robert."

Robert sighed impatiently. "I've already said I won't investigate in an unsafe fashion. Do you need me to swear an oath to that effect?"

"Wouldn't hurt."

"Really?" Robert questioned.

"The last guy to promise me that he'd leave things alone blew himself up."

"Oh. I didn't think of that. I swear that I will leave it completely untouched until you're sure that it's safe. Mallory, I promise."

"I believe you, Robert. Keep the thing closed and untouched."

"Alright. So, tell me how it all happened."

Mallory sat down and prepared to retell the tale of their adventure, when her phone chirped out a ringing reminder. She pulled it out, looked at the time, and groaned.

"Oh crap- I've got 10 minutes to get home. I gotta go."

"I better go with her, Robert. Even my parents will get testy if I'm late for dinner tonight. I'll call you later."

Kean and Mallory dashed out of the apartment and into the elevator as Robert shouted after them.

"You better call and tell me about it-I really hate being kept in the dark, you know."

Chapter 19

Heisenberg wandered around the room. He was in the dark about his current location and how he had ended up unconscious beside a train wreck kilometers away from his shop. . Somehow, affecting the magical tether lines attached to the Antikythera device had flung him to some strange part of mid-western Ontario. Now he was under house arrest by counterfeit police who claimed to be a part of a secret organization that was at war with some other secret group that his captors thought he was a part of. The situation was just getting more and more ridiculous.

Heisenberg scanned the entire house and surrounding area with his magesight, looking for any additional information. He found only mundane people and objects around him. Even the repulsive Mr. Worksley was absolutely plain and normal, which was a relief for Heisenberg. He didn't like the idea of being held by a group of paranoid mages. The paranoia was justified. The shotguns being carried by Boris and warren as they patrolled the grounds and guarded the doors were enough to worry about, without adding in the threat of magic.

Heisenberg weighed his options and started piecing together an escape plan. Getting past the guards wouldn't be too difficult, though using magic would be painful. Heisenberg felt the lurking threat of karma surrounding him, and it was much stronger than he had ever felt before. And with every entrance and window under video surveillance the resistance to spell casting was intense.. He wondered if the kids had noticed the feeling of resistance and pressure that was pushed back on a mage when they contemplated casting a spell while being recorded. Heisenberg had only stumbled upon the correlation a few hours before the experiment that brought him here.He hoped that he would somehow make it back to the kids to share the discovery with them.

Out of the corner of his eye, Heisenberg caught a dim trail of magic stretching from the southwest terminus of the house to the center of the house, snaking its way down to a space below him. He closed his eyes to focus his magesight, and followed the line down to a dark void below the main floor. There he found a stump of an object sitting in some kind of partially demolished crate. The object was emitting a feeble trickle of magic that was more of an afterthought than an actual effect. Worksely entered the room and spoke loudly, startling Heisenberg.

"Time to wake up. Dinner is now served, Michael. Please, join me."

They sat down at the dinner table, at opposite ends of each other. Between them lay a scattered array of dishes: a bowl of mixed greens, a roasted chicken, a smaller bowl filled with potato salad, and a full gravy boat. Someone had taken great care to present the food as if it were a home-cooked meal served in a fine dining style, but Heisenberg could see the remnants of the packaging and grocery bags on the counter of the kitchen. The meal had come pre-made from the local Loblaws grocery store.

Worksley grabbed the bowl of potato salad and ladled out a heaping scoop of it for himself.

"Go on, eat as much as you like. This is all for us."

"No food for the help, Mr. Worksley?"

"My underlings have their own meal. This is reserved for the elite."

Heisenberg doubted very much that Worksley was in any way elite, but he was too hungry to start a fight. He filled his plate with food and looked around for a drink. Worksley called in Warren.

"Bring a beer for our guest, Mr. Warren."

"Oh no thank you. I do not enjoy alcohol. It upsets my digestion."

Worksley frowned.

"All alcohol? How horrible. A fine beverage is one of the most enjoyable parts of life. Very well, bring our guest a soda, and I'll have one of the beers. The imported ones, of course."

Warren glowered at both Heisenberg and at his supposed leader, but he dutifully shuffled off to the kitchen and fetched the requested drinks. Heisenberg and his captor ate their meals in relative silence. When his plate was clean, Worksley let out an enormous belch and grinned contentedly.

"There is nothing more noble than a fine meal. Now that we have broken bread together, I think we can continue our discussion and find a peaceful solution to our situation. Isn't that right, Michael?"

"I'll do my best, but you are really overestimating the amount of knowledge I have about all of this."

"Claiming ignorance won't help you tomorrow evening. Please keep that in mind."

"Other than the end of my mortal existence, what is so significant about tomorrow evening? Why is it the deadline for my revelation?"

Worksley leaned back in his chair and took a deep drink of his beer, finishing it off. He wiped his mouth with his sleeve.

"Because tomorrow night, my mentor will arrive, and he has expectations that have to be met. He also has a much less…agreeable nature than I do."

"Ah. Your boss is coming."

Worksley blushed. "It's more complicated than that. Our relationship isn't a boring boss and worker deal."

"But he does tell you what to do, doesn't he? And he is the only one with the authority to kill me, isn't he?"

"Watch out, Michael, you're wandering into dangerous water. Don't think that you're safe and sound until tomorrow evening, unless I decide to let you stay that way. But why worry about the future, when we can just avoid all of that ugly stuff. Where is the Kingmaker now?"

"I have no idea."

"Who has the Kingmaker right now?"

"I don't know."

"What were the names of the people who robbed the train with you?"

"I don't know."

"Aha! So you admit you robbed the train!"

Heisenberg studied Worksley's animated features and thought about how to proceed. Denying all involvement would enrage Worksley. Playing along, on the other hand, might give Heisenberg a chance to trick information out of the greasy thug. Heisenberg slumped his shoulders and looked down at the ground.

"I give up. I did it. I helped rob the train. But I was only the hired help. They found me through a friend of a friend and paid me in cash to sneak onto the train and help derail it. They never told me their names, or what it was they were trying to steal. The explosion was bigger than it was supposed to be, and it knocked me out cold. The next thing I remember is waking up at the hospital."

"They tell me you were radioing someone at the hospital, trying to send a message of some sorts. Who were you trying to contact?"

", They were using a shortwave radio system to communicate during the robbery. They said cell phones would be too risky. I guess that I was trying to call them for help in escaping the hospital, but it's very hard to remember."

"Did you get an answer from your friends?"

"No, I don't think so. But I was quickly restrained and drugged immediately after sending a message, so who's to say what they heard? They weren't the smartest group anyway. They wouldn't have been much help."

"Or, they betrayed you and left you to rot. Have you considered that? They may have played the part of heroic do-gooders to you, but they're just thieves. Simple thieves with no moral code at all. Though I will say they are a little bit smarter than you give them credit for. They manufactured a pretty convincing fake of the Kingmaker. And not just a copy, but a copy of what the device would look like if it had been ruined in the crash. Clever. Too bad for them, and for you, that my mentor saw through the ruse immediately. He said it was 'emanating with a false energy'. So profound and mystical. Someday, I hope to have that much of a connection to the power of the Kingmaker. "

"Oh, so there's a fake copy? That's news to me. These guys weren't honest with me. I think you're right about them. I don't even know what they called their organization."

"It's a ridiculous name, arrogant and pompous. They call themselves 'Ex Libris', some kind of Latin mumbo jumbo. Everyone knows there is no power in the Latin language. The name has something to do with books, like they're librarians or something. I hate how smart they think they are."

"So they're your enemy? Do you spend a lot of time fighting with them?"

"We fight in the shadows, battling to control the powers and secrets of humanity. We, the students of Novalis, work tirelessly to retrieve the great works of the hidden world, and to use them to steer humanity towards a bright and brave new future. The stupid librarians only want to hide these magnificent things away so that society forgets about them."

"Novalis, eh? That's a neat name. What does it mean? Is it a martial art? Some kind of diety?"

Worksley grinned from ear to ear and stood up. "Come with me, Michael, and I will show you all that the great name of Novalis means."

Heisenberg followed Worksley up a narrow set of stairs in the kitchen. The stairs brought them into a narrow hallway on the second floor. Worksley pulled a key from his vest pocket and unlocked the wooden door to their right.

"Step inside and learn man's true history."

Heisenberg stepped past Worksley and walked into the small square room. The walls were lined with full bookcases and display cases, and above each of the cases were framed documents: pieces of ancient-looking parchment that would crumble to the touch, newspaper articles, drawings of mechanical devices, and several hand drawn maps.

In the center of the rear wall, a glass dome sat over an antique radio that rested on top of a stone pillar. A small metal plate identified the radio as "The Aetheron". Heisenberg had to assume that the radio had special significance to Worksley because it had been given a place of prominence and honour in his home-made museum. He wondered if Worksley had realized the radio's name was Latin. Worksley stood in the middle of the room and began his lecture.

"And here is the history and glory of Novalis. Please, take a moment to take in the full scale of what you're looking at. Some of these books are hundreds of years old, and they hold secrets most of the world thinks are lost, or were never real in the first place. With this knowledge we have searched for the great artifacts of the lost age. A time when men could craft machines of arcane might and bend the rules of the universe itself. These maps show the path that our ancestors followed in their quest for the devices.

And here, my finest item in the collection. The Aetheron. The communication device used by our founder, Georg Philipp Friedrich von Hardenberg, to reach out and discover the other mystics who were on the quest to regain man's lost glory. He drew those brave souls to him and they swore to work together to bring about a new age. In addition to searching for the lost artifacts, they used their advanced understanding of science and the natural world to experiment with their own creations that would manipulate the world around them.

Their first triumph was the creation of this radio. The power infused in it allowed contact between our two safehouses, years before any such communication was an option for the rest of the world. Sadly, we lost the paired radio to this one, when the safehouse in Zurich burned to the ground. Now this one only serves as a historical reminder."

"Is this your main safehouse? It seems a little out of the way for the headquarters of an international secret society."

"You have no idea where you are right now, Michael. You could be in the heart of Europe, but screened from the outside world by our elaborate technologies."

Heisenberg peered out of the tiny window. "I'm not so sure that they have old "welcome to Huron county" signs sitting around in the heart of Europe, but I could be mistaken."

Worksley answered Heisenberg with a scowl, but continued on.

"There should be another piece in our display. The Kingmaker should be front and center in the display, but your employer the Librarians have somehow been able to keep it out of our grasp."

"And how long have they been in possession of the device?"

"The Kingmaker has been hidden away and feared lost for several decades. We kept searching for it, of course, but the Librarians had found a very good spot to hide it. It was so well hidden that the Novalis elders couldn't detect the mystic emanations."

Heisenberg forced himself to casually walk around the room to hide his shock at this revelation. Someone at the top of this cult was a mage and could use magesight to find the Antikythera device. The idea of a cabal of secret mages made him very nervous. Heisenberg traced his finger along the spine of one of the books as he read the title out loud.

"The Quest Magikal. Sounds like a hit. Must be full of useful secrets for learning to do magic. That is, if magic actually existed. Unless this is a reference book for stage magic, in which case, I'd like to see some card tricks."

Worksley glared and snorted at Heisenberg. He pulled out a small revolver and pointed it at Heisenberg.

"You should watch your mouth and stop making fun of things you can't understand. We have powers that you can't even begin to imagine."

"Okay, okay, I'll refrain from teasing. Are all of the members of Novalis able to use magic?"

Worksley let the pistol's barrel drop and he slowly put it away as his anger subsided.

"No. The gift is incredibly rare, and almost impossible to witness. Only the great masters of the past had the full gift of spells. We study and practice in the hopes of gaining access to the same abilities, but no one has managed to do so. My mentor has seen the energies of the invisible world, but it only comes to him in fleeting glimpses, and not at his bidding. We were lucky that he had a vision while looking at the false copy, or we might have spent months thinking it was the real thing."

"And what about the people who hired me to help steal this thing? Why were they stealing it from themselves?"

"We'd like to know that too. From the records of the item transfer, the Kingmaker has been locked away as a part of the permanent collection of the Royal Ontario Museum for several decades, neither in the Librarians or our hands. Then, one year ago-"

Heisenberg interrupted Worksley's monologue."Just to be clear- the device was at the R.O.M.? Not a foreign museum, like the one in Athens?"

"Yes. Why?"

"No reason. It's just surprising that it was in the possession of a Canadian museum when there are much older museums that would have loved to have it."

"Many things about the Kingmaker are confusing to a small mind such as yours. As I was saying, a year ago, a scholar from Western University put in a request to study the Kingmaker, though we have no idea how he knew about it. The plans were formalized and the artifact was shipped by train 4 weeks ago. During the trip, you sabotaged the train's engine to cause a crash. In the aftermath of the crash, the Kingmaker was stolen and replaced by the decoy. Our own sources had d discoered the plan to move the device, but we arrived at the train crash a few minutes too late to catch the Librarians in the act. We found the decoy and took it, assuming it to be the remains of the real thing. We didn't see you lying by the tracks."

Then I wonder who found me? It would be nice to know what state I was in when they discovered me on the ground. Maybe visiting the crash site would jog my memory."

"We'll see about that, Michael. I have a feeling that you might be thinking about escaping, but I warn you, that would be a bad decision. A fatal one, in fact."

Heisenberg imagined creating a giant ball of spell energy, crackling with electricity and fire, and hurtling it into the chest of the detestable greasebag in front of him, but quickly wiped the thought out of his mind before the spell became an unfortunate reality. No matter how irritating it was to be threatened by an unwashed thug, Heisenberg couldn't justify blasting him with a potentially deadly spell.

"No thoughts about escaping, boss. You have the upper hand. I just want to help you out and get far away from here. No more weird jobs for me."

Chapter 20

After they had finished their long list of Saturday chores and gulped down their dinner with their families, the three friends had rushed to gather in Robert's room. They talked excitedly to each other as they looked at the map of Southwestern Ontario laid out on the floor. Robert was pacing about the room, waiting for Mallory and Kean to sit down and listen to his discovery.

"I found out how to use my wavereading!"

Mallory was hunched over the map, trying to make sense of the lines Robert had added to it.

"Your what?"

"My magesight now lets me see electromagnetic radiation. I've been able to focus the ability and make it useful. And I can direct radio waves! I trace a route for them to travel and I can correct the course as the wave travels along it."

But waves move way too fast for that, don't they?" Kean asked.

Robert shrugged. "You're right. It should be impossible to follow a radio wave. But all magic is impossible."

"Fair enough."

"So what are the lines on the map, Robert?"

"I'm glad you asked, Mallory, even though I was going to get to that next. When the two of you were investigating the device and triggering explosions-"

Mallory interrupted. "One explosion. And it was pretty minor."

"It blew out a wall, Mal. Keep going, Robert."

"The explosion was set off by the collision of a spell and a counter-spell, correct?"

Kean nodded. "Yup."

"My theory is that the conflict between the spells created a paradox. That's when two things that could not happen at the same time are somehow forced to occur. You were trying to destroy the existing spell, but there was some unknown force that required the spell to continue to exist. So, when the two forces collided, a small rift was torn open."

"You mean a spell scar."

Robert shook his head. "I've been thinking about the whole thing, and looking at what we've been calling a scar. It's not a scar. A scar would be the healed remains of a rip in the fabric of reality, but the tear that happened at the battle site wasn't healed. It was dormant and almost closed, but it was still a hole."

"A hole? Where does the hole lead?" Mallory said.

"That's a very good question. I didn't even realize that the hole could lead somewhere until you set off that explosion and created the micro-rift. The radio message that passed through the rift had direction and purpose. It also felt like it had travelled from a very far distance."

"How can you feel the distance travelled by a radio wave?"

"Honestly, I don't know. It's all hunches and gut feelings right now. Maybe it has something to do with the intensity of the wave and uniform amplitude degradation, or maybe it's a new instinct that I have. That micro-rift disappeared entirely when the energy discharged.It didn't collapse into a dormant state like the first one. And guess what? The first one isn't in the same place anymore."

"I know" Kean replied, and Robert looked a little disappointed.

"Really? How did you know?"

"We drove by on the way home. We both saw that the scar, or I guess the rift, had been moved by the explosion. I don't understand why, but it was."

Robert beamed with pride. "I have a theory. We have to accept that the rift was torn open, not by the battle with Herlech, but by the creation of the Old Alex Spell. More importantly, it was created by the sudden appearance of our Starborn friend Sterling. Sterling was the most out-of-place, the most improbable part of the spell.His existence on our planet pushed our reality to the breaking point. When Herlech started pushing even harder, the rift opened, and it stayed open until the cause was removed. While he was walking around with us, watching bad cowboy movies and eating everything that he could get his hands on, Sterling kept the rift open. He was a kind of anchor. So was my part of the spell. And Herlech's. When my part was stopped and Herlech was blown through the rift, Sterling was able to return home."

"If every cause of the rift has been fixed, why does it still exist?"

"Because there's one more anchor, one that we didn't connect to the big picture before. The device."

Kean shook his head and Mallory put up her hand.

"Question-why would the device keep the rift open if it's been sitting around in a museum somewhere since they found it in the ship wreck? And why did it suddenly become active and start messing with us?"

"It's not the same device, that's why. This once came from some other place. It came from a place where the Antikythera didn't sink, and so the device stayed intact and functional. And wherever it came from, Heisenberg is there now."

"So where is he?"

"I don't know. I just found the rift again, after searching for it all afternoon. When you set off that micro-rift, the energy it released dislodged the original anchor to the battle site. The rift's original shape was like pulling an elastic band into a triangle shape, with each point of the triangle being one of the anchors. Losing one anchor meant that the rift turned into a straight line between the remaining two points. One of those points is the university, and presumably the device itself. The other is somewhere to the southwest of Toronto."

Mallory studied the map and found a mark that didn't make sense.

"Robert, why is the tea shop marked with an anchor symbol?"

"That was an interesting discovery I found when I traced the lines of effect onto the map. Before you dislodged the anchor point entirely, it had been moved from the battle site over to the tea shop. I'm guessing that Heisenberg's experiment accidentally moved the anchor, as well as blew him through the rift to locations unknown."

Kean sat back and tried to process Robert's theories.

"But why didn't the rift pull all of us through during the battle? And if the AD is one of the anchors, why didn't we see it having an effect on the rift?"

"But we did. Heisenberg took us to look at the rift and it was pulsing open. And that started happening at the same time that the AD was triggered. We just didn't understand that they were connected. And this must mean that the doohickey triggers automatically on some kind of lunar calendar event"

"Mallory's right. I spent the evening sending out bursts of shortwave radio waves, and following them. Since waves came through the micro-rift, I thought that I could find the big rift by listening for the radio waves that disappeared without warning. So I pulled out my shortwave radio from our stage space downstairs and I starting exploring. I finally found the rift around here."

Robert pointed to the red 'X' on the map that had been excitedly circled several times. It was almost halfway between Stratford and Kitchener, southwest of a little town called "Shakespeare", sitting on top of the rail line.

"That's it. That's where the rift is now. And, it's more open and powerful than I've ever seen it before. I tried to navigate the radio waves through it, but it got very, very confusing, and gave me a headache."

"Like the one the AD gave you?" Mallory asked in alarm. The vision of Robert lying unconscious on the floor returned to her mind.

"No, not anywhere near that bad. This was more of a concentration headache. It was like I was trying to remember pi to the 30th place while trying to find Waldo. When I stopped looking into the rift, the headache went away."

Kean took in a deep breath and focused his magesight on the sealed box containing the AD. The faint magical tether line slipped out between the edges of the sealed box and extended from the box towards the southwest. Kean closed his eyes and followed the tether as it snaked off into the distance. He willed his magial vision to follow the line at a faster speed., The scenery hurtled by, traced in the faint bluish tint of a world recreated with magic. He arrived at the end of the trail and saw the rift, glowing and pulsing with increasing energy. Even at this great distance, Kean could feel the aching pain of potential backlash surrounding the rift. The power of the rift became too much for him to handle. He snapped out of magesight with a grunt.

"The rift's going to make something bad happen soon. We have to shut it down."

"Did you see the device's anchor line heading into the rift?" Robert asked.

"I saw it approach the rift, but everything was too bright to see anything in the rift itself."

"I was able to follow it right up to the rift and it goes inside. The Antikythera device is propping the rift open, and we have to send it back."

Mallory spoke up. "Are you sure that will close it? And what if sending the device back blows all of us up?"

"I'm not sure that it will close it for good. And yes, it might blow up."

"Well, that's reassuring. Great motivational speech, Robert."

Chapter 21

Heisenberg woke up in the tiny bedroom beside the museum room. The blinding sunlight pouring through the narrow window aligned perfectly with his face, and the heat and light of it forced him out of bed. Worksley had shoved him in the room after the tour last night, with a copy of "The Quest Magikal" as entertainment for the evening. Heisenberg had given up on the overly complicated and foolish book and its guesswork about magic after 2 chapters.

He had been very happy to discover a tiny en suite bathroom attached to his locked bedroom. Heisenberg had soaked a hand towel and given himself a quick wash of his face and neck, enjoying the momentary solitude despite the overall danger. He had fallen deeply asleep as the sun set and stayed deeply asleep until the sun had intruded.

Heisenberg gulped down a glass of water, emptied his bladder, and washed his hands. A series of loud knocks resonated on the bedroom door. A rattle in the door lock preceded the entrance of Worksley, who was still wearing the same clothes as yesterday. A waft of cheap cologne filled the room. It was almost covering up the base body odour that Worksley carried with him.

"Get up, Michael, if that is your real name. I have questions for you." Worksley snapped his fingers. "Escort our guest to the sitting room and secure him to the chair."

Warren pushed past Worksley and grabbed Heisenberg's arm to drag him downstairs.

"Easy now, friend. I'm happy to follow you. No need for the rough treatment."

Warren ignored Heisenberg's words and maintained an iron grip on his arm until Heisenberg was seated in the high-backed oak chair in the middle of the living room. Warren shackled Heisenberg's arms and legs to the chair again, twisting the cuffs as he put them on to make sure that they caused scrapes on

Heisenberg's wrists and ankles. Satisfied with his work, Warren handed the keys to Worksley and left the room.

"Who are you, Michael? We've done some investigating into your background, and here's the surprising discovery we made: you don't have a background. No electronic trace of you before the moment you arrived at the hospital. No birth record, no work record, no criminal record, nothing. I had Boris drive into Toronto and canvass your supposed neighbours and none of them had ever heard of you. If we had the time to wait, I would have your fingerprints and dental records looked into, but I'm going to guess that we wouldn't find those either. This really puts a dent in your story about being the hired help. How high up are you in Ex Libris, Michael?"

Heisenberg shook his head. "I'm not a part of them. I told you that."

Worksley took a lunging step to close the distance to Heisenberg, and then he uncorked a full arm slap across Heisenberg's face.

"Enough! In 12 hours Mentor Tweedsmuir will walk through that door and ask for the Kingmaker. He will punish whoever fails him."

Heisenberg wished he could rub his cheek to lessen the sting from the slap.

"Is it safe to say he's going to punish both of us?"

Worksley stepped back and tidied himself. "Any correction he offers me will be gratefully accepted. He is my mentor and I do as he tells me. You will be tortured until you reveal the location, or until you die."

"I wish I could help you, Mr. Worksley. I really do, to save myself from the horrors you promise more than anything else. But I don't know where the device is."

"For the moment, I'll give you the benefit of the doubt. Let's instead go back to the very start of the crime. You can explain the history of the heist step by step. Perhaps that will jog your memory. First of all, why are there no records of your existence?"

Heisenberg stared at Worksley searching for some kind of plausible cover story.

"Would you believe that I don't exist in this place?"

Worksley looked confused. It looked like hea was was trying to decide if Heisenberg needed another slap. Heisenberg continued.

"Look never mind that. It's too hard to explain. I really meant that I'm a foreigner, here in Canada illegally. I snuck in from Wales about 10 years ago, and I assumed a fake name to stay here. That's why I have to break the law to support myself. I can't get a real job. But I don't know anyone who calls themselves a member of Ex Libris. I don't even know if I've ever met a regular librarian, much less one who dabbles in the arcane. My friend Skins found out about the train job, and he gave me the details. Paid me in cash, half up front, and the other half due 2 weeks after the job. I suspect I won't see the second payment."

"And where were you supposed to meet Skins to get the second half of the payment?"

"I was supposed to call him 2 weeks later and meet him at a pub downtown."

"Then let's take a peek at your cell phone and see if there's a number for this fellow in there, shall we?"

Worksley scooped up the plastic hospital baggie containing Heisenberg's personal effects, and he dug out the beat-up blackberry from it. The screen had a spider web of cracks running across it, but it still turned on when Worksley pressed the power button. He scrolled through the contact list and asked about each entry. When he asked about the entry labeled "K", Heisenberg spoke up.

"That's him, that's Skins' number."

"Why "K"?"

"K for a thousand, as in a thousand dollars."

"Fine. Give "K" a call."

Worksley tossed the phone at Heisenberg, forgetting that his arms were immobile. The phone clattered to the ground and Worksley scurried after it in a panic. Heisenberg rolled his eyes.

"I cannot believe that I'm your prisoner. Are you sure you're the one in charge here?"

"JUST TALK WHEN THE PHONE'S ANSWERED!" Worksley shouted as he pressed 'dial' and held the blackberry to Heisenberg's ear. The phone dialed the number but a series of strange beeps and blips accompanied the normal phone sounds. The sound of the ringing was warbled and inconsistent, getting suddenly louder and quieter without warning. When the ringing stopped, the click echoed through phone, repeating several times. It was like the phone was connecting for a brief moment, but then disconnecting, over and over again. Heisenberg could feel that the signal from the phone was trying to route its way to Kean's phone but couldn't manage it. The creeping sense of backlash accompanying the phone call also told him that trying to reach Kean from his current location was coming very close to breaking the rules. Heisenberg shook his head.

"The phone isn't working. It was probably damaged in the crash. Look at the screen. I'm surprised it even started up."Worksley held the phone to his own ear and confirmed the the call had failed. He cursed and brought out his own cell phone, a cheap pay-as-you go phone with scratches all over it. Worksley typed the phone number into his own cheap phone and then tried to complete the call.

"It says the number is not in service."

"That pretty much confirms that my friend Skins isn't really my friend. I think I've been betrayed."

Worksley considered his options while absentmindedly picking his nose. As he dug deeper and deeper, Heisenberg became so repulsed by the man's lack of common etiquette and hygiene that he had to tell him off.

"Good god, man, I'm right here watching you. You have the manners of a toddler. And have you even considered having a shower before putting on the exact same clothes that you were wearing yesterday? And I have to assume you've been in that suit for several more days than I know about, based solely on the stink that accompanies you. How is it possible that someone living in a beautiful antique house, a person in a position of authority in their organization, lives his life like a brain-addled hobo? Wash your face! Brush your teeth! Are you afraid of soap and water?"

Worksley moved quickly, grabbing a short walking stick from its spot leaning against the wall. He struck the handle of the stick into Heisenberg's left temple. The world blurred for Heisenberg and he gulped in air and bellowed a shout of pain and surprise. A rivulet of blood ran from a gash in the centre of the rapidly swelling skin of his forehead, dripping down his face and into his left eye. Worksley swung the stick again,. This time the strike was aimed at the narrow part of Heisenberg's left forearm. The walking stick came up and smashed down on Heisenberg 3 more times, and he felt his hold on consciousness slipping away. As Worksley brought the stick up for one final whack aimed at Heisenberg's face, another of the security guards came running in.

"Sir! Sir! You need to come to the gate! There's a police officer there. Mr. Warren is trying to get the officer to leave, but it looks like the officer heard a scream from inside the house, and he wants to investigate."

Worksley dropped the walking stick and dashed over to the front window. He peered through the curtain and yelped in dismay. He turned and met eyes with Heisenberg, and Heisenberg could see the panic and fear in Worksley's eyes. Through the pain, Heisenberg managed to smirk.

"Would you like me to go talk to him for you, Worksley old pal?"

"Just shut up! You, guard the prisoner. Clean him up a bit and put a bandage on that cut. I'll go take care of the police."

Worksley threw the keys to the guard and walked out of the door. The new guard approached Heisenberg and examined the cut.

"You don't look like any of the guards I've seen so far. Are you new on the job?"

"You could say that. Are your legs hurt at all?"

"No, but why do you ask? Are you planning to continue where he left off?"

The new guard smiled and winked. "Not quite. Let's get you out of those shackles."

Heisenberg watched the guard quickly unlock all of the restraints and step back. Heisenberg wasn't sure what to do next: should he launch himself from the chair, knocking over the guard, and run for the front door? Heisenberg rubbed his wrists and ankles and slowly stood up.

"Are you ready to go? We don't have much time."

"But don't you work for them?"

"Actually, no.They really need to screen their prospective employees a little bit more thoroughly. When you hire in a hurry, you just can't tell what you're getting. Come on!"

"Well, I'm sure that it's ill-advised to put my trust in an absolute stranger who appears to be working for the fellow who was beating me moments ago, but perhaps I'm being a touch too cautious" Heisenberg said with a chuckle. "Can you at least tell me your name?"

"Sure. Isaac. And I work for the other team. Does that put your mind at ease?"

Heisenberg picked up the walking stick and broke it over his knee.

"Since staying here means more beatings, I say lead the way Isaac."

Isaac nodded and ran awkwardly off down the hallway and into the kitchen. He unlocked the back door and beckoned Heisenberg to follow him into the yard. They ran hunched over to the shed in the back corner of the yard, where the yard blended into the surrounding scrub land. Behind the rough wooden shed sat a mud-covered ATV.

"There's our chariot. Hop on."

Heisenberg perched himself on the second seat, behind Isaac, and looked around for a helmet.

"I can't find a helmet. This seems unsafe."

Isaac looked back at Heisenberg, with a raised eyebrow and smile on his face. He went to respond, but the sound of a pistol being fired was answer enough. Isaac started the engine and they roared away as Worksley and the other goons shot at them.

Chapter 22

Kean woke up Sunday morning to the sight of Mallory standing at the foot of his bed. He bundled the sheets around him and tried to keep a yelp of surprise from escaping out of his mouth.

"What are you doing in my bedroom?"

Mallory looked at Kean with wide eyes and spoke in a monotone.

"I watch you sleep sometimes, because it calms me."

"Really? Oh jeez, that's creepy. We have to talk about boundaries, Mal."

Mallory snorted. "You are so gullible, Kean. There is nothing calming or interesting about you while you sleep. Maybe if I had a drooling fetish. If that was the case, then watching you would be a thrill a minute. Nice jammies by the way."

Kean blushed. "Why are you in my room, Mal? I'm pretty sure you'd freak out if the situation was reversed."

Mallory thought about this for a moment.

"You know, you're right. I should have thought this through a little better. I got a little carried away. We have to get things moving and send the device back to where it's supposed to be today."

"And breaking in to my room was the best way to hurry things up?"

Mallory shrugged. "You can't hear the phone from your room when you're sleeping because you sleep too deeply. And your parents can't hear it at all from their bedroom, not that I'd want to be the one waking them up early Sunday morning. That's your job."

"You know too much about my family."

Plus, I had to get out of my house quick, or mom would have started asking questions. I'm supposed to be heading off to skating practice at the arena, and then going to the library to study until dinner time. Oh, and I wanted to freak you out for the fun of it."

Kean decided to get even with Mallory. He stood up and pulled off his pyjama shirt. He turned to face her and prepared to pull down his bottoms.

"Whoa WHOA THERE! No nakedness! Not cool!" Mallory exclaimed.

"You said we should hurry, and I'm hurrying. You could help by finding me some underwear in the bottom drawer there. Or you can dig through the laundry basket for a pair that doesn't smell too badly."

This last sentence drove Mallory from the room, followed by Kean's laughter.

"That'll teach her" he said to himself.

After a quick shower, a fully dressed Kean came out into the living room to talk with Mallory.

"Okay I'm ready to go. Did you call Robert?"

"I did. He's waiting for us to show up, and he'll put the box in the hallway when we get there. I have to call his cell so that we don't wake his mom up. And there's one little detail that's not sorted out."

"And what's that?"

"We need a ride. Think you can call Damien?"

Kean sighed. "Him again? He's just going to ask more questions, and I don't like lying to him."

"So don't. At least, not entirely. Leave out the really hard to believe stuff but admit the other things. Tell him we accidentally took something that didn't belong to us, and now it is way too big a deal to handle. That's pretty honest. Or we can wake up your parents and spin some ridiculous story to try and talk them into driving us to London. Or hey, let's hire a limo for the day and go in style!"

"That sounds expensive."

"That's because it is. Just call Damien."

Kean found his cell phone, unplugged it from the charger, and sent his cousin a text message. He put the phone down and got a bowl of cereal while he waited for a response.

"Do you want something to eat, Mal, or did you already help yourself while I was sleeping?"

"I already ate, and you don't have anything tasty."

They turned on the TV and watched local news reports while Kean ate. The explosion at the university was mentioned in the top of the hour wrap-up. The speculation was that it was a protest of some sort, though no one could identify just what was being protested. There was no specific mention of the device, but there was reference to "missing materials". The newscast moved on to the weather report, and the strange bursts of unstable weather that had been occurring over the last 36 hours. Small but intense cells of thunderstorm activity, sometimes with large hail, were popping up in the southwestern region of Ontario. The intensity and suddenness of the storms seemed to be surprising the meteorologist.She kept repeating that this kind of violent weather wasn't normal for the region at this time of year. Watching the map of the weather events, Mallory could see a rough pattern forming.

"Kean, look at that. The storms are all lining up with the path of the rift. And the most intense ones are centered on the spot Robert said the rift was at now."

"And look at the timing-the storms are speeding up. First few were 3 hours apart, but now it's down to an hour between each."

"We better try to close the rift down before we start seeing funnel clouds."

Kean's cell phone buzzed and vibrated on the table. He picked it up and checked the new text.

"Damien said okay, but we have to buy him breakfast and lunch. If it goes late, he'll want dinner too."

"Can we just make him a sandwich?"

"Don't think so."

Kean left a brief note for his parents that included a promise to call later, and went to step out of the door. Kean's mom stepped out from the master bedroom, yawned and shuffled down the hall towards the kitchen, with her eyes barely open a sliver.

"Oh, morning, Mrs. MacGrath. I hope we didn't wake you up?"

Mrs. MacGrath cracked open her left eye to see where the voice had come from. She stared at Mallory for a moment, and then continued on her path to the kitchen.

"Mom doesn't talk very much before she has a cup of coffee. We're kind of supposed to pretend she's not here until the coffee is ready."

A grumble and a nod from Kean's mom confirmed his statement. She turned on the coffee maker and shuffled through the open arch to the living room, where she sat down in the recliner. Kean stood in the kitchen with Mallory and waited. Mallory shot him a look, pointing at the clock. Kean held up his hands in a silent request for patience. The red light on the coffee maker went dark, and Kean went into action. Moments later, he delivered a perfectly prepared cup of coffee to his mother, who accepted it with a grumbled "thank you". Kean waited for a few sips of the coffee to make their way into his mom before launching into his request.

"Mom, we're going out for the day with Damien. There's a paintball place outside of town that we're going to try out. They give us all the safety equipment we need, so we'll be totally safe. I'll call you in the afternoon to check in, and we should be back in plenty of time for dinner. Is that okay, mom?"

After another sip, Mrs. MacGrath spoke up.

"Don't you have any schoolwork that needs to get done before march break? It's only a week away."

"I'm all caught up, mom. 100%."

"Okay. Do you have enough money for this?"

"Uh, yup."

"Have a good time, and call me after lunch time."

"Love you, mom." Kean said as he leaned in and kissed her on the cheek. "Come on, Mallory. Let's get over to Damien's."

"Hold on. Damien's going with you?"

"Yeah. He's driving."

"You're going to keep your cool, okay?"

Mallory looked at the mother and son talking to each other, and tried to decipher the point of this conversation. There was a tension between them that didn't make sense.

Kean paused for a moment. "I will mom. I'll keep everything calm."

"Good. You know I don't like surprises."

Mallory felt a sudden sense of guilt. "I'm sorry, Mrs. MacGrath. I didn't meant to surprise you. I just didn't want to wake you up, so I went straight to Kean's room this morning."

Kean's mom raised an eyebrow at Mallory. "What are you talking about, dear? Kean, are there interesting developments taking place in your bedroom on early Sunday mornings?"

"No, no, no, no" stammered a very embarrassed Kean. Mallory joined the chorus of denial.

"There's nothing funny going on, I swear. We're not like that. And definitely not in your house, while you sleep, 'cause that would be rude and insensitive."

Kean's mom laughed. "You two are adorable. You're both so easily embarrassed. I believe your early visit was entirely innocent. Now go off and have a good day, you crazy kids."

"Okay thanks mom." Kean said as he hurried towards the front door. As they stepped outside, Kean heard his mom shout after them "but you two would make a super cute couple". Kean groaned and rolled his eyes. Mallory snickered a little bit.

"I like your mom."

"I don't know why everyone thinks it's weird that we're friends, but not boyfriend and girlfriend. Is it really so strange?"

Mallory shrugged. "It's the easiest assumption to make. We spend a lot of time together and we obviously enjoy each other's company. We're teenagers so we're presumably full of lusty hormones, and I am very attractive. Stunning, even."

"That's modest of you."

"I call 'em as I see 'em. In fact, I'm probably way out of your league" she said with a wink.

They walked down the street for a while in silence, passing the muddy lawns that were patchy with the remains of last year's grass. The neighbour on the end of the street had replaced his front lawn with a landscaped rock garden, and one of the larger rocks had somehow ended up in the gutter in front. Kean stopped, lifted up the rock and put it back in its prescribed place.

"I don't feel turned on. Is there something wrong with me? Should I be trying to put the moves on you?"

Mallory wasn't sure how to answer the question at first, but she knew waiting too long to answer would make Kean really uncomfortable. She thought it was best to get it out in the open.

"Kean, do you like girls? Maybe you're not interested in them."

Kean blushed but replied. "I like girls. I like them a lot. I just don't chase after every girl around me. That would seem kind of gross. Especially you."

"You're not calling me gross, are you?"

"No! You're the opposite of gross."

"So I'm hot?"

"Oh geez, don't make me say that."

"Okay, okay."

Chapter 23

They turned onto the short cul-de-sac that Robert's apartment building resided on and walked up to the doors. They called Robert's cell phone, and the door buzzed open seconds later. Kean finished his earlier thought during the elevator ride.

"You're too important to me as a friend to even think about you romantically. We share so much history, and you're the one girl I trust completely to give me an honest opinion on anything. Including other girls. So it doesn't matter that you're really pretty. Does that make sense?"

Mallory rolled her eyes, sighed, shook her head, and then kissed Kean chastely on the cheek.

"You are the sweetest boy in the world, Kean MacGrath, and I am going to make sure any girl who tries to get their hands on you deserves your affection."

They walked out of the elevator and met Robert in the hall.

"Shh, be quiet. I want my mom to be able to sleep in. She worked pretty late last night."

Robert handed over the travel case containing the artifact.Mallory took the case from him.

"Don't you want to try to come with us? It would be nice to have a third set of bad ideas to choose from."

"I don't believe that it would be safe for me. The case is pretty good at dampening the emanations from the device, but in the last 12 hours, it's started to, well, leak a little bit. I had to leave it out on the balcony overnight."

"Did it trigger the same symptoms for you?"

"Yes, the headache started to return. The leaky radiation started to interfere with my ability to read any other waveforms around and that was terrible. I had a lot of trouble blocking it out."

Kean took a step back from Robert, and held his hand out to Mallory.

"Mal, give me the case. I think we need to check the device."

"What? No way. It'll melt Robert's brain."

"Hey! Listen to her!" Robert protested.

"I won't open it for long. I want to see what happens when we open the box while we're still in a pretty safe place. I'll go all the way down the hall and open it there. You stay here with Robert and keep an eye on him. "

"This is nuts."

Robert considered Kean's suggestion. "You know, it's actually a good idea. It's better to know what it's going to do now. There's a door that leads out to a small outside deck just down the hall there. We can see each other through the glass door, but my neighbours won't see you."

Kean walked down to the door Robert had pointed out, stepped through and turned around. 30 feet back down the hall, Robert and Mallory were sitting down and ready for the opening. Robert gave Kean a thumbs up, and Kean undid the latches on the box.

As soon as the seal of the container was breached, Kean could feel the pulsing energy of the device pushing its way out. He cracked the lid open and the glow of radiant magic bathed his hands. It was so strong that his magesight became active on its own.

The device itself was exactly as Kean had last seen it. It was undamaged by the theft and escape and perfectly intact. A blast of green-blue energy crackled and shot out of the device and traced a luminous path across the sky to the southwest as it shot out of sight. Kean closed the box back up and refastened the latches as a sudden clap of thunder overhead made him jump. He looked up to see a line of black clouds filling in the path of the energy bolt that had just erupted from the box. Kean turned his head back and saw Robert wincing in pain with his eyes closed.

"Well I guess that settles that. Robert's gotta stay here."

Kean cautiously walked back down the hall, watching Robert's reaction for any increase in pain from the device. The closed box seemed to be providing enough protection to keep Robert safe for the time being. Mallory helped Robert stand up.

"There's no way you can come with us, Robert. If the box is already becoming leaky, it's only going to get worse as we approach the rift."

"And it would be really bad if we had to open the box."

"Why in the name of everything logical would we even think about taking that thing out of the box again? It stays locked away until we...what are we going to do with it?" Mallory said as she realized their lack of planning.

"Throw it into the rift and duck?" Kean offered.

"Be serious."

"He is being serious, Mallory. And I can't think of a better solution, although you might see a better choice when you examine the current rift site. I'm going to stay at home all day and monitor the weather and energy patterns of the region. I want the two of you to keep me updated with whatever is happening."

"Even if it's something mundane, like 'we're stopping for a burger, roger?'" Mallory teased.

"Before you answer her Robert, I advise you to ignore her instead.. Egging her on might earn you a surprise visit where she breaks in to your house and scares the crap out of you when you wake up."

"Did that happen today? Why didn't she just call? Seems to be more complicated than necessary."

"Goodbye Robert, we'll call you with every little detail."

Mallory stormed off to the elevator in an attempt to exit dramatically. The subsequent waiting time for the elevator to arrive at their floor deflated the drama of her exit, punctuated by Robert giving them a cheery wave as they left.

Mallory and Kean left Robert's apartment building and walked through the pedestrian path to the street behind. The path ran through an overgrown corridor of trees and bushes engulfing the fences barely holding them at bay. Behind the fences on the far side was the back row of townhouses from a dense townhouse complex. The kids at school whispered that the townhouses were for poor families, and that the complex was full of criminals and lazy bums. Mallory hated hearing that kind of slander, but it stuck with her and that bad reputation was very hard to ignore. She felt nervous despite her rational mind telling her that there was nothing to worry about.

The concrete under their feet was littered with empty fast food cups, candy wrappers and cigarette butts. Kean pulled the box close to his body and moved a little more quickly through the path and into the street beyond. He turned to the left and walked into the townhouse complex. Mallory followed reluctantly. They walked to the inner row of units and stopped in front of the middle unit in the row.

"Is this Damien's place?"

Kean nodded. "Yeah."

Mallory didn't know what to say. The townhouse was in a bizarre state of repair.Some parts of it were clean and well-maintained, but other areas were rundown and filthy. A nice looking set of outdoor wicker chairs were arranged carefully near the front door, but just a few feet to the left, a pile of old magazines sat besides an overflowing can of cigarette butts. Through the large front window the kitchen was clearly visible and full of clutter. Underneath the window was a tiny patch of garden that looked cared for, but the plants in the garden were struggling to thrive in the grey light and poor soil. They heard high-pitched yelling from within the townhouse. The sound was muffled enough to obscure the exact words, but the rage in the voice was unmistakable. Mallory watched Kean flinch in response to the sound. The front door of the house flew open and Damien barrelled out of it. The shouting became decipherable as the source of the noise came to the threshold of the door.

"There is too much to do today and I cannot do it without your help, Damien. You're my son and you need to remember what you owe me. Do you think I can pick all of this shit up by myself with my medical condition? Goddamit Damien I'm sick and tired of you running off all the time. You're just like your father. Useless!"

The woman was shouting loud enough that the entire neighbourhood could hear her.Mallory took a step to the side to hide away from the awful woman in the doorway and Kean followed suit.

"Is that Damien's mom?"

"Yup. That's my aunt Rhonda."

"Is that normal behaviour for her?"

"Depends on what medications she's on, but yeah, it's pretty normal."

Damien walked right past the two of them, and muttered "let's go." As they walked away, Damien's mother kept yelling, repeating the same types of abuses and threats until they were in the car.

"I'm sorry that your mom yelled at you like that."

Mallory knew it was silly to apologize for someone else's poor behaviour, but no one deserved to have their mom yell at them like that, and she felt bad that it was happening to Damien. Damien just shrugged off her apology and raced the car out of the parking lot and towards the highway. He flicked on the radio and turned the volume up to fill the car with noise. "Negative creep" by Nirvana blared from the speakers and pounded their eardrums. Mallory started to feel slightly nauseous as the booming bass shook her stomach. Finally the song ended and the dj threw to the local news report. Damien turned the volume down but listened closely to the report about the suspected bombing and theft from the university campus. As the reporter covered the details of the robbery, Damien started to shoot glances at Kean. The news report finished and segued to sports. Damien confronted Kean.

"That was you two, wasn't it? You're the 'unidentified suspects' that they're looking for. What did you take?"

"What? No way, that wasn't us. I heard the explosion when we were there, but we weren't anywhere near it."

"Crap! It's that thing right there! The big metal box you hid in the back. What the hell did you take?"

Kean looked back at Mallory, hoping for some kind of help from her. Mallory just stared back, unsure of what to say. The car slowed down and off the road onto the gravel shoulder.

"I 'm not going to jail. I don't care who you stole this for, or how much they're paying you, but I'm not a part of this."

"No, it's not like that! No one hired us to steal anything. We didn't even want to take it, but we had to."

Damien snorted. "You had to?"

Mallory spoke up. "It's a really strange situation, and it looks terrible, I know, but you have to give us a little bit of trust here Damien and believe us when we tell you that we're trying to help people. This thing is dangerous"

"Dangerous? It's stolen and dangerous? Oh goddammit what did you steal, Kean? Some kind of nuke?"

"It's not dangerous like that. Here, just look at it."

Kean brought the travel case onto his lap and opened it up, despite Mallory's vigorous protests from the back seat. Another blast of energy escaped the case a few seconds after its opening. Damien stared at the Antikythera device.

"What is that thing?"

"A very old artifact that gives off some very bad energy. It's getting worse because it's not where it's supposed to be. We're going to go put it back in the right place and hopefully fix all of this."

To punctuate Kean's explanation, a bolt of lightning exploded from the sky above, a sky that had been almost cloudless and blue just moments ago. The bolt arced through the air and slammed into the ground 5 meters from the car. The smell of ozone filled the car.

"Did it cause the lightning too?"

Kean nodded and shut the case. "Yeah. It's causing a whole bunch of storms in the area, and the storms get much worse when the case is opened. "

"And the worst part of this is that we can't explain how it's happening to anyone. By the time we convinced them that we weren't crazy, there would be tornados or the sky would catch fire or some other terrible thing would happen."

"Mal, that's a little bit of exaggeration."

"I hope it is, Kean. I hope it is. Now can we keep going, Damien? We've got a world to save."

Kean laughed. "Melodramatic much?"

Damien joined in the laughter and started the car up again.

"I think the two of you are nuts, but I believe that you're trying to do some heroic garbage, so I'm in for the adventure. If the police ask, though, you forced me to drive you."

"With what, our magic powers?" Mallory teased. Kean shuddered and suppressed the urge to shoot Mallory a dirty look.

"So now that we're partners in crime, can I ask a sensitive question?" Mallory continued. Damien shrugged.

"Yeah, why not?"

"What's the deal with your mom?"

This time Kean did turn around and shoot Mallory a furious look of disapproval.

"Mal, that's none of your business. She's just under a lot of stress and we caught her at a bad time."

Damien gently pushed Kean back into his seat. "It's okay dude. You don't have to protect me, and she doesn't deserve anyone's protection. My mom is sick. Mentally sick and physically sick, but the physical part isn't the problem. She's paranoid and crazy, and I don't think I can take it anymore."

No one spoke. They didn't know what to say to Damien, or even if he wanted them to say anything. Damien continued explaining after a few kilometers of quiet driving..

"My mom has always been uptight, but it's gotten a lot worse over the last year. I remember when I was 12, I overheard my aunt, Kean's mom, talking about my mother at a dinner party at grandmas. She said that my mom was 'high-strung'. Your dad started to say something else, Kean, but your mom hushed him. So I've known for a while that there was tension between my mom and the rest of the family. And she hasn't made things easy on anyone. She had gall stones and the doctors removed her gall bladder 5 years ago. There were complications, and my mom has been in and out of the hospital every 6 months to try and fix the issues. I have the feeling that she's made the situation worse by demanding inappropriate treatment for her symptoms. If a doctor tells her to just change her diet and live a healthy lifestyle, she storms out and finds a new doctor to prescribe a new bunch of pills. The pills make her feel terrible, so she stops taking them correctly, and then the cycle begins again. She shouts at me, suspects everyone of plotting against her, and she accuses family members of all kinds of abusive things. Her last boyfriend egged her on and told her to sue each of her previous doctors, but he got arrested for selling stolen satellite receivers before she actually hired a lawyer. When we went to London last time, I was getting her file so that she can go to a new specialist. She didn't like the diagnosis the hospital gave her. Kean, she's getting worse. She's starting to get violent."

"So what's your plan?"

Damien sighed and shifted around in his seat.

"I'm going to live with my dad in Winnipeg."

"Wow. Big change."

"Yeah, but I don't have any other options, you know?"

"I could ask mom if..."

"No dude, that wouldn't be fair to her or to you. You'd just get more craziness from my mom."

"But leaving now would screw up the end of your school year. Why don't you stay with us until the end of the school year? Finish the year out, and then make a clean break by heading out west."

"I don't know, man. She's going to get pretty aggressive with your mom and dad."

"Mom's been dealing with her for a very long time, and dad knows some karate."

Damien gave a quiet laugh.

"Fine. I'll do it. We can talk about this with your folks when we get back. Unless we get arrested and sent to prison for grand theft."

"If we get caught, I'll confess that we forced you to drive us and you had no idea that we were doing anything illegal. Easy!" Mallory said.

"Will you do the same for me?" Kean asked.

"No way, bub. If I go down, you're coming with me. We're partners in crime."

Damien groaned. "Partners? Oh crap. I totally forgot about Paula. She's going to go mental when I tell her I'm leaving. Can you guys help me keep this quiet for a while?"

"You don't want to tell your girlfriend that you're leaving?" Kean asked.

"I'll tell her eventually, just not for a while. When I tell her, she'll get upset, and she'll keep crying and yelling and crying. And she'll want to come with me."

"Would that be bad? Don't you, you know, lo-"

"God no! I thought I did at first, but now it's more that I'm worried that she'll meltdown if I leave."

Mallory quietly interjected from the back seat.

"I don't mean to be rude or say anything insulting, but have you noticed that your girlfriend is a just a little bit like your mother, in terms of temperament and possible mental instability?"

Damien clenched his jaw and his face flushed in response. He abruptly pulled the car back off the road and into the parking lot of a strip mall. The car sat idling as he stared off into the distance. Mallory and Kean squirmed in their seats and waited for Damien to say something. Even if he was going to command them to get out of the car, it would be better than the awkward silence. The car commercial on the radio ended and was replaced by the noisy breakup pop song "Part of me" by Katy Perry. Mallory couldn't believe she was sitting in the car and listening to this song while Damien struggled with his future.

Damien shook his head and laughed. "Goddamit, I ain't going to sit here and get all worked up over some chick break-up song. That's it-I'm gonna break up with Paula. And then, we're going to get ice cream cones and get out of the city."

"You know it's only 9AM, right? Isn't it a little early for ice cream?" Mallory said.

"You don't want any?"

"I said no such thing. Let's roll."

Chapter 24

The car pulled out of the parking lot as Kean sighed and relaxed into his seat.

"You two are nuts, but I like you anyway."

"Don't be so quick to praise me, cuz. I want you to come to the door with me when I break up with Paula."

"What?!? Why?"

"Morale support? Cover fire? Or I'm afraid I'll chicken out when she starts getting weepy."

"Do you usually give in when she cries?"

"Yeah."

"Maybe you actually care about her and you feel guilty for upsetting her?"

"Hey! Are you trying to talk me out of it now? You hate her."

"I don't hate her, Damien, but I don't think she's been a good girlfriend."

"Me neither. And no, I'm all done caring about her feelings. I'm ready to be around people who can hear my opinion without crying and throwing something at my head."

"Just checking."

The car zigzagged through the streets of the non-descript subdivision that Paula lived in. Her house was a new two storey house, with a 2 car garage and about half a meter between it and the next house. Across the street were empty lots waiting for their turn to be transformed into a mirror image of Paula's house. Damien parked the car and got out, followed by Kean. They both looked back at Mallory, who quickly shook her head in response.

"No way. Uh uh. Break-up detail is not a part of my job description. You dudes are on your own."

Mallory tuned the radio to her own favourite station, CIUT FM from the University of Toronto. The early morning program today was a free-for-all of any and all musical genres, and she loved the unpredictability of the sounds. A pounding African rhythm filled the car and she closed her eyes and let the music vibrate through her whole body.

Kean and Damien slowly walked up the driveway. When they reached the porch Kean took a half-step backwards and stood directly behind Damien. Damien took a deep breath and walked onto the porch to ring the bell. In the moments after the sound of the bell rang through the house, Damien looked back at the car hopefully, like he might have a chance to escape this confrontation.

"Looks like she's not home. Better get on the road."

"Hey, ring the bell again. And give her a chance to get down here. It's pretty early. Where would they be?"

"Church. Or they went out of town."

"Damien, you're full of dumb excuses. Is there anything that will get better if you don't tell her now? Delaying won't change it."

"Tell me what?" said the surprising response from the opening door. Paula was standing there, dressed in a fluffy pick bathrobe, with a deeply suspicious look on her face.

Damien grimaced and stepped forward to tell his girlfriend that their relationship was over. Kean tried to be invisible as Paula started her crying and shouting. He hoped that her upset was slightly less because she had him there as an audience, but there was as equal a chance that she was performing on a more intense level because she was being watched. After the first salvo of accusations, insults, and begging, Kean sensed they were at the point where Damien's resolve would start to weaken, and in that weakened state he might try to appease Paula. Kean steeled himself for the negative response and said "Damien, we have to go now."

Paula launched a non-stop stream of hurtful and pathetic statements at Damien as he walked away, but luckily she stayed on her porch. Kean was ready for the possibility that she could lose that last shred of self-control and come hurtling down the driveway to launch a physical assault on Damien, but the attack never came. Damien scrambled into the car, dropping his keys and then scraping his knuckles when he rushed to pick them back up. He nervously jammed the keys into the ignition and gunned the engine. Kean barely had time to buckle his seatbelt before the car lurched forward. No one in the car watched Paula's reaction as they drove away, or heard her swear to destroy the person she was blaming for all of this, the "meddling bitch in the back seat", Mallory. The clouds overhead darkened, and a rolling rumble of building thunder followed them out of the parking lot and onto the highway.

The muddy fields of rural Ontario were the dreary scenery passing by the window. Mallory asked why they were driving through the country instead of on the highway.

"Highway doesn't get us any closer to your secret destination, wherever that is. Remember, you just pointed in a direction and said 'drive.'"

"I guess so."

"Damien is also forgetting to mention that he doesn't like the highway. It scares him" Kean said.

"Shut it, wiener."

"Didn't we take the 401 to London?"

"We did, and you didn't notice that Damien's hands were curled tightly around the steering wheel in a death-grip the whole way."

"Listen runt, it's a bad idea to tease the driver when you need him to haul your ass somewhere. I should just stop the car and turn around."

"Geez, so sensitive. We're paying you for this, remember?"

"The price just went up. You're buying me dessert."

"Sure thing Scooby."

Mallory left the boys to their playful bickering and called Robert to check up. Robert reported no new weather disturbances: the existing ones were still in the line leading to the probable location of the rift. He wasn't feeling any ill effects from the exposure to the device, and he was trying an experiment that looked promising.

"The storm looks amazing in my wave sense."

"Wave sense?"

"That's the newest name for my weird new eyesight, though it's more than just vision. I have to imagine that its very similar to being able to see the world in RADAR."

"Is it like magesight? Sometimes, I can trace out entire neighbourhoods from the magic lingering in the area."

"There are some similarities, but it's a different feeling. I was able to follow the storm line from my apartment all the way past Toronto. It took so much effort that I couldn't maintain it any longer and I lost focus. I was about to start tracing the line again when you called."

"Don't push yourself too hard. We'll need you to have a functional brain in your head to give us advice on what to do when we get to the rift. Uh oh."

Mallory pulled the phone away from her ear, ignoring Robert's repeated requests for an explanation. The car filled with the flashing lights being sent out from the police car behind them. Damien pulled the car over and stopped the engine as instructed by the cop. As the police officer sat in his car checking the car's details, Mallory imagined the Antikythera Mechanism case throbbing with a guilty hum in the trunk, pounding louder and louder like the tell-tale heart until it was impossible for the cop to ignore. She could see from the look on Kean's face that he was also starting to freak out.

"What are we gonna do here, Keaner?"

"I don't know. I just don't know. I don't want to mess with a cop. I can't go to jail. I'll get into so much trouble."

Damien sighed. "Relax you two. It's probably just a routine traffic stop. If you don't lose it, we can just answer his questions and go on our way."

"Are you sure?"

"I can't read his mind, Kean, but I'm pretty sure he's not real suspicious of us. We don't look threatening in any way."

The cop got out of his car and walked slowly up to the car. Damien rolled down the window.

"Hi officer."

"May I see your license and your proof of insurance, please?" was the gruff response from the police officer. The man was over 6 feet tall, and carrying a hefty amount of extra weight in a paunch around his midsection. The fat belly didn't distract from the thick, muscular limbs that were evidence of a natural inclination to muscle mass. The cop took the documentation when Damien offered it and turned around to walk slowly back to his car.

"He's going to check out my license and insurance, to see if I'm driving legally. And to see if I have any outstanding warrants for my arrest."

"Do you?"

Damien scowled at his cousin. "No dumbass, I am not wanted by the cops. I'm more of a law-abiding citizen than the two of you thieves."

"Shh! Don't call us that."

"He can't hear you from here."

The cop returned and started asking all three of them about what they were doing. The car was filled with an awkward silence as all three tried to come up with a plausible explanation. They were driving around the countryside without a specific destination, and that was exactly the kind of thing that made cops suspicious. Damien finally answered.

"Just driving out to the country to watch the storms roll in. Looks like a big storm front is building up."

"Little out of the way for weather-watching, isn't it? Your parents know where you are?"

"My mom said it was fine."

"So if I call her and ask, she's going to say the same thing?"

A wave of panic shot through the car. Even Damien shifted uncomfortably in his seat.

"Uh, yeah. She will."

The cop took a long look at Damien, and then turned his accusing stare to the other occupants in the car. Kean tried to smile and look natural, but he couldn't keep eye contact with the cop. Mallory glared back at the police officer. Being accused of wrongdoing when there was no proof of anything being wrong made her angry. The stolen device in the trunk didn't lessen her sense of outrage.

"Anything in the car I should know about, kids?"

"Like what, officer?" Mallory answered, with a sneer in her voice.

Damien turned around to give her a warning look. "No sir, nothing in the car. Just us and some fast food wrappers."

"What about the trunk? Any surprises in there?"

Kean forced himself to look down at the floor mat and not react to the question. He didn't know why the cop was giving them such a hard time, but something had caused his suspicion to rise. The case sitting in the trunk was obviously out of place, and if the cop caught sight of it, he was probably going to ask them to open it. Kean started to pull spell energy together. He was unsure of what he was going to do with it, but he wanted to be ready for whatever happened next. As the spell energy coalesced around his hand, a soft but definite noise thumped in the trunk, and Kean felt a sudden tug as something grabbed on to his spell energy and pulled at it. Kean also felt the ominous sting of backlash building up, much more quickly than it ever did normally. Kean waved away the small pool of summoned energy but the effect lingered.

The cop took a step back from the car in reaction to the sound coming from the trunk. His hand hovered cautiously above the handle of his holstered handgun.

"I am asking you for the second time, what is in the trunk?"

Damien answered. "Nothing! Just some rags and the spare tire and a metal shipping case my mom left in there."

"I want you, driver, to step slowly out of the car."

Damien followed the instructions of the police officer and stood away from the car. One by one, Mallory and Kean were also told to exit. When all of the occupants were free from the vehicle, the cop instructed Damien to open the trunk. Damien walked to the back of the car and gave Kean a last, helpless look before opening up the trunk. The device case had popped open and the Antikythera Mechanism was clearly visible. The air was filled with the smell of approaching thunderstorms, and the clouds overhead were thickening. The cop waved Damien away from the trunk and stepped up to take a closer look at the device. He scratched his head and muttered to himself, barely audible over the building hum emanating from the device. Mallory tugged on Kean's sleeve and silently pleaded for some kind of idea on what to do now. Kean saw that Mallory was beginning to summon her own ball of spell energy, and he shook his head violently.

"No" he whispered. "The device will tap into your spell, and the backlash will be massive."

Mallory huffed in frustration and gave up on her spellcasting. The cop turned back to all of them and asked "what the hell is this thing?"

"What thing sir?"

"Don't give me that, kid. You know what I'm talking about. It's some kind of machine, and it's giving off a noise and energy, like static electricity. Whatever it is, you shouldn't have it."

"It's just an antique that my mom owns. She's a big fan of old machines like that."

"Radios!" blurted Kean.

"Yeah, radios. She got her first one from her grandfather, so now she collects them. This is her newest one, and she must of forgotten it in the trunk."

Mallory had a bad feeling that the story had too many holes to be believed. Her bad feeling was confirmed when the cop shook his head and waved all of them back away from the car.

"Sorry, kid, but that doesn't add up. Why would your mother spend a fortune on a radio like this, but leave it sitting in the trunk of her greasy-haired teenage son's beat-up car? I'm going to bet that somebody somewhere is missing this thing, and you're going to have a lot of explaining to do. Now sit down and wait until I tell you to do something different."

The cop grabbed his radio's microphone and contacted the station. He rattled off a quick description of the Antikythera and asked for any reports of stolen property that might match it.

"That's it, we're doomed" Kean moaned quietly. Mallory looked up into the sky and nodded in agreement. They sat, dejected and defeated in the silence of the back country road, with only the frequent rumble of the worsening weather breaking the silence.

After 10 minutes, the cop's radio crackled back to life. The communication from the station was full of static and pauses, forcing the cop to listen intently and repeatedly ask for clarification. The words that the kids could pick out didn't give them any clue as to what their fate was going to be. The radio conversation ended and the cop walked over to stand in front of Damien. Reflexively, Damien held out his arms in preparation of being handcuffed. He was stunned to feel the cop pressing his license and proof of insurance back into his hand.

"Turns out you're right. That antique radio is registered to a Mrs. Rhonda Fergus, which is your mother's name. The station gave your mom a call, and she confirmed the whole story."

"Really?" Damien said, unable to contain his surprise. Mallory rolled her eyes at him and mouthed the words 'shut up' as clearly as she could.

The cop ignored Damien's doubt and walked back towards his car. Slowly Mallory and Kean stood up, wary of angering the cop by getting up too quickly but desperate to get back in the car and get away. Before getting back into the cruiser, the cop shouted back to them.

"Hold it!"

They all flinched and braced themselves.

"Your mother said that you have to be home in time for dinner, and you're making it. From the sounds of it, she has a terrible sore throat. Could barely talk. Pick her up something nice."

And with a tip of the hat, the cop got into his car and sped away, leaving the three kids standing dumbfounded. A moment later, a tinny voice bellowed out from the palm of Mallory's hand.

"Close the device case!" said the voice coming from the forgotten phone in Mallory's hand. Kean dashed over to the trunk and packed away the AD while Mallory held the phone up to her ear and spoke.

"Robert? Are you still there?"

"Yes, and it's lucky I stayed on the line. It sounded like the police officer was becoming suspicious, so I traced my way to his base station and tinker with the dispatcher's search. I put up a fake website listing the device as a radio owned by Damien's mom, and I intercepted the call to her. I pretended to be her and I backed up your flimsy explanation. I have to hang up now, because I'm feeling light-headed and exhausted from all of that. And there's a big karma debt I have to deal with as well. I'll call you back later."

The line went dead and Mallory stared at the phone in complete amazement. The crack of thunder overhead knocked her out of her stupor, and she scrambled back into the car. Damien and Kean followed, and they drove off down the road in search of the heart of the storm.

Chapter 25

The ATV bumped over the dirt clumps and ruts in the cornfield. Heisenberg held tight to Isaac to keep from being thrown off of the machine and into the dirt. The thin needles of rain carting down from the clouds overhead stung his exposed skin. He squinted to see the land in front of them, and the dark nebula of storm clouds moving in a slow circular motion in the sky.

"How long has the weather been acting so peculiarly?"

"It's been an unusual season for weather, but this unnatural pattern didn't start until today. And it centers on the site of the train wreck where you were found."

"I don't mean to be obtrusive, but how are you so well informed about the crash and my confinement?"

"It's my job, mister. I research and collate and cross-reference and archive."

Heisenberg tightened his right hand grip on Isaac's jacket, to free up his left hand to dab away the trickle of blood running down from his brow. The after-effects of Worksley's assault were making themselves known. The throbbing in his temples was worsened by the roar of the ATV. He focused on the conversation in hopes of lessening the building headache.

"It sounds a bit like you're a librarian, though one does not hear much of the espionage and subterfuge skills of the public librarian."

"We don't work in the public eye. But you're right; most of us are trained librarians. I am. My university training was lacking in counter-abduction extraction techniques though, so you'll have to forgive me if it seems that I'm making this up as I go along. That's because I am."

"You'll forgive me if I find that slightly discomforting."

"No worries! How are you feeling?"

"Dizzy and nauseous, with an increasingly powerful headache."

"I'm sorry I couldn't interrupt earlier, but I had to wait until the police car arrived."

The ATV slowed to a stop. Isaac carefully dismounted, and led Heisenberg over to a small pile of brush. With Heisenberg's help, they covered the ATV in a mud-coloured tarp. He gestured to Heisenberg to sit down beside him. Isaac pulled out a lunch kit, complete with a thermos full of dark, rich coffee. Heisenberg gratefully accepted the food and drink, along with the 2 extra-strength acetaminophen Isaac offered.

"So do you have the device they're looking for?"

Heisenberg appraised Isaac in light of the incredibly direct question.

"I can't say that I'm very comfortable with your question. I am very fond of the escape from a continued beating that you provided me, but I don't think we've been companions for a sufficient duration for me to open up unreservedly."

Isaac took a swig of his coffee and nodded. "That's a fair statement. Maybe if I tell you as much as I know about the device, the people who had you captive, and the people I work with, you'll be more at ease.

Your captors are a part of a very small secret organization that we call the Novalis Cult. They use a more complicated and unwieldy name for themselves, the "esteemed travelers who walk on the path of enlightenment in the steps of Novalis" was the most recent version of the name that we've confirmed, but they're pretty much a standard issue cult. An obsession with the occult and with finding a quick route to power over society. They claim to be an ancient society, but the earliest references we can find to any kind of group similar to them are in 1790. Their namesake founder was at Law school at the time, and he found a handful of German and Austrian weirdoes who all wanted to have magical control over the workings of the world. They spent most of their time drinking and chasing girls, but in 1794 something changed. They became more serious and focused as they worked on using a new and secret device to further their goals."

"And that's the Kingmaker, isn't it?"

"That's the name they gave it. Supposedly it has the ability to manipulate the people around it, primarily through inflicting illness or inciting heightened emotional states. They planned to use it as a means to destabilizing, then taking control of the court of the Prussian chancellor. From there, they would expand their political influence until, presumably, they held the whole world in their grasp. From the reports of the day, their initial attempt went very poorly. They put their plan into action without enough preparation, and the only victims of their plan were their own agents and a stone pantry wall that was blown out by an explosion. Several members of the cult were arrested, and the Kingmaker device went missing. Or, if you ask the right people, the device was secured in a safe place."

"So, I'll ask you: was the device lost or secured?"

"Publicly, it was lost. Privately, it was sent to the most secure archive that we have and it was locked away in a private section at the British Museum and studied at a very safe distance."

"So are you telling me that the Kingmaker worked?"

"It did, and it does."

"How? Does it release some kind of toxin? A hallucinogenic poison?"

Isaac watched Heisenberg very closely. "It's magic, and I think you know that."

Heisenberg blinked and sat silent under Isaac's scrutiny. He switched into magesight and scoured Isaac's aura for any trace of magical affinity, but found none.

"And what would you know about magic?"

"Nothing, really. It's an impossible subject to gather information on, and impossible to confirm anything. In fact, if we didn't have two hundred years of indirect observation of the Kingmaker, we'd have no idea of its actual power."

"Indirect?"

"If you watch it directly, it stops exhibiting any kind of active sign. But the moment you leave the room, it begins to emit radiation. Varying types, varying intensities. Nothing harmful, but still present. And if you happen to change the settings on the face of the device, you might trigger a much more pronounced reaction."

"That sounds like a very risky way to learn how it works."

"Oh we didn't do that, I assure you. We left the device untouched in the tiny forgotten vault in the British Museum archives, but accidents still happen despite our precautions. In 1952, a brand new curator by the name of Von Hoop, a Dutch fellow if I remember correctly, decided to peek into each and every vault. In the Kingmaker vault he caught the corner of his jacket on the doorframe, and while he tried to dislodge it, he knocked the device onto its side. When he righted it, he changed the position of the long metal hand on the front, and the device activated. Everyone within the building at the time fell sick with a mysterious illness that thankfully passed after a few days. The official explanation was a minor gas leak was the cause of the illness, but our monitors told us otherwise. And since that day, it's been entirely hands off, except for the times where we have to move it to keep it out of Novalis' possession."

"So who are "we"?"

"We don't have a nifty secret name. We're just librarians, albeit a very specialized type. Ex libris libertatem, de cognitione pax. From books freedom, from knowledge peace. That's our motto. We protect strange and rare texts from being destroyed, or misused. And in this one particular case, we store and protect what might be the world's only actual magical artifact."

"Misuse? That sounds a tad suspicious, if I can say so without offending you. Who are you to judge what acceptable use is and what's misuse? How would one prove to you that their intentions were above board so that you'd deign to give them access?"

"That question comes up all the time at our board meetings. Sometimes it feels like we spend more time arguing over accountability and transparency than actually researching. We don't restrict access, that's the thing. We find the source material, we make a complete copy of it, and we release it back into the wild, so to speak. We're not keeping anything hidden away from the general public. We're making sure that there's a complete record of the most obscure and weird texts, and we study those texts. For each of those rare oddities, we make a reference guide, and we watch for any public mention of the text. When it comes up, we make sure all of the information about it is released to the public, in the hopes of eliminating or at least lessening the chance of misinterpretation."

"So you put out a press release about the Necronomicon?"

Isaac laughed. "Not quite. We work really hard at not becoming a part of the narrative. Being named as the source of the information would undermine our goals. Instead we make the information available in the digital and physical archives at various institutions. The scholars usually find it quickly. Our reference sheet leads them to the source materials they need to understand the mysterious new text, and then everyone can judge the intent and value of that new text."

"The one exception seems to be the Kingmaker."

Isaac sighed and walked over to the dirt hill to his left. He looked out over the sloping landscape for signs of activity.

"You're right. We don't want to be the keepers of the Kingmaker. It doesn't fit with our mandate. It's not even a book. We have the book Novalis wrote about it, by the way. Almost entirely useless, except it vaguely confirms that Mr. Novalis, Georg Philipp Friedrich von Hardenberg, didn't make the device magical. No one in the cult made the thing to begin with.They thought it would have a greater chance of becoming powerful if they started with a relic from the ancient world, and they somehow got their hands on an old Greek computing machine. In the late 1800s, it was still fairly easy to buy whatever antiquity you wanted, I suppose. Then one of their order, a man that they never mention by name, a guy they don't even describe in Hardenberg's book, took the device away and worked on it in solitude. When he brought it back, it had newfound magical abilities. The unfortunate surprise for the leaders of the cult was that the man responsible was now stark raving mad and unable to explain how the thing worked. He vanished, and they were left with a complicated new toy that they didn't have the instructions for."

Isaac walked over the small dirt hill and pulled out a pair of binoculars. For the first time, Heisenberg noticed that Isaac had a slight limp.

"Are you hurt?"

"Pardon? No, I'm not hurt. Why do you ask?"

"Well, you seem to be limping."

Isaac laughed. "Oh that. I tend to ignore it, because it's just a part of my life. I have a rare genetic disease, MPS-VI. One of the many symptoms is joint stiffness, which means I move a little awkwardly. Looks like the crash site is guarded still, and I think they're Novalis men. Come take a look."

Heisenberg stifled his curiosity about Isaac's condition, and joined him to observe the crash site. Heisenberg had to flinch and shield his eyes as the rift came into view. It was pulsing and sparking with arcane energy. This confirmed to him that Isaac was completely mundane, because anyone with magical attunement, even a dormant mage, would have a hard time looking directly at the rift. And for the first time, Heisenberg felt the rift pulling at him. It wanted him to go back through. With some difficulty, he suppressed his magesight and used the binoculars to find the guards. Ducked down underneath a badly made lean-to, Boris sat smoking a cigarette. After a moment, the other goon from his initial abduction, Warren, came over the hill and joined Boris in their shelter.

"They look pretty settled in. What's your plan?"

Isaac walked back to their spot on the other side of the hill to remain unnoticed by the guards, and Heisenberg followed.

"That depends on you, Michael. I was hoping that you'd come up with the next step once we got here. Truthfully, this is the limit of what I know: the Kingmaker has gone missing during its trip to the university, most likely during the train wreck. There was a ruined copy of the device left at the scene, along with your unconscious body. Novalis has the copy, and until an hour ago, they had you as well. Since the train wreck, the weather patterns in this area have become unstable. There's an area just down the tracks that has some kind of unidentifiable atmospheric effect located there. Maybe it's radiation, maybe it's something…else, but whatever it is, living things don't want to go near it. I tried to sneak up to it, and when I approached it, I suddenly had a variety of very compelling reasons to not be there. It was almost as if my subconscious had declared that spot hazardous, and it pushed me away from it. Even the coyotes won't go near it, and there's a fat rabbit corpse right there for the eating. One old coyote keeps a vigil on that forbidden meal. It's kind of funny. I don't know if the Kingmaker is buried in the dirt there and spitting out harmful rays, or if there's an even more unnatural explanation. But, whatever is happening there is caused by the Kingmaker in some way, and it involves you, so I need you to help fix whatever it is. Before the skies open up and we are beset upon by a rain of frogs or a repeating tornado or some such terror."

Heisenberg cast a sideways glance towards the rift's location with his magesight active. The brightness hurt his eyes, but he was able to squint and block out enough of the arcane light to examine the area around the rift. The rift had an aura itself, and that aura was slowly expanding to encompass a larger area directly around the site. Heisenberg looked down and was alarmed to discover that a thick, knotted rope of magical energy stretched out from the rift and attached itself to his midsection. This was the source of the pulling sensation he was feeling.

"The Kingmaker isn't buried there. It's very far away from its home. As am I."

"You'll have to give me more than that to go on, Michael. Riddles are fun and all, but we're getting close to something awful happening."

Isaac's statement was punctuated by a terrible roar of thunder as a ball of lightning formed just a few feet away from the rift and exploded into electrical tentacles radiating away from the center.

"I need a minute to think about it. Believe it or not, this is also an unexpected situation for me."

Isaac turned his head to locate the source of a new sound that filled the space left by the thunder. Heisenberg needed a moment longer to hear it. A rumbling roar of the exhaust from a high-powered vehicle was now audible. The two of them crested the hill again, this time on their hands and knees to remain undetected. A large sport utility truck was now parked beside the lean-to. It was a gleaming bright red Hummer, and from the driver's seat a tall, muscular man emerged. Dressed in well-worn jeans, sturdy hiking boots and a dark blue navigator's jacket, the man swung himself out of the seat and down to the ground below. The two goons immediately stood at attention.

"That's the highest ranking Novalis member in Canada, Kenneth Tweedsmuir. If he's here, then things are about to escalate."

Heisenberg's mouth was wide open in absolute surprise. The Novalis boss's aura identified him as an unawakened mage. A powerful one.

"That guy is going to be trouble. Do you think we can drive over to the rift site without being seen?"

"Rift site, you say? I think you have some information you could share, Michael."

Heisenberg sighed. "Okay, here's what I think is happening but this is all guesswork. There was an event last September that caused a tear in the fabric of time and space, and the tear didn't close up after the event. I initially thought it was just a tear, but it looks like it was actually a hole in the barrier between one reality and another. It's a rift between my home and this reality. Somehow I was blown through it, and the Kingmaker was blown back through. From what you're saying, my reality's version of the kingmaker was pulled back through to here as well. The rift is being pulled open by the out of place items, and the stress of that pulling is causing the weather and the negative energy aura around the rift site."

"Are you certain that you're not crazy? Not even in the least bit?"

Heisenberg watched the pod of Novalis operatives scurry about in preparation.

"I might be totally stark raving mad, but until we get a more rational explanation that fits the situation, mine will have to do. If we're going to fix any of this, we have to approach the rift, and we have to do it before they get there."

Isaac carefully pulled himself back over the hill and back up to a standing position. He crept over to the ATV and removed the camouflage. He waved Heisenberg over to the passenger spot behind him.

"Get ready" he hissed. "I'm going to hopefully start the engine at the same time as the next thunder clap, but if that doesn't work, we'll have to take off quickly."

Heisenberg hated waiting for random chance to dictate their survival chances. He decided to give their chances a boost with a magical intervention, despite the threat of amplified backlash. As soon as he began gathering up the energy to cast a spell, he could feel the aggressive resistance of the universal constant pushing against him. The amount of raw magical energy in the area was overwhelming. It took his complete concentration to limit the amount he was directly responsible for. The tiny ball of magical potential in his hand was already digging into his flesh and nervous system, like a bundle of hooks and barbs ready to tear into him. He looked around the area for some simple way to increase the likelihood of a thunder strike. Heisenberg tentatively reached out to the storm itself, but the angry power within it threatened to shut his cognitive abilities down and send him into a catatonic state.

He shifted his attention to the tallest item in his surroundings, the rusty metal pole that formed the main support of the lean-to. As delicately and gently as possible, Heisenberg sent the tiny puff of magic from his palm to the support pole. The magic flew across the space between Heisenberg's observation spot and the Novalis campsite, finishing its journey at the halfway point of the metal pole. The arcane sphere unfolded and became a thin sheet of spell energy that crept up the pole and coated it. He took the top edge of the spell and elongated it into an impossibly thin, negatively charged thread of magi and sent that thread up into the black cloud overhead. If his rough understanding of electrostatic discharge was correct, this would give an easy path for the next bolt of lightning, a path so easy that the threshold for formation would be lower. And that would make the next bolt happen sooner than normal. Heisenberg's connection to the spell gave him a sense of the electricity building in the sky above. He murmured to Isaac "get ready-the next bolt's coming" and true to his prediction, lightning struck. A blinding bolt of pure white lightning came slamming down into the tent pole that Heisenberg's spell had transformed into a lightning rod. He tried to dismiss the spell as he felt the bolt about to strike, but the connection severed too slowly to spare Heisenberg the sympathetic reaction. Heisenberg felt his entire nervous system catch fire with electrical current, and he was on the verge of falling off the back of the ATV. Isaac caught Heisenberg just in time.

In the Novalis camp, chaos descended. The explosion of lightning had obliterated their lean-to and sent a small can of gasoline shooting across the clearing, leaving a trail of burning fuel behind it. The boss was shouting instructions to Boris and Warren while climbing back into his vehicle. Boris and Warren stood with panicked looks on their faces, trying to understand their new instructions. They couldn't hear what the instructions were due to the ringing in their ears from the thunderclap.

Heisenberg was grateful to feel the ATV start up without any reaction from the Novalis camp. Isaac slowly eased the ATV forward, heading on a diagonal away from the Novalis camp and towards the rift site. Sensation and control of his extremities returned to Heisenberg, though a piercing pain throughout his teeth had started to make itself known. He guessed that the dental pain was his karmic memento. He leaned over to the small right-hand rearview mirror of the ATV and examined his teeth. Heisenberg gave a little shout when he saw the pitch-black line that traced the top visible edge of each of his teeth, like someone had painted along his gum line. It gave his smile a terrifying appearance. He hoped that it would fade naturally, but there was every chance he'd have to scrub and bleach the dark stains away.

He gently tapped his right incisor, the darkest looking tooth, and was dismayed to feel it move slightly. The accompanying wave of pain told him his dental woes were just beginning.

The ATV dipped into the ravine following path of the train tracks. There were less than a dozen meters between them and the total obfuscation of another rising hill. A strange voice came blaring out from the ATV's CB radio at the loudest volume the device could manage..

"HEISENBERG? CAN YOU HEAR ME? ARE YOU THERE? ARE YOU ALIVE? IT'S ROBERT."

Heisenberg's heart was filled with a burst of joy and homesickness at the sound of Robert's voice. He wanted to grab the radio and tell Robert that he was here and he was okay. Isaac turned his head and looked at Heisenberg with alarm.

"We're spotted! Hold on!"

Heisenberg looked back down the tracks t see what Isaac meant. Robert's broadcast had caught the attention of the Novalis operatives, and they were all piling into Tweedsmuir's Hummer. He could also hear the echo of Robert's continued broadcast: every CB radio in the area was broadcasting the same signal. Isaac kicked the ATV into top gear and tore off down the track. Heisenberg grabbed for the CB radio's microphone several times unsuccessfully before he was able to compensate for the bumping and jostling.

"Robert! I'm here! I don't know how you're getting through to me, but if you can, focus just on this radio. Things are a touch heated here and there are some folks that shouldn't hear what we're conversing about."

Isaac veered suddenly away from the tracks and headed towards a thick stand of trees about a kilometer away. The ATV hit a deep rut and Heisenberg's left leg was jarred loose. He wrapped the CB cord around his right hand and grabbed tight onto the seat of the ATV until he was reseated properly. The radio crackled to life again, but a lower volume than before.

"Can you still hear me?"

"I can Robert, and it's fantastic to hear your voice my boy."

"I'm glad to hear yours. I can't wait until I tell Mal and Kean. I can't hold the connection much longer though. It's taking too much out of me to stay focused on you. And you're moving too, aren't you?"

"I am. Running from some ne'er-do-wells. I'll be near the rift site soon. And then we can find a way to swap me with the Antikythera device."

"I knew it! You're in a different universe."

"Well, to be accurate, I believe we'd have to use the world 'reality' since it shares the same physical existence as our own. Same planet, same galaxy, same universe, but different at the same time if you follow me. Are you at the rift on your side?"

"No. I was reacting badly to the AD. My new abilities are very sensitive to it. But Kean and Mallory are on their way now, with the device. I just talked them out of a traffic ticket, and possibly being arrested."

"Tell them that I'm on my way to my side of the rift, and we'll have to move quickly when we're all there. The men chasing me are very intent on retrieving the device and using it for their nefarious purposes."

"I'll tell them. Try to stay safe."

The radio went silent and the only sound was the ATV crashing through piles of dead branches and field trash recently uncovered by the melted snow. Isaac risked being caught to slow down and survey their surroundings. Satisfied that they had gone far enough away from their actual destination, he adjusted their course for the rift site.

They broke through the tree cover, emerging on the other side of the scrub forest. Isaac slowed the ATV down and told Heisenberg to be ready.

"The dead zone is just through the culvert drain there. We came around to the other side of it. As far as I know, they haven't found the dead zone yet. You'll have a bit of time to mess with the rift and fix the universe."

The ATV stopped and they walked down into the corrugated steel culvert drain. A thin dribble of brown water sat stagnant at the bottom of the large pipe, and the smell of the tunnel urged Heisenberg to traverse the span quickly and get away from it. The stench was a mix of decayed plant matter and dead animal flesh, married with the odor of urine and feces. Heisenberg gagged at the intensity of the smell.

"I don't spend much time in the country-are tunnels like this usually this pungent."

"Would you be surprised to find out that I'm not much of an outdoorsman myself? I am a librarian, remember."

They emerged from the other end of the tunnel with the stink still clouding around them. Directly beside the entrance, Heisenberg discovered one of the sources of the smell. A large skunk had been grievously injured, but had been able to pull itself to the crest of the opening before dying from its wounds. There were drag marks leading up to its final resting place, made by the animal in its desperate attempt to outdistance death. The last few centimeters of its final journey must have been excruciating. The direction of the skunk's escape led back to the rift and the dead zone around it.

"Well, at least the dead zone has kept the Novalis goons from finding the site. The next question will be if we can approach it under our own power?"

Isaac turned to face Heisenberg. Sweat covered his forehead and his breathing had a ragged edge to it.

"Are you feeling sick? Because I am. The idea of walking towards the dead zone is making my legs buckle. I can't even see it, but I'm terrified of it."

Heisenberg nodded and patted Isaac on the shoulder.

"It's not affecting me. You make your way back to the ATV and bring it around to the other side of the dead zone, just in case."

"Are you sure you're fine? There's something awful happening with your teeth."

Heisenberg rubbed his jaw. "Ah, yeah. That's an unrelated symptom. A reminder that this reality does not take kindly to my presence and my interference."

Isaac grimaced and turned around. Heisenberg went to walk towards the rift, shielding his eyes from the baleful glaring light arcing through it. An out of place sound stopped him in his tracks. He spun around to see the cause of the heavy thump was the meaty fist of one of the other Novalis goons slamming into Isaac's stomach. The goon's other hand was clamped over Isaac's mouth. Heisenberg lowered his head and charged the goon, but a surprise punch from a second thug forced Heisenberg to the ground.

Heisenberg looked up at the thick-necked thug who had just assaulted him. The goon had a Neanderthal slouch and the thick arms and eyebrow to match it. He returned Heisenberg's angry stare with a smirk. Heisenberg drew himself up on one knee, preparing to launch himself at the Neanderthal, despite the obvious mismatch in physical stature and prowess. The goon responded by showing Heisenberg the pistol in the other hand. "Sit" the Neanderthal grunted.

Isaac was dragged over and thrown to the ground beside Heisenberg. He looked even worse than he had a moment ago, and the punch to his gut had made breathing painful.

"How hard did he hit you?" Isaac asked between breaths.

Heisenberg paused to spit out a tooth before answering. "Not that hard."

The Neanderthal laughed and Heisenberg replied. "I'll have you know that I had existing dental issues that caused that tooth to fall out, so don't flatter yourself." He punctuated his claim by nosily spitting out a wad of bloody sputum.

"Listen, this is getting much too much out of hand. There's no need to resort to violence and other unpleasant and illegal activities to get what we all want"

Heisenberg hoped to somehow talk his way out of the current predicament. The Neanderthal's answer was a quick kick aimed at Heisenberg's ribs. Heisenberg pulled away to avoid most of the blow, but he was sufficiently deterred from trying to talk again. Within 5 minutes, the Hummer pulled up to the site. Tweedsmuir and Boris stepped out of the truck and walked over to the captives. Tweedsmuir stopped directly in front of Heisenberg and crouched down.

"Hello Michael. You're more resourceful than my lieutenant had thought."

Heisenberg looked over nervously at the Neanderthal, worried that any response he gave to the boss's statement would earn another kick. The Neanderthal was a few steps away, and paying little attention to the scene now that his superior was on site.

"Your lieutenant is the unpleasant Mr. Worksley, right? You may want to include a refresher course in hygiene as a part of his performance review this year."

Tweedsmuir kept a straight face. "I'll take that under advisement. Now, you need to give me the item in question."

"I don't have it."

Tweedsmuir held up his finger in warning. "No more games, Michael. We have very little time here before the police disturb us. In the short time that we have here together, you will discover a very painful series of sensations, and you probably won't live through it. Neither will your associate here, but that may mean nothing to you. So, let's avoid a mess and you can tell me right now."

Heisenberg considered launching some kind of gaudy spell to distract his captors and get away, but the very thought of using arcane energy caused his heart to race and a screaming pain to inhabit his head. The rift seemed to shriek at the idea of any kind of spell casting. He resigned himself to his inescapable future. He shook his head and braced himself for the consequences of his next statement.

"It's somewhere over there, but that's the best that I can tell you" he said with a wave of his hand towards the Rift.

Tweedsmuir snarled and stood up. He rolled up the sleeves of his dark red dress shirt and fished a small, highly polished wooden object from his pocket. With a quick flick of his wrist, he exposed the gleaming blade of a straight razor. As the blade of the razor descended slowly with ill purpose, Heisenberg panicked and tried to scrabble away. The Neanderthal appeared behind him and held his arms tightly, making any escape impossible.

Tweedsmuir swiped the blade menacingly in front of Heisenberg's face, almost grazing his eyelids.

"Now's the time to adjust your attitude, friend. You've already earned a cut, but the severity will be entirely up to you. Let's start the line here."

Tweedsmuir put the corner of the straight razor's blade at the edge of Heisenberg's jaw line, just below his right ear. He pressed in slowly, until a trickle of blood welled up around the blade and down his face.

"Wait wait wait! Just turn your head at look at the clearing over there. It's littered with dead animals, because the Kingmaker is emitting some kind of deadly radiation. That's where the device is, I swear. Just look at it!"

Tweedsmuir paused, leaving the blade in place. He added pressure to widen the cut slightly and looked to the Neanderthal.

"Do you see anything?"

"No sir. Nothing."

"Mr. Kreigs doesn't see anything, Michael. I believe you're trying to trick me."

The blade was pulled along the line of Heisenberg's jaw, and a bright scarlet line was drawn behind it.

"He can't see it, he's too stupid. He's not worthy enough to see the truth" Heisenberg said in a shrill and hysterical voice. He hoped that somehow this would convince Tweedsmuir to look at the clearing, and that the rift's energy was strong enough to become visible to an unawakened mage.

Tweedsmuir smiled. "Well if that isn't a ridiculous attempt at delaying the inevitable, I don't know what is."

"Please, just look. You're different than he is. Different than all of them. And you can feel it too."

Tweedsmuir took an agonizing amount of time to consider this statement, and Heisenberg waited for a sudden and savage slash from the razor as an answer to his desperate attempt. With his eyes closed tight in dread anticipation, Heisenberg didn't see the razor drift away from his skin and hang loosely at Tweedsmuir's side. After a moment of silence and stillness, Heisenberg re-opened his eyes. He saw Tweedsmuir now staring wide-eyed at the rift, wincing in pain from the brightness of it but too fixated to look away.

"What is it?" Tweedsmuir gasped.

Heisenberg weighed all of his possible responses, and went with the simplest. "Magic."

Chapter 26

Mallory's cell phone buzzed loudly and she snatched it up and answered

"Hello?"

The hurried response from the other end of the line made her gasp. "We have to hurry up and get to the rift NOW!" She shouted at Damien and Kean.

"What's going on?" Kean replied.

"Robert just talked to Heisenberg, and he's alive but in some kind of trouble. He's being chased."

Damien spoke up. "I can't hurry up if I don't know where I'm going. You just keep pointing at the storm clouds and saying 'go that way' but we're under the storm now and all the clouds look the same."

Mallory relayed the information to Robert, and promised to call him back the second that they arrived at the rift before hanging up. She turned and focused her gaze on the landscape approaching them off to the left of the car, mirroring Kean's search on the other side. The road they were on was lower than the farms on either side, so their view of the horizon was blocked by silos on one side and a dilapidated barn on the other. Mallory's magesight revealed darting clouds of raw spell energy peeking through the clouds before vanishing, over and over again.

She scanned the land and air for any kind of clue as to which direction the rift was. As they climbed out of the valley and crested the hill in front of them, both Mallory and Kean received the blinding answer to their search. The rift was a blazing scar on the fabric of reality, stretching hundreds of meters up into the sky in an iris shape. Mallory closed her eyes tightly and clamped her hands over them to block out all light. The light of the rift had overwhelmed her vision. She pointed off in the direction of the rift, hoping that she didn't accidentally whack Damien in the back of the head.

"That way. Take the next right and keep going. We'll tell you when to stop."

Damien followed the instructions, but kept looking back at Kean and Mallory with their eyes closed.

"Are you two okay? What the hell is going on?"

Kean blinked furiously to clear the tears from his eyes. "We're fine. Just keep going. Do you have sunglasses in the car?"

"What? Why?"

"Something you can't see is very bright, and I'm hoping that sunglasses might help. Probably won't but there's no harm in checking."

"In the storage box under the armrest."

Kean dug through the storage box under the armrest between the driver and passenger seat. The space was crammed with cds, old receipts, napkins and a flattened pack of cigarettes. Digging even deeper, Kean found the sunglasses and he put them on. Cautiously, he switched to magesight and tested the blocking power of the sunglasses.

"So does it work?" Mallory asked. She still had her eyes closed tight and she wasn't going to risk opening them until she knew the answer.

Kean looked at the extreme edge of the rift's light, and waited for a negative reaction. Though the sunglasses didn't block the light out, they did seem to reduce the intensity. It was almost as if they were shifting the light from arcane to something more mundane and manageable, like being at the beach on a bright summer day.

"It works. Do you have glasses, Mal?"

She whipped on her large, dramatic sunglasses with the bright red frames.

"Of course I do, and they're fabulous."

Kean shook his head and gave Damien his next set of driving instructions. 5 minutes later, they were at the edge of the rift site itself. All three of them got out of the car and stood at the edge of the area affected by the rift's energy. The grass surrounding the rift was scorched and brown, darkening to black at the center of the circle. The diameter of the circle of effect was about 10 meters, and the pressure from the expanding magic field told Mallory and Kean that the area would only keep growing and consuming more land. Damien stopped moving forward and refused to move any closer.

"I don't know what the hell is going on, but there's something bad over there and I'm not going. I'll be back behind the car."

"Stay in earshot, D. Things might get pretty strange and we might need your help."

Damien nodded and retreated back to the safety of the car. Kean crouched down and looked at the first stretch of turf in front of them. He noticed a small lump of brown fur just ahead. it was a dead mouse. He pointed to the corpse.

"This may not be a terribly safe place to be, Mal."

Mallory squirmed. "Ew. You're right, but what else are we going to do? Make guesses on how to fix things from the comfort of our seats in the car? Let's check the most important reaction first. What happens if we bring the AD towards the rift?"

Kean walked over to the trunk of the car and got the AD case out of it. Even the simple act of removing it from the car's interior caused the rift to spark and intensify. As Kean cautiously walked a few meters back towards the rift, an arc of arcane energy snapped out from within the rift and connected with the case. A jolt of unpleasant sensation ran up his arm, like an electrical shock. He hastily put the box down and walked back to Mallory.

"We better leave the box there until we know what we're doing."

"And when, precisely, will that be?"

Kean scowled at her. "You don't need to keep pointing out that we're making this all up. I've been here since it all started. I know."

"Alright, alright. So first idea-chuck the thing in the rift, and run away while hoping that the reaction isn't explosively deadly."

"And what happens after the device enters the rift?"

Mallory scuffed the ground and paced forward and backwards before answering. "It enters the rift, and the attachment to its home reality pulls it through. The whole tether theory that Heisenberg had."

"What about him? Will it pull him back through?"

"…I guess? Or maybe he has to jump through at the same time?"

From behind the car, Damien shouted. "Are you both nuts? Just checking."

Kean shouted back at him. "It's only going to sound crazier. Just focus on remembering song lyrics or something, and we'll tell you when things get normal again."

Damien shot his cousin the middle finger and hunkered down behind the car again. Mallory had picked up an old 2 foot long tree branch, and she approached the rift with the branch in hand. Kean was startled to see her so close to the rift, but he didn't have time to say a word of warning before she casually tossed the branch halfway into the rift. There was no sudden magical explosion or release of deadly energy. Both of the kids sighed noisily in relief. They watched the branch shook and shimmered as it slowly disappeared into the rift. Mallory dashed forward and grabbed the end of the branch before it vanished completely into the rift. The charred remains of the stick now in her hands left Mallory with a terrible feeling of dread. She brandished the stick at Kean, showing him the destructive nature of the rift. Kean responded by picking up thin metal survey flag pole that had been blown into the field from the hydro towers just beyond. He walked to the rift and stood beside Mallory.

"Have to test that again, to confirm the results. Maybe you should step back while I do this."

Mallory obligingly took a full stride step backwards. Kean extended his arm and slowly inserted the metal shaft into the rift.

He paused, and then reversed direction to remove the flag from the rift.It emerged unchanged.

"Huh" he exclaimed. "Wonder why this one is okay?"

"Metal versus wood?"

Kean thought about this, and decided that it would be worth checking that out. He took the charred branch stub and used some twine to tie it to the flag. The metal rod bowed erratically under the weight of the branch, but Kean was able to hold it more or less straight and he inserted the combination into the rift. It returned untouched again. He turned the test contraption around, and gently tossed it flag-first into the rift. This time, the flag pole twitched and crept further into the rift of its own volition, and when Kean snatched it back up, the section that had been fully inside the rift was completely destroyed.

Mallory and Kean analyzed the smoldering remains in front of them. Mallory was the first to come up with a theory.

"It's you. You kept the rift from destroying the thing. Here, put the pole in the rift again, but keep holding it."

Kean followed the instruction, and Mallory watched his arm intently for magical reactions. Though the arcane light from the rift was still painful to her magesight, she was able to ignore it and notice Kean's aura extending and surrounding the flag pole.

"I knew it! Your magic is keeping it safe. Anything non-magical that interacts with the rift will get destroyed, unless a mage is protecting it."

"Well, that's good to know, I guess, but does it help us answer our real problem?"

"One thing at a time. We need to get a rig together for further testing, and we need to contact Heisenberg. Call Robert."

"Wait. There's one other thing we can test."

"What?"

"What the inside of the rift looks like."

Mallory looked suspiciously at Kean. "Your cousin might be right. You're crazy."

"If we don't get a look at the internal structure of the rift, our plan might be doomed to fail right from the start."

"It's probably just a hole through to some other place. There's no "inside" to look at."

"Maybe. But what if there is?"

"Then you get lost, and I have to tell your parents that you've vanished from this plane of existence. And then they commit me to a psych facility. Or send me to jail for your murder."

A sudden thump startled both Kean and Mallory, and it took them a moment to realize that the sound had come from the bundle of nylon rope that was now sitting at their feet. A second line of nylon rope was tied to the bundle, and trailed back to Damien standing at the edge of the clearing.

"I got bored of hiding, so I started watching what you're doing."

"Can you see the stuff disappear?"

"Sort of, but don't ask me to tell you what I'm actually seeing. That makes my head pound. So no thinking for me, but rope-holding is fine and dandy."

"When this is all over, we have got to figure out why this isn't making you crazy."

Kean busied himself unbundling the second line and tying it tightly around himself. When it was knotted and secure, he gave instructions to Mallory and Damien.

"I'm going to poke my head forward and take a look. If I start twitching or I fall down, pull me right back out. I'll try to describe what I'm seeing."

Kean took a deep breath and leaned cautiously into the rift itself. He had to close his eyes as he passed through the bright corona of the rift, with its light so intense that it turned his eyelids into a translucent red mask. The intensity of the light diminished as soon as his head was fully into the rift. Kean opened his eyes. A million possibilities surrounded him, countless windows, doors and portals leading to unknown and unrecognizable spaces. Each possibility flashed by in an instant and was replaced by a new, more bizarre vision. There was no sense of space or limited distance, just an endless shapeless void defined by a perimeter of exits. Kean's head swam at the sight of this incomprehensible location. The rapidly changing light and sound of the space added to his disorientation. He felt his body start to betray him. His knees buckled, lost without a sense of equilibrium, and he fell face-first, further into the riftspace.

Mallory watched in horror as Kean's body went rigid and thenfell down. She grabbed tight to the rope. "PULL , DAMIEN! PULL!" she screamed, and they both dug in their heels and pulled to drag Kean out of the grasp of the rift. Mallory could feel the rift itself resisting her efforts, and she caught a hint of malevolence attached to that resistance. The rift was ready to punish every mage it could get a hold of, and it wanted to start with Kean.

Feeling the surprising difficulty of retrieving his cousin from the mysterious thing that he had slipped into, Damien twisted the rope around his elbow and stepped around the corner of the car to use the vehicle as additional leverage. The added force was enough to tip the balance, and Kean tumbled out of the unseen rift.

Mallory ran over to Kean's limp body and shook him. He groaned loudly, but stayed unconscious for another full minute. When he finally came to, Mallory was at the edge of hysteria and was ready to haul him out of there and to the nearest hospital.

"Kean! Are you okay? I am retroactively declaring that plan as totally stupid, and you're an ass for trying it."

"Ugg. Stop yelling at me. I'm fine."

Kean's claim of being back to normal was challenged by the wobbly legs that tried to stand him upright. He sat back down and rethought the situation.

"Okay, I'm a little groggy from going in there. But I'll be fine.We needed someone to go in there. It's not a straight pass-through to wherever Heisenberg is. There are millions and millions of directions to go, each with another portal at the end of it. There were so many possibilities that I couldn't handle it all. I couldn't tell which direction was up, or forward, and I had no idea of how t get back here. It was too much for me to handle, and I blacked out."

"It blew your mind, eh? Wonder if that's what the hippies are talking about?"

"Hippies? What are hippies?"

"Oh never mind. Watch an old movie or two sometimes Kean. Culture existed before 2005, you know."

"Can we get back on topic, please?"

Mallory dialed Robert and began talking at him the second that he answered the phone.

"Robert, we're here at the rift and we've done some exploring. The rift is going to freak out once the Antikythera mechanism gets lose to it, so it will have to be a fast process. The inside of the rift is immense and totally confusing, so anyone going into it will get lost and go crazy. Kean almost went crazy."

Kean interjected. "Hey!"

"Quiet, I'm on the phone. So anyway Robert, we're ready at the rift to do whatever the next step is but we don't know what that is. And, things are getting pretty wild, in a magical vortex slash cataclysm sort of way, so we better find a solution soon. Oh, one other thing-if a non-magical item goes into the rift, it's destroyed. But if a mage is holding it, it survives unharmed. That might turn out to be important. So can you get a hold of Heisenberg again and tell him we're here?"

Mallory nodded and passed along Robert's answer to Kean. "He's contacting him now. Get ready."

Chapter 27

Heisenberg hoped that the stunned surprise being broadcast by Tweedsmuir would have distracted the Neaderthal enough to allow for an escape attempt, but the goon's meaty mitts were still clamped onto Heisenberg. The noise of the clearing was increased by the puttering sound of Isaac's ATV, being driven by Boris.

"Found this on the other side of the tunnel. Almost flipped the damned thing getting' it over here."

The ATV's radio crackled to life again. "Heisenberg, are you there? They're ready to help, but they don't know what to do next. Hello?"

The sound of Robert's ghostly radio voice woke Tweedsmuir from his dazed state. He stormed over to the ATV and picked up the microphone. "WHERE IS THE KINGMAKER?" he bellowed into the receiver.

Robert sounded meek and frightened as he answered. "Who is this? I don't know what you're talking about."

Tweedsmuir jerked his head towards the ATV as an instruction for the Neanderthal, and the goon responded by dragging Heisenberg over. Tweedsmuir wrapped the cord of the microphone around Heisenberg's neck and shouted back at Robert.

"Your stupid friend is right beside me, and he's choking to death. I am going to strangle the son of a bitch and then I'll cut him up, unless you tell me where the Kingmaker is."

Heisenberg was still able to breathe, albeit with some difficulty. "Robert, I'm here and I'm in a bit of trouble. The angry fellow is looking for what we've been calling the Antikythera Device, and he's quite serious about doing some very unpleasant things to me if he doesn't get it."

"What should I do?"

Tweedsmuir yanked the microphone back to his mouth, increasing the restriction around Heisenberg's throat.

"You take the Kingmaker, and you walk it over to this spot, and I will consider letting you live."

"He's on the other side of the rift, there" Heisenberg croaked.

"And so? What does that mean?"

"No one knows how to get through it. It was an accident the first time."

Tweedsmuir screeched with impatient rage. "That's garbage! Stop lying to me." He punctuated each word with another pull on the cord.

Robert interrupted. "I, I think I have an idea, but I have to check with the others. They're the ones actually at the rift site. Hold on."

The pause was an eternity for Heisenberg. The plastic cord cut into his throat and made the blood pound in his ears. Finally Robert returned to the conversation.

"Okay, we're ready to try bringing it back. There's a shield of some sort on this side, protecting the rift from intrusion. Seems to be blocking most forms energy except for the energy the rift is generating. We can hear a very loud noise that is increasing in intensity, so be ready for a sudden loud noise when the device passes through. Are you ready for us to throw it into the rift, Heisenberg? You have to be there to catch it. Anything non-magical that interacts with the rift is destroyed, so you have to be ready to catch the device."

Heisenberg caught the pleading tone in Robert's voice, the hope that a second message was being heard. Heisenberg braced himself for the blast of karma that was going to thunder down on him, and he drew a tiny bubble of spell energy ttogether. He took as deep a breath as he could muster and told Robert "I'm ready" as he flicked the spell energy into two little bundles of paired ovals. One pair shot towards Isaac and the other into Heisenberg's own ears. The spell-crafted earplugs slipped into place and blocked out the sound around them a split second before Robert sent a terrifying blast of high-pitched feedback through the ATV's speaker and the sound system of the SUV. The sound even came out of the microphone in Tweedsmuir's hand, surprising him with an intense shooting pain in his eardrums. Tweedsmuir's grasp on the cord went slack, as did the gorilla grip of the Neandethal, and Heisenberg threw all of his weight behind sending his shoulder into Tweedsmuir's gut.

Heisenberg broke free of their restraints and stumbled towards the rift itself. The backlash slammed into him, a blunt painful force with no definition, and he stumbled to his knees and continued to crawl towards the rift. The appearance of a pistol barrel in front of his face forced him to stop. Tweedsmuir was livid, jamming the gun into Heisenberg's face. He was screaming at the top of his lungs, part in anger and part because the noise blast had temporarily deafened him. A trickle of blood ran out of Tweedsmuir's left ear.

"You're going to stick your hand in there, and it better come back out with the Kingmaker, or I'm going to shoot you in the stomach. Just like your friend there is about to get shot. Boris! Shoot the other one! Boris! Damnit! SHOOT HIM! WHY AREN'T YOU KILLING HIM?"

Heisenberg laughed at the ridiculous question, despite the danger of his situation. He looked at the goons standing outside of the area of effect and wondered why they were standing so still and rigid. The Neanderthal toppled over like a felled tree, followed by Boris and the others. In the space behind where the Neanderthal had been standing, Isaac stood smiling beside another similar looking fellow, both of them with tasers in their hands. Tweedsmuir had noticed all of this as well, and he went to point the gun at the two men when he too went rigid and unresponsive. From the edge of the area of effect, a second new arrival waved from behind the sights of a taser rifle.

"Michael, meet my brother, Gabe, and our friends Andy and Ron. This might be the first ever rescue performed by a librarian cavalry."

Gabe elbowed Isaac in the side. "We're not on horses, dummy."

"It's a turn of phrase. 'Here comes the cavalry' to denote a sudden appearance of a fast-moving ally or remedy to a predicament? Sound familiar?"

"Sounds laboured. Anyway, hi Michael, nice to meet you. Let's figure out a solution to this cataclysm before the world comes to an end, okay? Ron and Andy will tie up these dopes."

Heisenberg held up his hand to stop Andy from moving forward.

"It's too dangerous for you to get any closer. I'll drag their boss over to a safe spot."

Andy lowered his taser rifle to his side and looked quizzically at Heisenberg.

"If it's dangerous, why are the two of you able to withstand it with no ill effects?"

Heisenberg winced as the general backlash pain in his body lessened and concentrated into a ringing in his ears. He shook his head and spit out a second bloody tooth.

"Not entirely unscathed. But Tweedsmuir and I are of a special sort of people who can endure the radiation being spit out from the rift. The rift that you can't see, and yes, I understand that sounds daft."

Andy shrugged and threw a roll of duct tape over to Heisenberg. A few passes of the tape around Tweedsmuir's wrists immobilized his hands, and Heisenberg dragged him to Andy's position outside of the rift circle. Isaac and Gabe came over to join them.

Heisenberg watched the brothers walk over and noticed the differences between them. Gabe was taller, and he walked with an ease that Isaac didn't. It was hard to tell the age gap between them, but if he had to guess, Heisenberg would pick Isaac as the older brother.

When all of the Ex Libris operatives had gathered round, Heisenberg summarized the situation as best as he could. He paused his explanation to use a can of spray paint retrieved from Tweedsmuir's SUV to mark the actual location of the rift. Being able to identify the location seemed to help them understand, or at least accept what was happening. They peppered Heisenberg with questions, most of which were too complicated to answer. Heisenberg felt perilously close to giving away too much about his own magical ability. He held up his hands in surrender.

"Fellows, I'd like to give you a better explanation, but you'll have to make do with what I've told you already. The long and short of it is, I need to go back through the rift to my home, and the Kingmaker has to come back here. And hold on a second, I think there's something more."

Heisenberg remembered the lump covered in a dirty blanket in the back of the SUV. It had looked out of place when he had gotten the spray paint, much too dirty to be thrown casually in the back of Tweedsmuir's pristine and well-maintained vehicle. Heisenberg went back to the trunk and moved the blanket to reveal the decayed remains of the Antikythera device. He scanned it with his magesight and confirmed that a gossamer thin tether line extended from it towards the rift. He picked it up and walked back to the crowd.

"I believe this has to go back with me as well. This is my home's version of the Kingmaker. The boat it was on sank in the Mediterranean Sea, over 2000 years ago."

Isaac frowned. "If that's the same as our Kingmaker, then it's much older than we had guessed. Based on the mechanics, we assumed it was made some time in the 14th century C.E. "

"It's a marvel of computational design, and you're right, it shouldn't have been possible before the Common Era. There may be another interesting story involved with its initial fabrication, but I suspect it has nothing to do with our current scenario. Right now, we need to swap the working one with this broken copy."

The ATV radio came to life again. "Heisenberg, I hope that worked. Can you tell me if it worked?"

Heisenberg walked over and answered. "It did Robert. Good job."

"Great. Hey, wait. What if you're still under their control and they're forcing you to lie to me?"

"Robert, that's a reasonable suspicion but thankfully unfounded. I've been rescued by a group of librarians, and I'm ready to come home."

Robert gave a little yelp of happiness, and then he repeated all of the details of Mallory and Kean's investigation of the rift.

"So, without a guideline, I'll most likely get lost in the rift as well" Robert said.

"We could hope that the tethers would propel all of the out-of-place elements to their respective homes through magical elasticity, but the risk of being lost in the interstitial space is too high."

Robert's normally impressive vocabulary knowledge failed him. "Interstitial?"

"An empty space between other spaces full of matter."

"Oh."

"The pressing issue is how we can establish a guideline between the two realities."

"Hold on. I've got an idea."

5 Minutes of silence passed by as Robert worked on some kind of solution. He came back to the radio and told Heisenberg to get as close to the portal as possible without entering it. Heisenberg did as he was told and he waited.

"In a second Kean and I are going to try something. I don't think I can maintain the radio link at the same time, so I'll be out of contact for a bit."

"Oh yes, remind me later to ask for an explanation on how exactly you're communicating with me."

Robert pressed on, ignoring Heisenberg's statement. "Okay, here we go in 3…2…1"

On the other side of the rift, Kean threw the knotted end of the nylon rope into the rift as hard as he could. Spiraled around the rope was a beam of radio waves, warped and repurposed by Robert to allow him to direct the rope on its journey through the interstitial space. The battle to direct the rope through the space left Robert exhausted and aching, as if he had been wrestling with an invisible opponent for hours, even though mere seconds had passed by. His efforts were successful, and the knotted end of the rope appeared in a flash of light on the other side of the rift. The sounds of surprise emitted by Isaac and his companions told Heisenberg that they had seen the light too. It had been powerful enough to cross the arcane barrier and become real to the mundane viewers. Heisenberg picked up the rope and wrapped it around his body. The tugs of resistance coming through the rope told Heisenberg that the other end was in someone's hands. He hoped that they could both hold on long enough to get through.

Isaac spoke up. "I don't know what you're doing there, Michael, but it's giving me a very bad feeling. I can't even look at you right now."

Heisenberg turned around and, sure enough, all of the Ex Libris guys were averting their eyes from the rift site. He had to guess that impossibility of the rope wrapped around him vanishing into nothingness was too much for their minds to handle. He decided to press ahead.

"I'll go through and get the Kingmaker. I'll rest it on the ground here before going back through. When everything is back in its right place, the dangerous energy should dissipate, but check before you get the device. Wish me luck! Robert, if you can hear me, I'm coming through now."

With the Antikythera Mechanism tucked under his arm and both hands on the rope, Heisenberg took a deep breath and stepped forward into the rift. The sensory assault slammed into him and threatened to knock him completely unconscious. His knees buckled but he stayed on his feet. Heisenberg forced himself to look only at the rope in front of him and ignore everything else around. The one sensation he could not block out was a frightening disconnection from his magical senses. He felt utterly isolated from the magic he normally felt surrounding him, as if there was nothing arcane in existence. The powerlessness of that feeling spurred Heisenberg on, moving as quickly as he could without indulging in full-blown panic.

Time lost all meaning in the interstitial space, and emerging from the other side was like stepping off the end of a death march across the desert. Exhausted, he was still overjoyed to see Kean and Mallory, and their faces mirrored his own. Both kids made a move to embrace Heisenberg, but he warned them off.

"No! We're only halfway done. I have to get the Kingmaker back to the other reality. Bring it here!"

Mallory dashed back to the metal box containing the Kingmaker. She hefted it up in her arms and ran back towards the rift. The energy emanating from the rift pushed her about and resisted her advance, while the arcane tether tugged at the Kingmaker and pulled it closer. She staggered in a zig-zag path until she finally returned to the mouth of the rift. Heisenberg dropped the Antikythera mechanism to the ground and took the Kingmaker case from Mallory. "Be right back" he said with a wink, hoping that the kids hadn't noticed his ruined teeth and general physical state of disrepair and injury.

The trip back through the interstitial space was hurried along by the intense pull of the tether of the Kingmaker. Its magical nature amplified the power of the bond, and it drew Heisenberg directly towards the other reality. He partially emerged from the portal and held the Kingmaker case out in front of him.

"I know you can't look over here, but I'm back and I'm putting the Kingmaker down now. Once it's down, I'll go back through. And gentlemen, it was a pleasure meeting, and being rescued by you."

Isaac waved back in response, still unable and unwilling to look at Heisenberg as he stood half there. Isaac didn't notice Tweedsmuir drawing his knees up under himself. Tweedsmuir launched himself towards the rift. Heisenberg saw the enraged Novalis leader running towards him, and he reacted by throwing the Kingmaker case as hard as he could manage.

"Isaac! Take the case-I'm throwing it at the ATV!"

The case sailed out of reach as Tweedsmuir was a step away from Heisenberg. Tweedsmuir howled with frustration as his prize escaped his grasp. Isaac heard the case land and he hurried over to reclaim it. Heisenberg yelled "get it out of here!" and Isaac complied, starting up the ATV and driving away with the Kingmaker. Tweedsmuir lowered his head and screamed incoherently as he slammed into Heisenberg.

The collision drove both of them into the rift. Tweedsmuir wrenched one of his hands free from the sloppy duct tape handcuffs, and he brought that free hand up to Heisenberg's face. "I'll tear out your goddamned eyes!" he screamed. Heisenberg twisted his body and tried to keep a gap between the gouging fingers and his face. The rope slipped from his grasp, and was loosely coiled around his left leg. If it was dislodged, Heisenberg and his assailant would be trapped in the rift. Heisenberg rolled in the opposite direction and managed to throw Tweedsmuir off of him. He grabbed the rope back up and moved as quickly as he could towards his home. Tweedsmuir sprung up and chased Heisenberg, staggering back and forth with each step as if he was on a ship in the middle of s turbulent sea. The villain's eyes were locked on his prey, oblivious to the incomprehensible landscape around him. As Heisenberg reached the exit to his reality, Tweedsmuir grabbed him by the back of his coat and went to pull him back into a grapple.

"Stop it, you fool! We have to get out of here or we'll both be destroyed" Heisenberg pleaded with his attacker. The energy within the space had turned vicious and threatening, and just being in there was causing a tremendous amount of pain and fatigue to Heisenberg. From the look on his face, the same pain was washing over Tweedsmuir, and the villain looked around for the source of his hurt. His eyes went wide and his grip on Heisenberg went slack as Tweedsmuir tried to reconcile what he was seeing with his understanding of the natural world. Heisenberg felt the surge of arcane energy return to the rift, with a powerful malevolence aimed at the intrusive trespassers within the space. The magical energy coursed through the air, clearly visible, and it leapt in an arc into Tweedsmuir. Heisenberg was horrified to see the violent shift in Tweedsmuir's aura as his magical abilities and sense were made active without his consent. He grabbed the now awakened mage and pulled him through the rift to the other side.

The two mages crumpled to the ground in a pile. Heisenberg coughed repeatedly and sucked up air, gasping out hellos in between breaths.

"Tie that guy up. He's a baddie" Heisenberg wheezed.

Kean immediately went over to Tweedsmuir and started lashing his arms and legs. The stunned mage gave no resistance whatsoever. Kean looked at the prone villain and saw nothing but emptiness in his eyes. Tweedsmuir's jaw hung open and a line of drool was slowly dripping out from the corner of his mouth.

"Heisenberg, this guy is in pretty rough shape."

Heisenberg struggle to his feet and brushed himself off.

"At least that means he won't be trying to kill me again anytime soon."

Heisenberg walked over to the prone man and examined him. The shift in Tweedsmuir's aura displayed his new-found magical capabilities, but the power within him was unfocused and erratic. There was no real consciousness guiding the arcane energies. The rift had driven Tweedsmuir into madness and catatonia.

"It broke him. Rest the man's rotten soul, it broke him in two" Heisenberg said, as the world swam in front of his own eyes. He fell forward as his body lost muscle tone for a moment. Kean ran over and tried to help.

"Oh jeez, Heisenberg, you're in rough shape. What did they do to you?"

Heisenberg shook the cobwebs out of his thoughts and replied.

"Oh, a little light interrogation, a little life-threatening straight razor work, and some not insignificant karmic backlash. As you might have guessed, the universe was intensely unhappy with me being in the wrong reality, and it punished my magical use accordingly. I have a considerable amount of time in the dentist's chair waiting in my future. Is the rift closing yet? Is the area safe for non-magical creatures?"

The sudden change of topic confused Kean for a moment, and it was Mallory who answered.

"It's much, much smaller, and not anywhere near the blinding super-painful lightshow of weird magic that it was before. It's still there, though, and that is a little bit worrying."

Kean clued in to the conversation. "The area feels less dangerous, but that just might be to us. Hey Damien-can you come over here, or is it still giving off a bad feeling?"

Damien cautiously approached the edge of the area, and moved a few steps closer tentatively.

"No, the bad vibes are pretty much gone.

Heisenberg sat up slowly and did his own estimation of the rift. Mallory was right, it had closed almost entirely and the energy emanating from it had dropped dramatically, but there was something that wasn't quite right about the situation. He peered more intently at the rift, peeking between the seams of the scar to see inside the rift. Inside the rift, the storm had followed him from the other reality, and it was coalescing into an angry darkness. The dark energy sent a creeping tendril out of the rift and it latched onto the Antikythera Mechanism sitting a few steps away from Heisenberg.

"Something's not quite right. Do you feel that?"

Kean and Mallory looked around. "What? Feel what?" a Bewildered Mallory asked.

Heisenberg's lightheadedness returned and kept him from immediately responding. When everything came back into focus, he explained.

"The threat of backlash is still very high, and there's another sensation associated with it."

Kean nodded. "I see a black band of energy tied to the AM that leads back into the rift. It's like a dark tentacle, and it's pulsing."

"Gross. Oh, double gross, it's reaching out to us" Mallory said.

True to her description, the main dark tendril had small whip-thin sub-tendrils that were unraveled from the main line and twitching about in their direction. Mallory and Kean seemed to be the targets and they backed away from the strange and ominous energy.

"There is still some kind of imbalance or misalignment in this reality" Heisenberg said.

"What the heck does that mean?" Kean replied as he backpedaled away from the slow but persistent tendril.

"Something's still not right. We better figure it out, or something bad is going to happen" Mallory translated.

"That's what the other sensation is-foreboding! The feeling that things are about to get much much worse."

"That's great Kean. We were definitely in need of some linguistic clarity and not actual solutions. Kudos!"

"Mallory! Kean! Bickering won't help" Heisenberg chastised them.

The tendrils suddenly shot forward to their intended targets and connected to them. As soon as the tendrils attached themselves to Kean and Mallory, the tentacles moved to their chests and flattened into circular crests, with hooked talons on the edges to stay securely in place.

"Ah! This thing is attached to me. How do I get it off?"

"Is it hurting either of you?"

Kean swatted ineffectually at the patch of black energy affixed to his chest.

"No, but that doesn't make this cool!"

Heisenberg tried to gather some spell energy, but the effort pushed him to the edge of passing out.

"Use a spell to sever the connection, one of you. Do it quick and as small as you can."

Kean was the first to react. He pulled a ball of spell energy together and transformed it into a shimmering long-beaked sandpiper. The magical bird flew over to the midpoint between the rift and Kean, and it snapped its beak onto the tendril and cut it. The cut ends writhed and twisted blindly, but the attached crest stayed in place. Kean sent the bird over to the other tendril and severed the connection between Mallory and the dark storm. He pulled the bird back and had it try to dislodge the crest on his chest, but an immediate shock of tearing pain put an end to that attempt. He dismissed the bird and waited for the karma to hit. The backlash energy quickly accumulated and he braced himself for the moment where it hit critical mass and bashed into him, but the collision didn't happen. Instead, the backlash energy was redirected into the dark storm. The black cloud consumed the backlash, and grew larger.

Kean backed away from the rift. "That was unexpected and a bad sign. Damien, come help me get Heisenberg back to the car."Kean bent down to grab Heisenberg's right arm. He waited for Damien to take the other arm.

"Come on, D, gimme a hand here."

The stammered response from his cousin made Kean turn his head to see what was happening. Damien was pointing at the rift, with a look of pure terror on his face.

"Wha...what...what..is...THAT?"

All heads whipped around to look in the direction Damien was pointing. The dark storm of energy had firmed up into a solid mass and was breaching the rift. The leading edge of the cloud had formed into a massive arm, 2 meters long and undulating with dense muscle tissue. The fingers on the hand were twice as long as they should have been, with short claws on the end of each finger. The fingers dug into the very air around the rift and the creature pulled itself out of the rift. It stood 3 meters tall and it absorbed the light around itself to appear absolutely black. The monster took a plodding step over to the prone body of Tweedsmuir. Its hands reached down and closed around the inert mage, and the monster slowly clenched his fists to crush the mage. The flesh of Tweedsmuir transmuted into an elemental grey stone, pockmarked like volcanic rock, and the monster pulverized the rock into a dust that the rift inhaled instantaneously. A burst of backlash energy escaped the ashes as they disappeared and the monster ate that ball of energy with its giant fanged mouth. Just like that, Tweedsmuir ceased to be.

"Damien, we have to go now!" Kean screamed, trying to pull Heisenberg towards the car on his own. His shouting roused Damien out of his frozen state of terror, and he ran over and helped his cousin retreat to the car.

Mallory suppressed her own fear and scanned the monster with her magesight. The monster was magic made flesh, a physical form comprised of arcane energy. She looked more closely at the energy itself, and discovered that this was a creature constructed of karmic retribution. The main tendril attached to the Antikythera Mechanism was anchored in the center of the monster's chest, and it throbbed with a disturbingly organic rhythm. She noticed that the black spell crest burrowed into her torso throbbed in unison with the scene in front of her. She dashed forward, within a meter of the monster itself, and she snatched up the AM. The monster turned it's body towards her and made an unnatural howling sound, like the sound of massive freight cars slamming into each other as their brakes screech with a metallic scream.

Mallory went pale as she made eye contact with the howling fiend. A wave of heat from the monster washed over her.

"Time to run. Now."

Chapter 28

They raced to the car and feverishly hurried to get in and get away. Kean helped Heisenberg into the back seat as Damien jumped into the driver's seat and started the engine. Mallory was a pace behind them, and she made it into the passenger seat as Damien shifted out of park and slammed on the gas.

The car whipped out of the clearing and kicked up a cloud of dirt as it tore down the road. Mallory and Kean kept a vigil out the back window, looking for a sign of the lumbering monster following them. Mallory probed the edge of the parasitic black mass on her chest with a tiny scalpel of magical energy, and instantly regretted it. The thing ripped and gouged into her flesh with its talons. The pain was so intense that her eyes rolled back into her head.

"Oh crap-don't do that. Ugg" she said as she closed her eyes and waited for the pain to recede.

"Do what? Are you okay?"

"Tried to mess with the black lumpy thingie on my chest. Was a bad idea. Don't try to pry it off. Little dizzy and kinda want to barf right now."

Heisenberg closed his eyes and took some measured, steady breaths to gather his own composure. "Is it still following?" he muttered.

"No, we're out of its sight for now. But it wants this thing" Mallory said as she lifted the Antikythera Mechanism up. Heisenberg scanned the ruined device and traced the arcane lines connecting it to their reality.

"I'm not quite sure what's missing. This broken machine is in the right reality, but somehow the universe's expectations have not been satisfactorily met. And it's attached to the two of you, which is incredibly alarming."

"What?" Mallory exclaimed, and she switched over to magesight to find that Heisenberg was right: the device was now tethered to both her and Kean. "How did this happen?"

"That, my dear, is a very important puzzle we need to solve."

"Hey, anybody got an idea of where I'm going? Am I driving back to Kean's house, or what? And who is this old dude?"

"Old? Now's not the time for insults. My name is Heisenberg, and I am the employer and friend of these two."

"Actually, you were our employer, but your business kind of doesn't exist anymore."

"What do you mean?"

"It blew up" Mallory answered.

"The tea shop?"

"The whole building. That's why we thought you were a goner. Just a smoking hole in the ground was left."

Kean had turned his attention back to scanning the horizon behind them. The sight of the pitch black backlash demon rising up into the air and flying in pursuit behind them sent him into a full-blown panic attack. He flailed his left arm back, smacking Heisenberg and Mallory to get their attention.

"Look! LOOK! It's still following us."

The engine whined and Damien mashed on the accelerator and sent the car hurtling down the road at top speed.

"What kind of a storm cloud can chase a car, and why does it feel like that cloud is going to kill me?" Damien wailed.

Kean looked around the car for some kind of answer to their crisis. He stared intently at the Antikythera mechanism. He visually traced the lines connecting it to him and to Mallory.

"It's not back in the right place. That's the problem. Damien, ignore the evil cloud behind us and get to the university!"

"Well that's not a sentence you hear every day!" Mallory joked nervously.

"See, even though the Kingmaker wasn't supposed to be in this reality, the universe was somewhat pacified by the device being in the same location that this broken one was supposed to be in. When we stole the Kingmaker, we disrupted that. We created sthat magical tension, but it was lost in the background because of all of the other, bigger problems. Now everything else is fixed, except for that."

"I don't think the angry flying monster would agree that this is one last little problem."

Heisenberg groaned and hefted himself up from the seat into a sitting position, ignoring the protestations of his battered body, to get a look at the karmic demon pursuing them. The air around the monster shimmered with heat distortion. The monster wasn't flying through the air as much as it was clawing its way forward. He caught a glimpse of a long tentacle darting out from the mouth of the creature and quickly reeling back into the maw. It reminded him of a snake's tongue searching the air for signs of prey. Heisenberg tried to gather spell energy, but his body refused to allow him. The pain from his accumulated backlash punishments and the physical toll of the inter-reality travel stopped him from accessing his magic. He slumped back down.

"We should consider some of our options in deterring this beast from consuming us, because I believe he's getting closer. And I am currently unable to provide any direct solutions, if the two of you catch my meaning."

Kean nodded towards Damien. "He's been okay so far, handling all of the weird stuff."

"That doesn't mean it's a particularly good idea to talk openly about things that don't like being talked about. Let's not tempt fateful retribution, alright? Kean, can you think of something to deter our inky chum back there?"

Kean furrowed his brow and concentrated on the magical energy around him. He summoned a pack of arcane vultures and sent them to fly at the monster to disburse it. The massive wings of the birds buffeted the monster, but had little effect on its speed and direction. Kean changed tactics and sent the flock into the monster itself. The vultures slammed into the monster and sunk into it, as if it was made of a thick, viscous tar. The birds emerged on the other side of the monster, still covered in the black ichors. They turned around and shot towards the car. Kean struggled to control the birds, but the link between his mind and his conjured minions had been compromised. He pushed outwards and tried to dismiss the birds outright, but found to his horror that he was no longer able to dispel them. The birds smashed into the back of the car, one after another, making the vehicle shudder and swerve dangerously all over the road.

"What the hell?" Damien shouted as he fought to keep control of the car.

"Okay, on the list of bad ideas-direct assault" Mallory said.

Kean felt the incoming threat of backlash move towards him, but reverse direction at the last moment. The backlash condensed into a ball that looked similar to spell energy but of a different polarity. The backlash sphere was inhaled by the monster behind them and the fiend's body seemed to flare and become more solid than a moment before. The fiend slowed down slightly and the distance between it and the car increased.

"It ate the backlash energy and slowed down" Kean shouted.

"Why? What does that mean?" Mallory answered.

"It's powered by the dissonance between what should be and what is."

"Being inscrutable is really unhelpful, Heisenberg! Make sense!"

"The creature is a manifestation of karma itself. The predicted outcomes have been subverted for too long, and now this monster has come into being to erase the imbalance and the things that caused it."

"Erase us?"

Heisenberg nodded. "I think that's possible. So the creature is made to consume backlash, to destroy it, and its power is determined by how much karmic imbalance is happening around it."

"So we just keep whipping spells off around it, and it'll stop to eat all of the backlash? That works for me!"

Mallory looked over to Kean, and noticed something that he had missed in his excitement. The inky black crest attached to his chest had thickened and spread, now reaching his collarbone and his navel. It throbbed, and the talons that kept it in place pushed deeper within his skin. Mallory reached over and touched the pulsing mass. A chill ran through her hand and left a cold sense of loss as she yanked her hand away. Mallory compared the sensation of touching Kean's parasite to touching her own, and the difference was noticeable. Hers was still firmly attached, but it wasn't doing anything else.

"Kean, don't freak out, but the spell made that chest hugger stronger, and I think it's draining your life or something."

Kean went as white as a sheet. "Don't freak out? That's the worst thing to say! It's sucking my life away? How do you know? I feel fine, I think. Hold on, maybe I don't. Oh jeez."

"Don't cast anything else and you should be okay."

"And what are you basing that on? Do you have a hotline to cosmic mystery solutions that I don't know about?"

Damien yelled back. "If he's dying, can he do it quietly? I'm freaked out enough on my own, and I need him to stop panicking."

"Nice sympathy, cousin. If I am dying, you're going to feel so bad."

Heisenberg took a closer look at Kean's parasite. He could see the talons and the increased sign, but nothing indicated there was a health effect to it.

"Both of you, please quiet down. Everyone in this car is alive and well, but veering off the road into a ditch would quickly change that. Damien, keep your eyes on the road. Kean, relax and let us take a look at your guest."

"Guest?"

Mallory responded. "He means your parasite. That's what the thing is, a parasite connected to the big guy back there."

"Mallory, how did you discern that there was a harmful consequence of Kean's actions? I can't see any indicator."

Mallory frowned and considered Heisenberg's question. "Well, it felt cold, and that was the first clue. Not just a plain drop n temperature, but an absence of the heat of the living. Kean felt far away from me. The feeling reminded me of Whisper."

Heisenberg touched Kean's parasite, but still felt none of things Mallory had felt.

"You know, the two of you could ask before touching me. It would be polite."

Heisenberg laughed. "Fair enough. Technically, a parasite is a separate organism, but it is a part of your person right now, so we should follow the rules of etiquette when it comes to personal space."

"I am so glad this is funny to you. Come on, I'm still freaked out!"

Mallory felt a flush of warmth return to the air around Kean. She reached out to confirm. "He's fine now. The cold has gone away and he's normal. Well, as normal as he ever is."

The car passed through a country intersection with a flashing caution light in the middle, and in front of them there was the first sprawl of the city of London. Almost out of sight behind them, the karmic demon clawed along the sky and earth in pursuit. Damien stared in the rear view mirror.

"Have I lost my mind, or are we being followed by a brush fire?"

The other occupants of the car all turned to look. With every step and grip, the monster was leaving small flares of combustion. Even when it's clawed hands dug into the air, a flash of fire hung in the spot where it had touched.

"Was it doing that before?" Mallory asked.

"No, I don't think so."

"Guess that's another reason to avoid casting. The more karma it eats, the hotter it gets."

The car radio suddenly came to life, with Robert's voice coming through it.

"Hey! What's going on? It's really difficult to find you guys."

Unsure of where to direct his response, Heisenberg spoke loudly into the general area of the radio.

"It would be best if you called us on the telephone. Anything out of the ordinary complicates our current predicament."

The radio went silent, and a small burst of karmic energy shot back through the car. A moment later, a white-hot fire flashed into existence at the foot of the fiend. Mallory's phone rang and she answered it.

"Robert! There's this thing and it…well there's no way I can explain it without triggering some unpleasant effects. Let me put you on speaker."

"Okay. Are all of you okay?"

"For the time being, but we're being chased by something. We need to get back to the lab at the university as soon as possible."

"You're going back to London? That might explain all of the strange news. Reports of wild fires caused by lightning, and one station is reporting it as suspected arson."

"The thing chasing us is setting those fires. It's going to get worse if we don't hurry."

"I have an idea. I'll help you get there quickly. I'll watch the traffic and I'll direct you to the fastest route."

Robert started giving them turn by turn instructions. They found green lights at every intersection, and at Robert's prompting, they picked up their speed until they were flying through the city streets.

"The police have all been routed to the northern edge of the city, so you're clear from where you are to the university."

"Thanks Robert. Remind me to ask how you did all of that."

"It wasn't easy. I have to lie down for a minute. Call me back if I can do anything else t help."

They made it onto the campus, pulling into the north-west entrance beside the Shulich medical school. Damien slowed the car down to keep from hitting any of the students teeming around the buildings and streets. He edged forward to the stop sign, ignoring the directional signs that pointed out he was now going the wrong way. A roaring sound filled the car, like the sound of water rushing over a waterfall combined with howl of a storm wind, and the sound reached its crescendo when the karmic demon slammed into the ground directly in front of them. It looked at the occupants of the car and gnashed its gigantic teeth together.

Chapter 29

Damien screamed and threw the car into reverse. "Oh god OH God-why does a storm have teeth? What the hell did I just see? Oh god."

The car hurtled backwards and turned down the service driveway running behind the sSocial Science building. The thunderous steps of the demon followed them as it closed the distance. Mallory pulled a massive ball of spell energy together and cast an entanglement spell. She took the two tall maple trees flanking the entrance to the driveway and drew chalk lines intertwined through the branches. She pulled the lines and used them to bend the tree limbs together into a knotted lattice directly between the monster and themselves. To increase the spell's effect, she drew a wire running from each of the lampposts to the latticework, and sent electricity coursing through the branches.

"Go! Go!" she shouted at Damien, but the driver didn't need any urging. He mashed the gas pedal and drove at top speed down the narrow driveway. Mallory saw the monster wade into the trees and start dismembering the obstacle. It cut easily through her spell lines, but jolted to a stop when the electricity hit it. They made it around the corner and out of sight before the connection to her spell were too damaged to maintain. The spell ended and the rush of karmic energy once again passed by its legitimate target and flew off to the beast. Mallory wanted to shut her eyes and pretend like the parasite on her chest wasn't burrowing deeper into her skin, but she forced herself to watch it and look for any clue as to how to remove it. She could feel the cold touch her, radiating towards her heart with alarming speed. The connection between the parasite, her flesh, and the tether to the Antikythera mechanism was too strong. Through chattering teeth, she gave the group orders.

"Heisenberg, are you mobile?"

Heisenberg sat fully up and tried to answer her, but the world turned grey and swam before his eyes.All he could do in response was weakly nod his head.

"I was afraid of that. Damien, you stay in the car and guard Heisenberg. If things calm down, find some water and food for him, but not until there's no danger."

Damien looked around and listened to the shrieking and screaming from the students. Whatever they were able to see when they looked at the monster was frightening enough to send them running in terror. Damien agreed to stay behind.

"Keaner, grab the device. We have to hightail it over to the building on foot. Make the thing search for us."

Kean grabbed the Antikythera Mechanism and followed Mallory in a mad dash away from the car to the nearest door of the UCC. The crackling sound of errant electricity still filled the air behind them, mixed with the noise of a panicked crowd of bystanders. Mallory threw open the door and raced down the stairs.

"Come on, this should get us into the tunnel system."

"Do you remember the way?"

Mallory grimaced before rushing through the next set of doors.

"A little late to ask for directions. Hopefully we'll catch sight of a tether line back to the lab, or find the tunnel we used the first time."

Mallory stood at the intersection of two tunnels and weighed the choice of direction. The thundering beat of her heart hit a skip and she felt a wave of lightheadedness wash over her. The icy cold talon of the parasite felt like it was slipped deep into her heart, and it was threatening to stop its beating. She took a deep breath and tried t calm down.

"I need a moment Kean. The parasite and I are in a disagreement about regular heart rhythms being a good thing."

"Oh my god-let's get you to a nurse or something. There's an emergency station up on the main floor of the UCC I think."

The building above them shuddered like an earthquake had just rolled over it. Mallory shook her head.

"Doesn't look like we have time for that. I think my heart is beating normally again. But I am not going to cast a spell at that thing again unless things are really about to totally explode."

They dashed off down the tunnel corridor that headed off to the left. The ground above them shook intermittently, sometimes farther away and sometimes so close that it felt like it was right on top. The karmic demon was still following them, but it was having trouble exactly locating them. The proximity of the demon had raised the temperature of the air a few degrees. Both of the kids were starting to sweat.

The tunnel twisted sharply to the left, and exited into an unfamiliar open room. The comfortable bench seats and television monitors in each corner gave away the room's function as a student lounge. From far overhead, a trickle of weak sunlight made its way down to them.

"I don't remember this room from the last time. I think we went the wrong way, Mal."

"Looks like. We're now in the…Lawson Hall student excellence centre? What does that even mean?"

"THERE YOU ARE!" boomed Robert's voice from each television screen at the same time. Mallory and Kean both screamed.

"Robert! Do not shout at us! We're being chased by a sentient cloud of angry backlash magic and it wants to destroy us, so we're just a little on edge."

"Sorry, but I couldn't determine the volume needed to communicate with you. Is this better?"

The sound of Robert's voice from the screen was matched up to a wireframe animated version of Robert's face. It made the conversation disturbing.

"Robert, we went the wrong way and the demon is after us."

"Demon? Is this a religious confrontation?"

Kean replied. "No, just a figure of speech. Big creatures made out of inky blackness, with sharp teeth and claws sound like demons."

"This is not important right now. Robert, find us a route to the North Campus Building, and hurry!"

There was a slight pause that was filled with a resonating rumble from somewhere above, followed by an almost imperceptible popping noise. The sunlight faded.

"Robert, things are getting really spooky here. That thing looking for us consumes any backlash it's near, which is good because it slows the thing down. But it's bad because the monster gets stronger and hotter when it eats karma" Kean explained.

"Oh, and Kean and I have magical parasites burrowed into our chests, parasites that are connected to the monster and parasites that drain our life away if we cast spells. The more backlash we create, the more life they suck away."

"Did you try to remove them?"

"Gee Robert what a great brand new idea. OF COURSE we did. Even probing the thing with magic caused it to dig even deeper into my skin and cause enough pain to make me pass out. Now where are we going?"

"Okay, the map is now loaded. I had to dig into their internal data facility to find a tunnel map, because-"

"I DO NOT CARE" Mallory howled.

"Sorry, sorry. Follow the lights."

The florescent lights running along the top of the walls began to dim and brighten in waves, illuminating the path they were supposed to take like the lights on a runway. Motion from high up above them caught Kean's eye and made him look up. The small pane of reinforced glass that formed the skylight had been breached. Through the melted hole in the center, thick black goo was running down the wall. The black mass was both liquid and elastic, like a pool of mercury set free to leak down a wall.

Mallory hadn't noticed the goo yet, and she was walking purposefully towards the door directly under the spot where the ooze was about to drip. Kean yanked her back from the door just as the goo hit critical mass and plummeted to the ground right in front of her. As it touched the ground, it began to reform into the karma demon. A wave of intense heat assaulted Kean and Mallory. The heat started to sear their skin, but their magical auras pushed back against the heat and kept them safe from the burning. Their route to the NCB was blocked, so Mallory improvised and ran down the opposite hallway.

"Robert, it found us. Need a new route. Can you follow us?" she yelled.

The tiny speaker underneath the surveillance camera in front of them answered. "I can. Can you go back above ground?"

Kean pulled ahead of Mallory and held open the next set of steel doors.

"We have to stay down here. Too many people above. We're insulated from the heat it's giving off, but a normal person could get killed."

"Okay. You'll have to take a roundabout route then. And I'll plot a course that avoids anything explosive."

"If you can think of any way to slow the thing down without setting off a firestorm or stopping our hearts, I'd be glad to hear it" Mallory said as she passed the doors and took a right turn to follow Robert's light path. The hissing sound of the monster's radiating heat scorching the tunnel behind them was punctuated by an inhuman howl. Mallory locked eyes with Kean for a moment and saw the same terror in his eyes that was in her heart. The howl behind them suddenly changed in tone, becoming a exclamation of pain and surprise. When they passed through the next set of steel doors, Kean closed them and jammed a chair leg through the door handles to brace them shut.

The new location looked vaguely familiar to Kean. "Hey, isn't this the University College basement? We went through here last time, and there was a tunnel right over there that led towards the NCB."

The direction that Kean was pointing was opposite to the doors Robert wanted them to take.

"That tunnel will take you through the physics building. Right by the labs in the basement, labs full of pressurized gas, radioactive and unstable isotopes, and a very long list of items that should not be exposed to excessive heat." Robert's voice was hard to understand, coming garbled through the PA system, but his tone of frustration came through loud and clear. The lights at the other exit door blinked impatiently, and the kids obliged and went that way.

"Are we gaining distance on that thing? What was that scream about?" Mallory asked as they bolted down a sloping hallway and through another door, a single steel door with a security window in it. They were standing in a mechanical room that was full of pipes and conduits. The weak light in the room seemed to direct them towards the center of the cramped room. Mallory paused for a moment as she waited for Robert to give her a response that wasn't coming.

"Would be nice to get an answer to my question" Mallory grumbled as she squeezed through the rows of machinery.

"There isn't a radio or a camera in here, so Robert can't talk to us" Kean offered as an explanation.

"He could call on the phone."

"Remember that cell coverage is pretty bad on campus-I bet there's no signal down here at all" Kean replied while pulling up the trap door in front of him. The single pulsing green light beside it was the only indicator that this was the right way.

Mallory hissed. "This looks totally sketchy."

Kean hopped down into the dark hole in the ground. "Come on."

Mallory let out a strangled cry of frustration and fear and followed Kean down into the maintenance hatch. The tunnel below was too short to let them fully stand up, and running down the compact space while carrying the Antikythera Mechanism was sending Mallory's back into spasms. "Here, your turn" she said as she handed the thing off to Kean.

They emerged from the cramped maintenance corridor and found themselves in a room full of old pinball machines, ugly brown carpeting, and a dusty old bar. The closest pinball machine flashed its lights in a repeating pattern. A harsh electronic voice came out of the game's speakers.

"Hey guys! I can talk to you again! That last area was incredibly difficult to interact with. It blocked most of my abilities."

Mallory looked askance at the machine. "Robert, is that you? Why do you sound like a monster truck rally announcer?"

"It must be the voice chip inside the game. Are both of you okay? The monster is stationary for the moment. I connected it to power lines and tried to pull him into the power grid. It drained the creature of some energy, but the wires melted around it so I had to stop."

Mallory noticed that she was breathing heavily and her legs felt wobbly.

"I have to take a quick break."

Kean and Mallory sat down on dusty wooden chairs and looked around the room.

"Robert, where are we?"

"It's the old location of The Spoke, one of the university's bars. They moved it out of there about 15 years ago, but the space hasn't been reused."

"Why?" Kean asked.

Robert went silent as he searched for an answer, and the pinball machine went through an automated routine of popping each bumper and resetting each target. The clatter stopped as Robert resumed talking.

"There is a building plan for the site. They're going to knock the existing structure down and build a new one, but the funding has been delayed a few times. I guess they don't want to renovate a building that will be torn down eventually. When you're ready, the next exit is over there, by the bathrooms. And I think you should try to be ready now. It's moving again."

Another howl filled the air around them. The sound of violent smashing echoed all around them. Mallory and Kean were already back on their feet and running when the door behind them exploded open. A cacophony of alarms started blaring as they left the abandoned tavern and ran down the tiled hallway to the next building, The Ivy school of Business.

They went through the entrance to the business school and were confused by the room they found themselves in. Giant vats of water covered almost the entire floor, rising up a meter from the ground. Lights suspended above the vats bathed the water in bright light. Floating in the water were massive lily padswith wide lotus flowers nestled in between the pads. A narrow walkway ran the length of the room, splitting the room in two.

"What the heck is this?" Kean exclaimed.

"Bio-filtration project. Supposed to clean the water" Robert explained.

Mallory reached the other side of the room. "Why is it in the business school? That's crazy" she said as she pushed on the door, only to find that it was locked.

"I don't know why it's there-would you like me to look it up?"

"Robert! The door is locked!"

The double doors behind them were covered in darkness. The monster entered the room, snarling and scraping its claws on the ground. The vat closest to the beast started to boil, sending steam billowing into the air. The monster took one step further into the room and Mallory lost sight of anything else in the room as the steam obscured everything.

"Kean! Where are you? Robert-we're trapped! HELP!"

Mallory pounded on the locked door in front of her. The ground beneath her feet suddenly disappeared, and she fell into a lightless space, tumbling and screaming in terror.

Chapter 30

The bottom of the unlit pit was full of foul-smelling water and slime that coated Mallory when she landed in the middle of it. She felt a pair of hands pulling and grabbing at her, and she flailed about in reaction to the perceived assault.

"Hey! Cut it out, Mal. It's me. Get up, we have to keep going."

She squinted in the darkness and could barely make out Kean's face just out of arm's reach. A loud clanging noise resonated from above them as the grated floor returned to its closed position.

"This must be a drainage ditch or overflow for the room above. Probably taps into an existing watershed branch. That explains why the artificial ponds were in the basement of the business school" Kean mused as he helped Mallory to her feet and made his way forward.

The room opened up into a sloping concrete chute leading down the hill towards the creekbed at the bottom. Weak halogen lights cast a puny amount of light down the space. The floor was treacherous, and both Kean and Mallory had to hold on to the metal grating on the wall to prevent losing their traction and falling down uncontrollably. They half-walked, half-slid their way down to the bottom of the slope. The water drained off through openings at the floor level, and a dry, narrow tunnel led off to the left. They nodded at each other and hurried off down the narrow tunnel.

The screeching noise of metal grates being forced to open told them that the monster had made it into the drainage canal. The smell became unbearably horrible as the murky water was heated and vaporized. Mallory caught sight of a ladder leading up to an open hatch, and she climbed up quickly. Once at the top, she grabbed the device from Kean to allow him to climb up too. He pulled his right foot up out of the tunnel as the monster reached the ladder. The viscous black monstrosity swiped at his calf with its clawed hand. His denim pant leg smoldered along the ripped claw mark, and the swipe pierced his skin and left a gash on his calf. He ignored the pain and ran blindly down the hall with Mallory beside him.

They dashed through the basement of Delaware Hall residence, and Robert finally reconnected with them. He lit the escape path out of the residence and into the staging building next door.

Robert spoke through the PA system. Even taking into account the diminished quality of the speaker he was using, there was a noticeable strain to Robert's voice.

"I found you again! You vanished completely and I couldn't' find any trace of you. You're getting near the building. Once you get through staging, there's a big set of double doors that will lead into the NCB. Do you need floor by floor directions?" "Robert, we're almost there now. Are you holding up okay?"

"I'm fine. I'm more worried about you and Kean."

"We're fine" Mallory answered, shooting a quick look at Kean. His pale skin and limp told Mallory that he wasn't fine at all. She fell a step behind him, trying to assess what was wrong with his leg while still moving towards their goal. She saw the serious cut in Kean's leg. The heat from the monster had partially cauterized the wound, but it still looked inflamed and very painful.

"Keaner, are you going to hold it together for just a few more minutes? We're almost there, buddy."

Kean gritted his teeth and nodded. "I'll make it."

The doors to the NCB were propped open and had signs warning of danger due to construction posted on them. Mallory first went towards the stairs, but looking at Kean's wounded leg made her change her mind. She decided that they had to risk the elevator. As she waited for the elevator to arrive, she pulled the entrance doors shut and looped one of the construction safety ropes through the handles to tie them shut. The elevator chimed its arrival behind her and she worked feverishly to tie off the knot. The sight of the monster loping down the hall towards her made her hands shake, but she fought through the fear. Hoping that the doors would buy them an extra moment, she ran into the elevator as the doors started to close. The elevator shook and creaked as the fiend slammed into the doors at the bottom.

"Guess my delaying tactic didn't work so well."

The walls of the elevator began to radiate heat, and the stench of melting metal and plastic filled the tiny space. The doors opened on the second floor and Mallory and Kean rushed out of the elevator as the fire spread through the elevator. Fire alarms started wailing throughout the building. They ran down the hall as the karma demon oozed out of the elevator shaft and solidified, showering the foyer with sticky burning embers.

Mallory turned to look at the beast. It uncurled its newly reformed limb and a sinuous tentacle shot out of its wrist. The tentacle struck Mallory's parasite and fused with it, giving the monster a direct hold on Mallory. She screamed and batted her fists uselessly at the black mass. Kean turned around and saw the trouble Mallory was in. Reflexively he swung the only weapon he had, the Antikythera Mechanism. It cut easily through the tentacle, turning any part of it that it touched into nothingness. The tension holding Mallory in place disappeared and she stumbled backwards. A pair of new tentacles snaked out towards them, but Kean held the AM in their way and back around the corner.

"It can't effect the AM, or even interact with it at all. I wish I understood why" Kean shouted as he pulled Mallory with him towards the lab. The hole in the wall was still there, though there were signs of repairs having started recently. Kean and Mallory stepped into the tiny closet turned lab and placed the Antikythera Mechanism back onto the display pedestal. They watched the tether between the AM and the karma demon fade away, but the same didn't happen for the lines connecting them to the beast. The parasites were still firmly attached, and the howling fiend crashing down the hall towards them was still hungry for their blood.

"The thing is still trying to kill us. Any new ideas, guys?" Mallory asked as she stepped back into the hall and looked around for escape routes.

"Head to the roof-there's too much fire below you and the monster is blocking the only fire route down from where you are" Robert replied. Kean groaned and limped to the staircase, followed by Mallory. The smoke and heat from the stairs below confirmed Robert's assessment, so they climbed up until they reached the roof. The flat, gravel-coated rooftop was asymmetrical in shape and gave them a clear view of the lack of escape options.

"Mal, just climbing down and trying to run won't help. I can't handle any more running."

"It would catch us anyway."

Mal's cell phone started relaying Robert's voice to them.

"I have one idea. It will hurt."

"Great sales pitch Robert, but lucky for you, we're out of options. Let's hear it" Mallory answered as the karma demon pulled itself through the doorway with its jaws wide open and dripping rivulets of black ichors down its chin. The kids hid behind a piece of blocky machinery near the roof edge.

"The thing is made of accumulated karma, and it has no way of resolving the paradigmatic conflict."

"What?"

"The universe's expectations. The monster needs a way out and it doesn't have one. The whole roof is surrounded by geothermal pipes, containing water. The whole system is designed to regulate and distribute heat. Lots of it."

"And that thing is super-hot. So we push it into the water? That's the answer? Why didn't it fizzle out in the fake pond room?"

"Not enough water, I guess" replied Kean. "Besides, we don't have another choice. Okay Robert, how do we do this?"

"I'll start. Use spells to direct it into the water system and hopefully everyone survives."

Robert's voice cut off abruptly as his focus shifted away from the communication and exclusively towards the power system of the geo-thermal pumps. He sent waves of spell energy through the machine, activating it's cooling functions and intensifying it tenfold. He ordered the rooftop vents to open fully, and reversed the fan direction to start drawing air in. The monster roared in response as the machine started to tug at its flesh, but the monster was still able to move towards the kids in their hiding spot. Mallory began drawing a massive amount of spell energy to her hands, and she saw Kean doing the same. She was terrified that casting the spell would stop her heart entirely, but the thought of being consumed by the karma demon was even more terrifying. She peeked out around the corner of the machinery and lined up her spell shot. She paused as she caught sight of another spell zipping up and channeling into the rooftop. Kean shouted out "It's Heisenberg's spell!" and Mallory was overjoyed to see the mage's spell colour coursing through the newly arrived magic. The addition of Heisenberg's magic forced the monster to a standstill. The creature bent down and went to all fours, using its claws to grip the roof and resume its approach. Simultaneously, all of pipes supplying extinguishing foam for the fire suppression system burst open and the foam coated the monster completely. The magic directing the foam onto its target was vaguely familiar, and the shimmering, multicoloured hue to the foam reminded Mallory of the other mage on campus, the kindly art curator.

Kean could feel the beast weakening through his parasitic connection, and he knew it was time for the final push. "Mallory NOW!" he yelled, and both of them let loose with their spells. The engines driving the vent fans whined as the mages supercharged the system, and the fans were seconds away from exploding from the strain. The air temperature dropped suddenly as the battle reached a tipping point. The karma demon began to be disassembled by the arcane-powered machinery, and the fans pulled chunks of the black goo into the vents. Each piece pulled off gave the entire monster less cohesion, and it rapidly fell apart. A massive discharge of heat exploded from the spot where the monster had been crawling toward them, and the spike in temperature pushed Mallory and Kean into semi-consciousness. Kean felt his heart hammering away in his chest. The parasite was still half-embedded into his torso and it was trying to finish its deadly mission. The edges of his vision started to turn jet black. The last of the karma demon was sucked up into the system and a painfully loud hissing sound filled the entire area. The now super-heated water in the system was racing through the pipes, looking for some kind of escape, and it found one in the physical plant. The superheated steam exploded out of the multitude of pipes carrying it, and shot upwards out of the giant ground-level exhaust fan. A column of black and grey steam shot up into the sky for 30 seconds, completely emptying the entire geo-thermal system.

The silent aftermath was disquieting. It forced Mallory to hear the irregular rhythm of her heart. The parasite was dissolving, but one wicked talon still dug deep into the muscle of her chest and into the space near her heart. The sky above the campus was filled with a sheet of blinding lightning, chased by a booming roll of thunder that sounded like the end of the universe itself. As the sound of thunder faded away, sheets of warm heavy rain started to fall. The first drops of water hit the parasites on their chests and dissolved them completely. Mallory sighed in relief as her heartbeat returned to its steady, regular rhythm.

"Kean, are we dead?"

Kean blinked the torrential rain out of his eyes.

"Nope. But we are going to be soaking wet in about 10 seconds. And we're still on top of a burning building, so I wouldn't say that it's clear sailing."

"You're such an optimist."

Chapter 31

The cozy cottage filled with the inviting fragrance of hot chocolate and warm spiced cookies as their host Mary-Anne prepared a snack to warm everyone back up. Mallory and Kean were bundled up in thick, soft blankets, and Mallory's hair was bound up in an impossibly fluffy towel wrapped around her head. Damien sat in the big recliner in the corner, watching the rain out the window with his iPod blocking out the sound of conversation. Heisenberg was resting on the loveseat near the fireplace, and even in his exhausted state, he tried to jump up and help Mary-Anne when she came back into the room.

"Oh sit yourself down, pal. I am perfectly capable of hosting my own gathering. Now take a mug of cocoa and a few ginger snaps before you pass out."

Heisenberg sat back down and took the offered food and drink. "Yes ma'am. I wouldn't dare suggest that you were anything other than capable."

The rest of the refreshments were handed out, and as soon as Mary-Anne sat down, Mallory started asking questions.

"How did you know we needed help? Did you suffer any kind of injury from the confrontation? Did you know Heisenberg before today?"

"Oh this is the Heisenberg, eh? I've heard mention of him in certain discussion groups, but no, I've never met him in person."

"Technically, I am not the Heisenberg."

"Oh, be overly precise if you must, but I believe we are who we say we are. As to your question about how I knew you needed help, well, the very air was thick with magical tension or 'backlash' as you like to refer to it. It was pulling at me and making my skin crawl. The gap between what was tolerable to the universe and what was actually happening was growing wider and wider, and if something didn't release that tension, there was about to be some kind of terrible mess. Oh, and then I saw the screaming bystanders, exploding power lines, and giant monster. Those were clues, too."

Kean stretched out his sore and aching body, wincing as he disturbed the gash on his leg.

"Yikes, that thing stings. Why do I end up with all the scars?"

"Well, I'm not going to show you, but I have a scar too, from the parasite. Right above my heart, already healed up and glowing with magical residue."

Compulsively, all of the mages in the room switched to magesight to look for the trace of magic in the scar. Mallory noticed their concentrating and scowled. "Stop it, you arcane perverts" she said, pretending to be annoyed.

"So, that fight left a pretty big mess. It was even bigger than our last fight."

"You've done this before, young man? What kind of dangerous life are you living?" Mary-Anne asked incredulously.

"In the lad's defense, this event was caused by the first conflict, and that was the product of an errant spell created by an accidental combination of three different magical effects. These two brave children saved the people of the city from a very unpleasant magical plague, of a sort."

"Robert helped too. This time, he had to stay at home. The other reality's device gave him migraines."

Mary-Anne raised an eyebrow. "Other reality? This tale is becoming very exotic."

Mallory's phone buzzed as she received a text message. She read the message and immediately started laughing.

"It's from Robert, but his mom had to type it for him. He says he "over-exerted himself and gave himself another migraine, so it's too painful to touch anything electronic. He's going to be fine, and he's looking forward to talking to us tomorrow at school. The storm looks like its passing, and everything is back in its rightful place" and his mom added a question mark to that last part. So it sounds like Robert has a bit of a backlash hangover."

Heisenberg smiled and raised his mug to the room.

"Don't we all? Here's to successfully surviving another wild calamity."

Kean chimed in. "And a nice long break from doing anything like this again."

"Agreed!" they all cheered.

Epilogue

The scaly charred skin at his neck burned in the direct light of the strange sun above him. He had fallen into a routine of practical survival: hide from the light during the long cursed day, and scrounge through the scorched earth during the brief hours of coolness at night. Herlech Gate had become more of an animal than a man, after being blown through the tear in the fabric of reality and into the land of madness. The glimpses into a million different realities had pushed his mind to its breaking point, and he had stumbled through the nearest exit and into this harsh desert wilderness. Now he found solace in the unthinking process of finding food and avoiding death.

But moments ago, something had called to him. A stirring of sensation that had been lost to him over the months in isolation. The fleeting, teasing taste of arcane energy had pulled him out of his rocky hiding place and into the blazing red sun. He darted from shadow to shadow, lurching with the uneven gait caused by poorly healed wounds. d fixed his eyes at a distant point in the sky. A ball of karmic energy emerged from a rip in the space far above him and shot across the sky. It rammed into a distant speck of light and flared as it consumed the tiny planet. The sun above him flared in concert with the explosion, and the air around him became too hot to breathe. Herlech dropped to his knees gagging for air.

The temperature dropped suddenly all around Herlech, and he gratefully gulped down breathable air. He felt the strangest sensation of being watched, despite a certainty that he was the only sentient creature in this entire wasteland. He stood up and looked directly ahead to a shimmering heat reflection of himself. Herlech wondered if he had finally lost his mind completely and was now going to spend the last few hours of his existence running from illusions.

The duplicate spoke in a soft monotone voice.

"I have awoken. I am hungry. You will open the way."

Each word sent sensations of fear and hunger over Herlech. The power barely contained within the words spoken by this creature pushed Herlech to his knees and he cried out "what are you?"

"I am the End of All."

The shimmering creature in front of him unleashed a torrent of dark magic energy that flooded into Herlech and filled his body. For a second, he saw the true creature behind the form in front of him, an unknowable alien being filling the entire horizon without nearing an endpoint, and then his mind was lost, completely and utterly.

####